The Endless Pursuit

A Mystery and Horror Story You Won't Believe

by

Paulina Paulson

The contents of this work, including, but not limited to, the accuracy of events, people, and places depicted; opinions expressed; permission to use previously published materials included; and any advice given or actions advocated are solely the responsibility of the author, who assumes all liability for said work and indemnifies the publisher against any claims stemming from publication of the work.

All Rights Reserved
Copyright © 2019 by Paulina Paulson

No part of this book may be reproduced or transmitted, downloaded, distributed, reverse engineered, or stored in or introduced into any information storage and retrieval system, in any form or by any means, including photocopying and recording, whether electronic or mechanical, now known or hereinafter invented without permission in writing from the publisher.

Dorrance Publishing Co
585 Alpha Drive
Pittsburgh, PA 15238
Visit our website at *www.dorrancebookstore.com*

ISBN: 978-1-4809-9930-5
eISBN: 978-1-4809-9948-0

Dedication

This book is dedidcated to:
My granddaughter, Dean-a Charbonnier.

Chapter 1

I learned of his death when my daughter called me one cold, bright January afternoon with the disturbing news. Becky, my middle daughter, kept in touch with her father over the years, not out of love, but out of need. She wanted a father in her life so desperately that she would try to visit with him a few times a year, but the visits were always unnerving because she would always find him in drag. He treated her nice when he was fully dressed in woman's wear. That's the only time when he was relaxed in his body. His mind didn't have to struggle with the relentless pursuit of having to satisfy his desires. He was plagued constantly with the nagging haunting to dress. The haunting never rested. Only when he gave in could he then play drag all day long. After all, he would surely go mad otherwise. Being in costume released all his anxious inhibitions. That's when he was able to put on the façade of being the most charming woman he could muster up. It was only then that his deranged mind was released into a world of bizarre behaviors, the only time he could let go and truly find contentment, the only time he could find peace. It was like playing a game, and games were always fun.

So, he finally died. After so many years, his tortured mind was, now, long last at rest. He died alone in a hospital with only doctors and nurses aware of his condition. He was 74, and diabetes had ravished his body since he was 18. That's when he was diagnosed with juvenile diabetes. He was a college student, excited about the prospects of his future, so unaware that this insidious disease was lurking in his body, getting ready to explode with blood sugars so high, it almost killed him. The doctors immediately put him on insulin shots for life. Over the years, the disease took its toll. First with kidney illnesses, followed by pancreatic episodes of pancreatitis, leg abscesses, blurry eyes, poor circulation, numbing fingers. Toes had to be amputated and when he refused to have his foot removed because of massive infection, it was the beginning of his demise. Without mercy, diabetes killed him. So there he lay, all alone on his death bed with no one to comfort him.

As for me, there was no love lost, not after all he had put me and the kids through during those horrific divorce years and all the troubled years that followed. Becky was the one the hospital called to notify the first of kin of her father's death. Becky phoned and said, "Mom, Dad died yesterday in a hospital way up in northern Maine. I just got the call from the hospital. Cause of death, diabetes." I was dumfounded and could only answer, "Oh," but no sound came out. The solitary thought that ran through my head was he can't hurt us anymore. There was no sense of sorrow for this man who inflicted such tremendous tribulation on me and our three beautiful children. The torment he had put us through for so many years could now be relinquished. So why was I not experiencing euphoria? In spite of it all, my sentiment spilled out as pardoning sorrow. It should have been implacable, revengeful, unforgiving gratitude that he had finally died. Where was this painful heartache coming from? Was I so Christian that the thought of him burning in hell for the next billion years was more than I could fathom? I continued to struggle with the resurrection/hell thing. I had so many questions about what happens when you die. I had voiced so many times in bible study class these same nagging questions without ever accomplishing a resolve. So, where was Hank? Was he being judged now and suffering eternal pain, was he sleeping, was he waiting to be judged? My mind was out of control with so many thoughts racing through my trembling body that I couldn't catch my breath. As despicable as this man was, even this retched soul shouldn't suffer for eternity, if there was such a place.

Crushing tears tore down my cheeks. As I moaned, tremendous sorrow swept over me. And this time, Becky heard me say, "Oh, my God, he died?"

How awful! How do you feel, Becky?" Becky answered, "I'm alright. I haven't even cried yet. I thought I would, but I haven't. At least he's out of his misery. Should I call his family and let them know of his death?" Becky continued to ramble on as my mind wandered and entered into a silent daze where nothing my daughter was saying could be heard in my head. Everything went silent, even Becky's voice. Common sense was stifled, and only thoughts of ridiculous grief washed over me, absolute ridiculous grief!

I shook my head trying to get back into the moment. I still had trouble hearing Becky speak, when I said, "Wait a minute while I put on my hearing aids. I can't understand anything you are saying. Please wait, and don't hang up the phone. I have to know everything."

By this time, my voice had reached fever pitch and was registering at .50 decimal points. I was telling myself to calm down, Mary. I quickly ran to grab my hearing aids and when I began putting them on, I thought, 'oh damn it, of all times for the batteries to fail.' By now my hands were shaking so violently, I couldn't get those tiny batteries into the microscopic mini round button holes. That's when I yelled out, "Calm down, Mary, for pity's sake!" Tears were now at full throttle and the size of golf balls. With blurry eyes and shaking hands, how on earth was I going to get my hearing aids on? I ran back to the phone and yelled into the receiver, "Becky, don't hang up. You have to speak really loudly because I can't get my hearing aids to work. Please talk loudly and tell me everything."

Becky yelled back at me, "Mom, you have to calm down. I can't talk to you when you are like this, please settle down. I'll tell you everything, but first, you have to promise me that you will listen to me without any interruptions."

"You're right," I said. "I promise I will listen and calm down. Please tell me everything, and don't leave anything out."

Becky went on to say the hospital had actually called her at the request of her father when he was dying. He wanted to see her.

"So, Mom, I drove up to Maine taking three days off from work to see him. When I got there, he was in his final days. I hated seeing him like that, but he was glad I was there, so I realized I had done the right thing by taking the five-hour car trip to reach the hospital. He wasn't in drag, but he still had his fingernails polished with bright red nail polish. I was so mortified that I went to the drug store to purchase some nail polish remover and returned to the hospital, hoping that he would let me remove the color from his nails. Thank God he agreed.

"Oh, Beck," I murmured. "How awkward for you. Did he at least say something to you before he died?"

Becky answered, "Yes, he told me he loved me, and I told him I loved him, too. He had tremendous difficulty talking and couldn't say anything else to me no matter how hard he tried. The next day, he couldn't talk at all, not even a groan, and then that night, at 2 am, he passed. The hospital immediately called me then, and I put in a pretty rough sleeping night. Actually, I couldn't sleep at all, so I got up and read my bible until 5 am and then decided to begin my day. I'm so sad, Mom. He was a tortured soul and hurt so many people since the divorce that I can't imagine the thoughts that must have been going through his head as he lay on his death bed. That would have been his final moment to make amends to everyone he had hurt over the years, but he offered nothing. He only said he loved me. Shallow words because he could have made a real difference in my life. He never sent me a birthday card, a Christmas gift, wrote me a letter, called me on the phone, or invited me to visit with him, nothing. Shallow words for sure."

"Oh, Becky," I said, "You have to know that he was incapable of reaching out to you in that way. He was so filled with hatred about the breakup of the marriage that he couldn't find himself. I'm not defending him. He could have at least reached out to you kids. But instead he chose to harness all that anger year after year. What a lonesome, isolated life he led. I'm so sorry, Beck. I wish I could take away your sadness. If I could, I would. Unfortunately, this is earth, not heaven, so wishing can't make it so."

• • •

After my phone call with Becky, I began to think back of how many times the same conversation Becky and I had just had had, in fact, taken place with all my children over the years. Forty years of remembering how things could have been rather than how they were tumbled randomly through my head. How does a mother converse with her children about their father being so heartless. Somehow you search for the words to soften the blow so the kids don't harbor ill will and contempt for their father. You try to raise your kids to be kind and generous and loving, even while their father was none of the above. So how do you manage their fragile lives and train them to mature into decent individuals capable of performing well in the world with goodness and love? I struggled with this exact thought every time I was forced to have this demanding conversation time and time again while raising my children.

Now, going back to the days of yesteryear, some forty years ago when these dreadful memories were so raw in my head, I'm reminiscing it was my fault for all this trouble because I probably should not have married him in the first place. But then my beautiful children would not exist, and I can't imagine my life without them. They are my life. At that time, the situation was so dire, I was not thinking straight. I had just turned thirty. Of course I should have married my husband. After all, I did love him, and he did love me.

• • •

We first met at the Skating Club of Wilmington. It was public skating every Tuesday, and I loved to skate, so I decided to go to the Skating Club for a night of skating. All my friends were busy that night, so I ended up going alone, but that was okay because I knew I would enjoy the evening trying to spin and waltz jump and skate backwards. That's where I met my husband to be. The speed skaters had just left the ice after their ten minutes of dedicated music, and the announcer at the organ called out, 'Couples Only.' As the organ began to play a waltz, Hank asked me to skate as a couple, and I said yes. I knew he was attracted to me, and our conversation was light hearted and fun. He skated well as did I and after the ten dedicated minutes of couple skating, the public skating was ending for the evening. He walked me out to my car and asked to see me again, so we settled on the next Saturday night. The rest is history. Now 14 years married, here I am, asking for a divorce. That was the beginning of the end for me and the kids.

Chapter II

It all started when Hank and I had been married for ten years. Life was good. We had three beautiful children; two little girls, Rebecca, age six, Izzy was seven and our son, Kenny, just turned four. I was so proud of my kids. They were so good, well-mannered, so devoted to me, wanting to please all the time. They were beautiful, too. Both Izzy and Kenny were natural blondes, Izzy with gold eyes with green speckles, and Kenny's eyes were light hazel brown. Our Rebecca had golden brown hair with huge liquid deep brown eyes, and her smile always displayed dimples. She was the sweetest of all the children, never making any waves, always going along with whatever was asked of her. Our oldest, Izzy, was a firecracker, filled with determination to always lead the way. She was headstrong, but she also was amazingly charming. As for our son, he was the apple of his father's eye. He had wanted a son right from the start and on May 11th, 1971, Hank's dream came true, a little boy weighing 8 lbs. 10 ounces and 20 inches long. He was a big baby for me to deliver, but all went well. When we brought him home, we were both delirious with joy. We felt we were leading the most enchanted lives anyone could imagine. As I said before, life was good. We had just purchased our very first home in the small community of Randolph, a small town just ten miles west of Boston, and it was a beauty. It was a large four-bedroom colonial. It had two staircases, five fire places, a portico off the dining room, and a huge brick floor screened-in porch. The kitchen had been newly renovated with a huge patio off the ten-foot sliding glass doors. The property was situated on two acres of beautifully landscaped grounds, nestled on a shaded street lined with 100-year-old maple trees. It was this side of heaven. We had a new house, new baby, were wealthy beyond our years, and now blessed with three beautiful children.

Our two little girls were now in grade school, and our precious Kenny would be attending kindergarten in another year. I was a stay at home mom and enjoyed my son's company beyond measure. He had the most charismatic personality, was absolutely silly happy, and had the patience of Job. I remember he would stay in his play yard while I did the usual morning chores around the house, and he was never trying to climb out. He was entirely captivated from head to toe by whichever toys he had to play with and would never try to climb out of this blissful space. Every morning when it was time for me to take a break, I would always take Kenny out of his playpen. He would be giggling. I couldn't resist playing with him. He constantly said the cutest things. I recall once I asked him to hang his wet bathing suit on the clothes line to dry after a glorious day at the beach at our summer home in Maine, and his giggling was excessive as he tried to do just that. He was jumping as high as he could to reach the clothes line and just couldn't reach it, no matter how hard he tried or how high he jumped. His little head kept bobbing up and down by the kitchen window as he clumsily jumped with relentless giggling until I yelled out, "What are you laughing about?"

"Look at me, Mom, I'm jumping for joy." What a delectable, endearing, sweet personality he had. Everyone who met him fell in love with him instantly and all the little boys always wanted to be his friend. He was just that kind of a kid. His dad at that time used to take him to work once a week. It was an enormous manufacturing plant where Kenny would run his little heart out and never reach the end of the factory. There were all kinds of barrels to climb into and play with and all the men would always let him sit at their work benches as they turned their wire jigs into steel shelving for Stop and Shop. Sometimes they would even let Kenny try his hand at turning the jig himself, claiming he was going to be a great engineer when he grew up. What a beautiful life we all had. I felt so blessed and thanked God constantly for giving me such beautiful children and such a precious life. Complete happiness was pervasive throughout our home, and I couldn't imagine life getting any better than this.

But that's when it all changed. One evening after we put the kids to bed for the night and Hank and I were getting ready to retire, Hank seemed to be quite agitated. He was sitting up in bed, waiting for me to join him after brushing out my hair from wearing an all-day ponytail. As I climbed into bed, I sensed something was not quite right. He took my hand the moment I climbed in next to him and said so seriously, "I have something I need to tell you." Such an ominous beginning of a conversation was always disturbing, and I immediately said, "What is it, you're scaring me."

Hank said, "I don't want you to get upset, but there is something that has been building up for years now, and I just have to get it off my chest. I just can't live with this secret anymore."

My heart sank, and a look of dismay pressed on my face so startling, I actually could feel my face turning warm and red. I did tend to be easily excitable. I was so naïve in those days and so protected from the real world, I had no idea of the perverse nature of things that people could actually pursue as entertainment. I was always thanking God for my blessings and had no idea of how truly ugly the world outside of my domain could in fact be.

"What is it," I said again. Hank began breathing deeply now, and I could tell that something was dreadfully wrong.

"What?" I said for the third time. "Tell me. I can't stand this. Please, Hank, tell me."

By now Hank was struggling and tried desperately to spit it out but his words came out in slow motion and did not tell the entire story.

Hank said, "I dress."

I remember thinking, what could he possibly be trying to tell me. Of course he dressed. We all dress. This isn't making any sense to me. I said, "What are you talking about? Of course you dress. You're really beginning to scare me now."

Hank tried to continue and took the deepest breath I have ever seen anyone take in my entire life. He then spoke methodically and meticulously saying, "I d r e s s u p l i k e a w o m a n."

I questioned, "Why would you want to do that? Nobody dresses up in women's clothes, do they?"

"Well, I do, and I can't help myself," Hank replied. "I have been doing it all my life, even before I married you. I used to play under the kitchen table at home when friends of my mother's were visiting. Looking at women's legs fascinated me. I remember once when I was only eleven, and my mother was not home, I decided to dress up in my mother's clothes. I never did that before, and I got excited just thinking about how much fun it would be to admire myself in front of the mirror. When I had finished putting on some of her wardrobe I would think to myself how beautiful I looked. It wasn't until I hit puberty that things really began to get out of hand. One day while my mother went food shopping, I was dressing up and almost got caught. I put her bra on and stuffed it with socks and then I had the idea to put a Kotex pad into my pants. My genitals felt complete. I knew something was wrong with me, that I shouldn't be dressing, shouldn't be enjoying such a fantasy and tried to stop before my mother returned home. At first, I could control the time being dressed, but after a while, my perversion became obsessive. I had just made the transition back to being a boy, when I heard her footsteps coming up the stairs. My heart was in my throat, and I remember saying to myself, this cannot be normal behavior. Why am I doing this? Of course, I am in puberty! That's the reason. It all made sense to me now. I convinced myself everything would work out okay, and I would indeed be normal again. I really didn't want to grow up being labeled some kind of weirdo."

Hank stopped talking, and I could see he was troubled as he sighed a deep breath of relief; he had finally spilled the beans.

Looking back now, I realize that I was suddenly forced to deal with this outrageous behavior. I sat on the bed with a puzzled expression, not knowing what to say or do. My mind was telling myself, okay, so he did this when he was growing up. So be it. It is what it is. It was a little bit strange, but okay, that time in his life had passed and so why was he telling me this now? Our life is perfect, so why ruin it with this hogwash? It was terribly upsetting to hear such a strange story about his youth and to tell you the truth, I was deeply concerned and greatly upset. I said, "Why are you telling me this now? I don't understand. If this happened in your youth a long time ago, why do I need to know this now? You're truly upsetting me now. What purpose could you possibly have for telling me of this appalling secret? I just don't get it."

I was young and stupid, so naïve! I did not have an inkling about drag, cross dressing, or what a transvestite was. It just wasn't talked about in those days.

Hank finally continued to reveal the ugly story of his life, a life I could not even begin to fully comprehend. Hank said, "I still dress all the time, but it is even worse than before. I go to sex parties where men are all in drag and want to have sex with each other. I haven't had sex with any of them yet, but I am so afraid that this ugly situation could escalate into something much worse. I need your help, Mary."

As I listened stupefied to Hank's enhanced affirmation, I began to cry. I at last realized this was not simply a stupid, nonsensical series of erratic behaviors performed in his youth. These circumstances were so much graver, and I began to cry. This situation was more than troubling. It was a life-long habitual habit that took life into an underground world of secretive perversion and constant deception. How could I ever trust him again after learning of this secretive life that he was living in our marriage? I gulped my tears down my throat trying to talk and yelled, "Why, why? I thought you said this was simply something to do with puberty."

"Well, it is worse than that," Hank replied. "It's really gotten out of control now, and I want to stop. I really do want to stop. No matter how hard I try, I simply cannot stop myself. I really believed that once I married you and could make passionate love to you that this all would go away. It hasn't. In fact, it got even easier because now I could use your bras and makeup every time you were not at home. The reason I'm telling you now is because I can't live with myself anymore. I have to stop this insane pattern of perverse dressing. Can you please forgive me and try to help me work this through? I need professional help and am afraid to go it alone. I need you with me. I need you to come with me so we both can talk to a professional. I need you in my corner by my side. I love you so much. I do not want to lose you and the kids over this."

I was silent. My head was whirling uncontrollably. My charmed life came to an abrupt and sudden stop. My life was spiraling out of control. I could not even speak for several moments, let alone think. Deafening silence filled the room. After what seemed like an eternity, I somehow found my chocking voice and could respond. I threw my arms around him and said, "How awful for you. You've suffered all these years with this horrendous secret. I explained to him that of course I was with him and would support him in whatever way I could. We love each other. We'll get through this together".

My head did not want to give up, but my heart was damaged beyond repair. My perfect life was over.

Chapter III

The year was 1975 when Hank confessed his tragic secret. Life was simpler then. There was no internet, Facebook, twitter, social media. The Brady Bunch was the number one family sitcom on TV then, depicting a beautiful family impressing strong family values on their children. The economy was thriving, government was enlisting young folks to join the Peace Corps and give back to their nation. Everyone wore suits to work, women dressed in dresses all the time, children proudly recited the Pledge of Allegiance in school along with a silent moment of prayer to begin their school day. Neighbors welcomed newcomers to their neighborhoods. Not anything like it is today where neighbors don't even acknowledge each other, let alone welcome them. There were neighborhood Christmas carolers and neighborhood block parties and barbeques and little league and girl scouts and boy scouts and priests who would play baseball with all us kids after school. How Hank could be dressing all those years ago during such a wonderful time in America, I simply could not understand. It simply didn't register. It absolutely made no sense at all.

• • •

Seething from last night's conversation with Hank, I started grabbing the phone book as soon as the girls left for school, Hank was off to the plant, and

Kenny was settled in the playroom. I started flipping through the yellow pages wildly, looking for a doctor to help us get our lives back to normal. William Hawkes, MD. PhD. glared out at me loud and clear because his practice specialized in cross dressing. I knew I was in the right place. Last night was the first time I ever heard the term cross dressing and now here it was, in black and white. How bleak my day seemed. I knew what I had to do. I was desperate for answers, hoping beyond hope this doctor could help us. I still loved Hank and wanted to help him. He seemed so earnest and was so fearful that I might leave him that I had to assure him all would be well. We will get through this together no matter what. I immediately picked up the phone and started dialing Dr. Hawkes. Please pick up, please pick up. Don't go to your message machine. After three rings, a soft spoken women answered with a pleasant voice, asking how she could assist my call. Thank goodness. God was with me this morning. After explaining my situation, she assured me the best thing to do was for the both of us to meet personally with Doctor Hawkes. I explained that my husband was in crisis, hoping to get in to see the doctor soon, but that was not a possibility. The woman explained cross dressing was not an emergency, stating that she was sorry I was so upset, but clearly understood my painful anxiety. I was able to get an appointment in ten days; and considering the large practice the doctor had, I felt as though she understood my urgency. I hung up the phone and began my day as usual, but had a tough time focusing on my chores, errands, even Kenny. He was the joy of my life, and even he couldn't pull me out of this funk I was in.

    I managed to get through the rest of the day, putting on a false front with all the neighbors, waving as I picked up the morning mail, saying hello to my next-door neighbor when she saw me and Kenny enjoying a little swimming pool fun in the back yard that afternoon. The day dragged on, but I was able to get through it without messing up too much. I did burn the cookies I was making, so when Becky and Izzy came home from school, they would not be having warm, fresh baked chocolate chip cookies. I scrambled to make chocolate pudding instead, hoping it would set up in 20 minutes. I rushed to put them in the back of the refrigerator, hoping the coldest part of the refrigerator would serve its purpose.

Sure enough, the school bus pulled up right on time, and the girls scampered off the bus, running up the driveway singing hello, hello, hello, hello. How cute. They are always starving when they first come home from school, and both girls quickly gobbled down the chocolate pudding still warm but thankfully set up. As I listened to their gibber jabber, I thought of how perfect my life was yesterday afternoon. Now it was a disaster. I just had to get through the next ten days and then everything would be okay. I was hopeful the doctor would calm me down and would assure me stressing that he could help my husband with his behavioral problem. Behavioral problem! I still couldn't use the term cross dressing. As I shook my head, the girls began to laugh, saying, "Mommy, why are you shaking your head?" That's when I realized this ten day wait was going to be much harder than I had originally realized.

The days gradually trickled by albeit painfully slow, as I thought I might go mad waiting. At last the 10th day of waiting had arrived, and Hank and I were driving to the doctor's office. We said hardly a word during our twenty-minute drive. I guess everything that had to be said had been said ten days earlier. Somehow silence for twenty minutes moves at a snail's pace. Be positive I kept repeating in my head. This is the beginning of the rest of my life. Be positive and by all means, maintain your composure and don't start crying or raising the pitch of your voice. It was a beautiful summer day with clear blue skies and a slight breeze. The flowers were in their full summer bloom, and everyone was hurrying about doing their daily routine. Daily routine, what was that? My routine over the past ten days was so fractured that my house started to take on the look of being a bit disheveled. Hank broke the silence saying, "We're here." He held my hand as we walked toward the doctor's office when he softly whispered in my ear, "I love you. Thank you." It was not until that very moment that I realized how much Hank must have been hurting.

• • •

"Hello, Mr. and Mrs. Clark," Dr. Hawkes said as he reached out his hand with a friendly hand shake to both Hank and me. We followed him into the inner office and made ourselves comfortable. The office was warm and friendly with cocoa painted walls and shades of browns all around the room. It was well put together, and the sitting area was perfect for intimate conversation. Dr. Hawkes cut right to the chase and after a full hour of non-stop talking, the session came to an end. Both Hank and I felt confident that this doctor could help us, and our spirits began to lift as though a heavy weight had been removed from our lives. The doctor explained that he would like to begin weekly sessions with Hank on Tuesdays and Fridays and asked his secretary to set up a schedule for the next three months. I remember thinking, how many months? I had just learned what cross dressing was and didn't fully understand the breadth and scope of the treatment needed to get this behavior terminated. Hank understood clearly and agreed to shift his work schedule to accommodate the good doctor. He was committed, and so was I.

• • •

It's been three months now, and our lives seem to have recovered to some degree of normalcy. The kids are happy, Hank continues to work hard at the business getting new accounts weekly, and the house returned to its clean and pretty look again. All is well, or so I thought. The phone rang, and it was Dr. Hawkes' office explaining that Hank had missed the last two sessions and was anything wrong? My eyes opened wide, and I didn't know what to make of the phone call. I asked to speak with the doctor personally and in a moment, was put through to his office.

"Hello, Mrs. Clark, I'm glad we found you at home." He continued, "I'm very concerned that Hank has missed his last two appointments. He is making steady progress, but still needs to continue with our sessions. Is anything wrong that I should be made aware of?" My head was trying to take in all the good doctor was telling me, and my mind was searching last week's schedule to assure myself that this could not be right.

"Doctor," I said, "I was not aware that Hank missed his last two appointments. He never told me. In fact, he intended to keep his appointments as he left the house last Tuesday and Friday. What does this mean?"

The doctor went on to explain that he didn't want to jump to any conclusions without first talking with Hank. If I could ask Hank to call his office, the doctor assured me he would get to the bottom of this and not to worry. Did he know who he was speaking with, asking me not to worry? That's all I did over the last three months was worry every time Hank left for one of his sessions. How would Hank return? Would he be pensive, upset, or confident with how the session performed that evening. I told Dr. Hawkes that we would be in touch with his office and thanked him for contacting me at home. Now came the wait. Wait until Hank came home from work. He wouldn't be joining us for supper this evening because he had a dinner meeting with a client, so he probably would not return home until 10 o'clock. It's only two o'clock now. The kids aren't even home from school yet. How could I be that patient waiting eight hours to discover the truth? Only the truth could set me free, and that wasn't going to occur until Hank arrived home. Waiting was always hard for me.

It was now nine o'clock, and Hank was still out. I was hoping the dinner meeting might have broken up early, but apparently it would run its usual timeline. All the kids were in bed peacefully sleeping, and I was in the den watching TV. Another hour, I thought, and Hank will be home. I was anxious not knowing how to begin the conversation, so I started to rehearse what I was going to say when all of a sudden, a horrific thought entered my mind. What if he was dressing on his appointment nights? Please don't let it be so, but I couldn't shake off the feeling of being lied to and once again, the trust factor reared its ugly head. It was now the beginning of fall and the house took on a slight chill, so I decided to turn the thermostat up so the kids wouldn't wake up to a cold morning.

Just then the door opened, and Hank came in. I glared at him with complete disgust. The thought of his lying and dressing was repulsive, and I didn't know how I was going to react to the truth.

"Hello, honey," Hank said as he kissed me on the lips. I just sighed with a fake smile, and Hank could sense something was up.

"Are you okay?" Hank questioned as he quizzically looked at me.

"No, I'm not okay; the doctor telephoned this afternoon, asking about your two missed appointments. Can you explain?"

"What are you talking about?"

That's when I realized he was lying. The nightmare had begun. If lying was the trump card, how could I ever trust he would continue with his therapy sessions? Instead, my mind was silently shouting, he's dressing again, he's dressing again. Perhaps he was dressing for the last three months all the while pretending he was attending his therapeutic sessions. How many lies had he told me? After all, he had been lying about his dressing now for over ten years, so why would I think he would just stop that behavior now. He was a good liar, or I was a damn fool. No more Mrs. Naïve. I challenged him, and the conversation became heated with accusations being flung that were hurtful and mean spirited. Hank alleged his innocence, but in the end, finally gave into the truth, stating that he was sorry, but he just couldn't help himself, that he did miss his sessions, that he did cross dress instead, that he did drive into Boston in drag for all to see. I was horrified. Tears filled my eyes as I turned and told him to sleep somewhere else tonight and that I was going to bed. I left Hank standing there, saying not a word.

It was the weekend now and family activities were planned with the kids, so I tried to put on a cheerful face. When Hank walked into the room, I couldn't help but glare at him, trying hard to smile for the kids' sake. I wanted to ask him so many questions about last night and knew now wasn't the place. The kids were all giggling at the table, talking about going skiing with Daddy today and were happily gobbling their pancakes, loaded with butter and maple syrup. Hank started teasing the kids, telling them the first one to finish their breakfast could ski down the big hill with Dad today. The kids all opened their mouths wide to finish, and Daddy claimed it was a tie. Very diplomatic, as usual he could always pour on the charm when needed. To my amazement, the weekend flew by without any issues. But as soon as the kids were all nestled in their beds Sunday evening, I approached Hank with a resolve to get to the bottom of this.

"Hank," I said. "We need to talk." I continued on trying not to take on a superior attitude but was insistent that he answer every question put to him. I was amazed when he cooperated and spilled out his guts. By the time the evening had ended, a new arrangement was made that he would look for another doctor to work with. Dr. Hawkes just wasn't working out for him anymore, and Hank felt he could not continue to make progress if he stayed with him. We agreed that he would begin to find another doctor, and we went to bed not saying another word.

Chapter IV

Another year has gone by, and Hank's therapy has taken a turn for the worse. He claims he is still seeing the new doctor, but I feel he is still dressing on many occasions because he's stopped coming home for supper more and more. At first, I truly believed that the business was growing so fast that Hank's work load had increased to monumental proportions. The business just hit the two-million-dollar mark, so of course his plate was full. In the beginning, he would arrive home by ten o'clock but after a few months, the time would stretch out to eleven, twelve, even one o'clock in the morning. When he started to arrive home after midnight, that's when the situation hit the fan. We began to argue more and more in our waking hours. I would be asleep some nights when he got home as late as two or three in the morning, so I knew this lifestyle had to be confronted. Our fights became almost a regular occurrence and sometimes when the kids were present, they would be so agitated with tears and shouting that the situation was more than I could bear. It almost seemed as though Hank would deliberately pick a fight, so he would have an excuse to leave. Of course, I realized that leaving meant he would be dressing for the remainder of the day.

The fights became so prolific that I resigned myself to not drilling him every time he came home late. Instead I would pretend to be sleeping. I just couldn't face reality. My health began to suffer. Excruciating headaches plagued me from my shoulders up, and even my eyes and ears and cheeks ached. My jaw was locked to the point that I could not keep my dental appointment to have my teeth cleaned because I could not open my mouth wide enough. My right leg from the knee down was numb with pins and needles for three months now, and I slept all the time. It was so bad that one day, I was making the kids' beds and before I knew it, the kids were home from school, trying to wake me up while sleeping in one of their beds. Instead of making the beds, I was sleeping in their beds. I knew I had to see a doctor because I was having such trouble functioning. Hiding the truth from the entire world was becoming a monumental task, a task I just couldn't handle anymore. I was so disgraced by what my husband was doing. Instead of being angry, I was humiliated more. I felt he was committing adultery, making love to other women. God forbid if someone should learn of what our marriage was really like. After all, everyone thought we lived a charmed life, and everyone looked at us as the luckiest family, the perfect marriage. I knew better. My life was a horror show. My health was rapidly declining, and I didn't know how much longer I could hold on.

I began seeing my doctor regularly now because I was so ill. I was on a massive dose of anti-depressants and at one point, my doctor was thinking I might have MS because I was so sick. My doctor ordered a spinal tap, but it came back negative. I never told my doctor of my failed marriage because I was so ashamed of what my husband was doing. It wasn't MS. It was major, deep depression, and the black hole was so deep that I felt I would never escape this tortured life. I prayed constantly, asking God to please take away this anguish, but my life continued to tumble downhill.

• • •

The last two years of our marriage were even worse because I just couldn't cope anymore, and my depression continued to spiral downhill to the point I was in the deepest black hole ever. The hole just kept growing deeper and deeper. I felt I was falling into the depths of hell. Why couldn't the doctors help me? There had to be some kind of medication that would be affective. I became desperate and began to increase my daily dosage, hoping that the increase would lift me out of this black hole. But even that didn't work. I knew I had to scale back to the prescribed dose because I was beginning to trip over my tongue. I knew what I had to do. I had to leave Hank. My marriage was in shambles. I was a shell of myself. I was a shattered wreck. My life was in ruins.

Looking back now, I realize I must have been a heck of a lot stronger than I realized because as sick as I was, nobody recognized my ailments. I was still able to hide all my symptoms from the world. I was so ashamed. Instead, I should have been so furious. I should have let my doctor and the whole world know how horrendously, horrific my marriage was. And it was horrible because of Hank. His rapacious cross dressing had reached fever pitch, and something had to change. The more money he made, the more arrogant he became, and the more arrogant he became, the more I began to hate him. He was impossible to live with anymore. I knew I had to leave him. And it had to be today.

• • •

It was Tuesday morning, and I was exhausted after putting in a very restless night. Hank was still sharing my bed and when I rolled over last night, I could feel his body had been completely shaved from head to toe. I was repulsed and immediately pulled away from his side. His legs were smoother than mine. This was a first. Things were really getting out of hand. This madcap of continuous surprises made me so jittery, I felt as though I would jump out of my skin. I couldn't calm down, not in this panicky state. My nerves were rattled beyond repair. Cross dressing had reached its pinnacle. This obsession of Hank's was utterly out of control. Did he actually want to be a transvestite, or was he really trying to be a woman? Perhaps he was trying to be a woman and a man, or was he just trying to be a man in drag? Which was it? Was it one or the other, or was it all three? The preponderance of questions kept swelling in my head. What this actually was was a sick perversion that I couldn't manage anymore. This repugnant, shocking belief of what was happening to my husband was self-inflicted, while what was happening to me was being forced down my throat. I loathed what was happening to me. I loathed him. The thought of spending one more night with him in this house was beyond repulsive, it was nauseating. I began to gag with dry heaves and kept gagging four more times. My body was now revolting. It was telling me loud and clear that I had to stop vacillating and come to terms with some kind of a decision. I had to do something.

It was 2 in the morning, and I couldn't get back to sleep, not with Hank in my bed, so I got up and went downstairs and slept on the coach. My head was pounding. It hurt so badly. It was just like it was before I began taking my depression meds. My head ached from my shoulders to my head with aching teeth, ears, eyes, and cheeks. My anti-depressants stopped working. I couldn't even see straight because my eyes were so blurry. I was so sick. How in God's name was I going to get the kids off to school and still maintain my composure? My mind was shouting, calm down Mary, calm down. Take a deep breath, Mary, for pity's sake. I needed a solution right this minute. Please, dear God, help me! I'm reaching out to you. Please take this burden from me.

Why was I so afraid to make a decision? I was completely stuck. It probably was because Hank was so controlling. I didn't stand a chance of surviving if I left him. As difficult as it was to live with him, I knew it would be much worse if I left him. I knew he would make my life miserable. And my kids! What about my kids? They were so innocent. What would happen to my kids? How could I do this to them? But then again, how could I not. Suddenly, shame flooded over me like a raging waterfall. I was drenched in condemnation, and my self-control was slipping into a black lagoon. I, at long last, decided. I absolutely am leaving him t o d a y.

The kids came running down stairs, laughing and chasing each other, all excited because today they were all having a Halloween party in school. I had baked them all a dozen cupcakes with chocolate frosting and the words BOO written on their cupcakes and when they saw them, they squealed with delight. Kenny said, "Can you put ghosts on my cupcakes, Mommy?"

Izzy and Becky called out, "Me, too, Mommy, I want ghosts, too."

"Alright, you little monkeys," I said. "I'll put ghosts on all your cupcakes if you all promise to eat all your breakfast with no talking."

My head was splitting, and the thought of the three of them hovering over me while I was making ghosts would have done me in. I said, "And the first one that talks doesn't get any ghosts on their cupcakes."

They all scurried to their chairs and began eating their breakfast with the biggest smiles on their little faces. Not a creature stirred, not a sound was heard as I started to frost the ghosts on top of three dozen cupcakes. Boy, did I love these kids.

Breakfast went well as did the ghosts and when the school bus picked them all up at the end of our driveway, I breathed a sigh of relief. Now I could tell Hank that I wanted a divorce. As he came into the kitchen and poured himself a cup of coffee, I said, "We have to talk. I can't continue on like this anymore. You're killing me. I want a divorce. I'll leave you to your dignity and go out this morning while you pack up a bag and when I return, I don't want to see you here. We'll work out the details later."

I left the room feeling very brave but very scared, scared to death, as a matter of fact.

I drove to Dunkin Donuts and ordered a large coffee and a plain donut. I sat in the far corner, hoping none of my neighbors would pop in for their morning fix. Luckily, I remained anonymous. Dunkin Donut's coffee was always scalding hot, so I knew I could nurse this cup of coffee for a while before returning home. I wanted to cry and had all I could do to hold back my tears. I knew customers were looking my way, wondering how pathetic I looked. But I didn't care. It was more important to proceed with my plan than to worry about people staring at me. I was hoping the caffeine in my coffee would ease the dreadful pain in my head. The headache that just wouldn't quit was now consuming me, and I could feel my resolve slipping as well. I was just praying that Hank wouldn't be there when I returned home.

As I drove up the driveway, I saw his truck wasn't there. I instantly thought, thank goodness, I was safe. The kids had only a half day of school today because of their Halloween parties, so I knew they would be coming through the door any minute. I hurried inside and was stopped dead in my tracks. I couldn't believe the wreckage I was seeing. The destruction was beyond hellish. Hank had destroyed our home. All the rooms were covered with shattered glass and chards an inch thick on the floor.

As my eyes tried to focus on this horrendous destruction, I began to realize that Hank had broken every piece of glass in the entire house. All the dining room china and crystal had been crushed and even the leaded glass in the china cabinet doors had been smashed. The huge mirror on the dining room wall with gold leaf corners lay on the floor in ruins. My heart sank. This mirror was a wedding gift from my grandmother, which I treasured dearly. Hank knew this and had chosen to wipe it out anyway. How cruel. All the expensive vases and pottery, as well as the china lamps in the living room, were shattered into a million pieces, and all the art on the walls were slashed with a knife, leaving gaping holes in the canvases. The kitchen was beyond recognition with every single pot and pan thrown against the walls, which dented the damasked wall coverings. All my Lenox dishes were broken, each and every one of them. All of my specialty pottery pieces and serving pieces and trays were shattered as well. The silverware drawer had been yanked out of the cabinet, and all the silverware had been crushed with bricks. The beautiful six-foot bay window was decimated, frame and all, without a single pain of glass remaining. And the TV room was annihilated. The ceiling to floor drapes lay on the floor, rod and all. Even the upholstery had been slashed. What a disaster! It sickened me.

How could he do this to us, to our beautiful home? He had to be a madman. No, he was a madman masquerading in drag. Shock couldn't describe my feelings. I was so shaken with terror. Hank was terrorizing me. The house was a war zone. I was frozen in my tracks, stunned beyond belief. Then, to add insult to injury, my kids came running in all excited about their school parties. All three started crying the minute they saw the destruction. I didn't know what to do or say to calm them down. Without thinking, the words just fell out of my mouth, "Kids, let's all get in the car and go see Memere. There's been a robbery."

The kids, still crying, turned and went outside. I still had the keys in my hands locked in a tight, clinched fist. The keys began cutting a tear in the palm of my hand. I followed the kids out to the family car. As we drove away, I thought 'the nightmare has begun.'

• • •

My mother lived in the next town over, and it took us about thirty minutes to make the drive. As we pulled up, I could see my mom in the yard, raking up leaves into a great big pile. It was a glorious fall afternoon, almost an Indian Summer, and when the kids saw the big pile of leaves, they scooted out of the car and made a mad dash to the inviting pile plowing into them with giggles and yelps. I felt relieved that my kids were back to playing. Mom was surprised to see us.

"I thought it was a school day," Mom said.

I answered, "Kids had a half day today," and then went on to explain we were all celebrating Halloween early and thought we would surprise her. Halloween is supposed to be filled with surprises, right? How ironic! Mom hugged all the kids, and we all walked into the house for some yummy hot chocolate.

Before Mom entered the house, I pulled her aside and explained what had happened. Her face dropped in astonishment. I tried to assure her it would be alright. Hank was just a little bit nuts right now. I knew he didn't want a divorce, and he simply exploded. I wasn't home when he destroyed the house. Thank goodness. I was upset when I saw the destruction, but seeing it made me realize I was doing the right thing. I tried to downplay how extensive the damage was. I'll explain it all to you when the kids are not present.

"What a control freak," my mother said.

"Mom," I asked, "can we stay the night?"

"Of course, you can. Let's go in and have some hot chocolate. We'll barbeque hamburgers tonight. The kids will like that," Mom said.

The kids played happily all afternoon in the leaves and on the swings in my parents' back yard. It never ceases to amaze me how resilient kids can be. All they had seen and the shock they had experienced this afternoon seemed to just magically disappear. I wish the same could be said for me. When Dad came home from work, he was delighted to see us all and went out to start the barbeque for supper. Kenny went with him, saying he was the big man of the house, and he was going to help Pepere. My parents made supper fun singing songs, telling funny stories, and playing guessing games. After dinner was done, Dad brought out marshmallows for roasting over the grill. The kids were happy as clams.

• • •

The kids went to bed early that night after I read bedtime stories. As soon as I came back down stairs after tucking them in, my parents called out to me to join them in the kitchen for some coffee. It was then that I could explain to them exactly what had happened, and it was the very first time I told them about Hank's cross dressing. Of course, they were shocked, but they offered encouragement and said we could stay as long as needed until things settled down. It was a long conversation, and my parents offered parental advice, as was to be expected. One of their friend's daughters had recently been divorced, and she seemed to be making out quite well in spite of the divorce. My parents offered up her attorney, and I accepted. We agreed I would try to make contact the next morning.

All of us were pretty worn out by then, and we all turned in for the night. Once again, I couldn't sleep. I was hoping I would since I was so completely and utterly exhausted. But no such luck. I ended up tossing and turning for several hours. It must have been about 3:30 in the morning when suddenly, I heard some noise from the front yard. I wondered what could possibly be making such a noise from the street this time of night. It sounded like a bang of some kind. I pulled myself out of bed and crossed the room to look out into the front yard. It was almost a full moon, so the glow of the moon made it easy to see the street quite clearly, even though it was the dead of night. I couldn't believe what I saw. It was Hank with another man I did not recognize. They were quietly walking up my parents' driveway when suddenly, I saw Hank hop into my Thunderbird, start the engine, and take off down the street. I couldn't believe my eyes. It was bad enough he destroyed our home. Now he we was stealing my car under the cover of darkness right under my nose. The bastard! How was I going to get the kids to school now? No house and now, no car. I was right when I thought he would make our lives miserable if we left him. Did he really think that ruining our home and stealing my car would win me back, or was he just that incredibly mean when it came down to his controlling personality? I knew my parents would be very upset to learn that Hank had stolen my car overnight right out of their driveway. I was so depressed. The situation had turned from triumph to agony. As I walked back across the room, I thought to myself, I've lost two battles now. How difficult will winning this war be? For me and the kids, the beginning of the end had just begun.

• • •

Chapter V

Everyone managed to sleep well last night except me. I desperately needed to get some rest. Perhaps when I get the kids back to school and we are all back to a regular routine, I'll begin to feel better. I was up before any of them, so I started the coffee and was hoping for a few moments of peace and quiet. I was thinking how I was going to plan my day now that I didn't have a car. I had about $50 in my wallet, along with my charge cards, so perhaps the best thing would be to start with *first things first*. I needed clothes for the kids. We left in such a hurry yesterday that it never occurred to me that we would need a change of clothes. I guess I'll just have to borrow Mom's car and drive back to the house and pack up some clothes for me and the kids. The kids have a holiday today because it's All Saints Day, November 1st. I decided to make a list spelling out the most urgent items that needed to be addressed. I had to prioritize, so why was my mind not cooperating. I was tired, so tired. I started to yawn as I sipped my coffee and wished away my life. It was too early in the morning to focus on anything practical. I'll make the list after breakfast. Maybe I'll be able to think better with a full stomach. I couldn't move. I just sat there like a fool, like a completely dumb fool. I leaned back in my chair and realized that instead of chastising myself, I had to grow up, start being an adult, and stop being a cry baby. I had to take charge. I made myself some breakfast and did feel better after eating. I swallowed down three Tylenol because my head hurt and decided I would try to make that list now.

1. Call Attorney
2. Borrow Car
3. Drive to House
4. Pack up Clothes
5. Go to Bank
6. Return to Parents

That works, I thought to myself. Just then, the kids were coming downstairs saying they were hungry, what's for breakfast. I said, "How does pancakes sound, chocolate chip pancakes. Let's see if Memere has chocolate chips."

All three kids yelled, "Yeah!"

Izzy said so enthusiastically, "I love chocolate chip pancakes. They're my favorite."

"I know," I said. "That's why I suggested them."

That's when Mom popped her head into the kitchen.

"What's all this commotion I hear going on in my kitchen?" using a teasing voice. The kids all laughed, and Mom gave each of them a big squeeze.

"I was just starting to make the kids chocolate chip pancakes," I said. "Would you like some, Mom?"

"Never you mind making pancakes," Mom said. "Why don't you enjoy that cup of coffee all by your lonesome in the den, and let me spoil my grandchildren." I had to agree, that sounded real nice, so I nodded and left the kitchen for a little bit of solitary confinement. Mom started cooking, and the kids helped set the table for breakfast. They excitedly pulled out the plates and some silverware, got some butter from the fridge, and went searching for some maple syrup while Mom made pancakes on her griddle. All three kids were now sitting at the table with their mouths watering, waiting patiently. Mom started dishing out the pancakes, which didn't look too appealing to the kids. As a matter of fact, they looked a little burnt. She started plopping pancakes onto each of the kids' plates and when she got to Kenny, she said, "They look a little burnt, but I bet they still taste yummy." Then she said, "Pancakes aren't really my forte." Just then, Kenny looked up at Memere and said, *"What is your forte?"* He had the most charming sheepish grin on his face. Everyone started laughing. That's my Kenny, always finding levity in any situation. His precious personality always came shining through like a lightning bolt.

With breakfast finished, it was time to start our day. So while the kids were washing up, I made my first phone call to Attorney Durkson. He answered immediately. I was surprised. I asked to see him explaining as succinct as I could the need to see him quickly, and he said he had court at two o'clock, but if I could find my way to his office this morning, he would be happy to discuss my case. I was thrilled. Finally, I found someone who was in my corner who might actually be able to save me and my kids from experiencing any more catastrophes. I quickly ran upstairs to get ready for the day, explaining to Mom and the kids I had an appointment with Mr. Durkson, and asked the kids to be really good doo bees for their grandmother while Mommy was gone. I promised them I would be back for lunch and if they were especially good, we would all go to McDonald's for happy meals. The kids all yelled yeah. As I dashed out of the house, I was feeling the most positive I had felt in a long while. Maybe this is going to be a good day after all. It has to be better than yesterday. It just has to be.

It took a little while for me to find Mr. Durkson's office, but I finally managed to find a place to park my mother's car and entered the office building where the attorney's suite of offices was located. He greeted me warmly and after a half hour discussion of what had transpired over the past few days, along with the fact that Hank cross dressed, he agreed that we had to get into court quickly. The plan was to get me and the kids back into our home, hire a service to repair the damage Hank had done, and get me a car and some child support. It was obvious I couldn't run the household on just $50. It was then he requested a $1,500 retainer and explained he did not accept credit cards, but a check would suffice. I knew that kind of money was only in my savings account and explained that I would need to go to the bank to make a transfer of funds before writing a check. That response was agreeable to Mr. Durkson. We made another appointment for next week. By then the pleadings would have been filed in the Middlesex County Courthouse and hopefully a date set for a court appearance. It looked pretty promising. For the first time in years, I felt I had a future and that things might just begin to go my way. I left for the drive back to Mom's to pick up the kids for lunch.

Becky, Izzy, and Kenny loved their happy meals and after lunch, we all drove to my bank to transfer funds. I left the kids in the car with Mom while I hopped into the bank quickly. I was at the teller window with my transfer request when yet, another bombshell hit the fan. The teller was informing me that all the savings account had been depleted by Mr. Clark, my husband. I reeled with disbelief.

"Well then," I said. "I would like to make a withdrawal from my checking account." The teller pulled up that account on her computer and turned to me and said, "Your checking account has only $25 remaining. Your husband withdrew those funds this morning as well."

Embarrassed, I said, "Oh, I forgot Hank was doing the banking this morning. Thank you anyway," and left the bank completely dejected. Battle number three had been won by Hank. Was I ever going to begin winning one of these skirmishes with Hank? I walked solemnly from the bank and returned to the car. My mother saw the disappointment on my face and asked, "Is anything wrong?"

"I'm just tired, Mom, that's all. Let's drive back home. I think I need a nap. I didn't sleep well last night."

As we drove home, I was thinking, I can hardly keep my eyes open. I knew I had to get home quickly, or I might start driving erratically. Somehow I managed to make the trip without an incident. God was on my side at least for those few moments. My heart was breaking, my head was splitting, and terror was creeping into my soul. I kept telling myself, hang in there, girl. Remember the positive meeting you just had with Mr. Durkson. Just get you and the kids home safely to Mom's house. It will all work out in the end once we get into court. Just hang in there.

• • •

That afternoon, I slept for over two hours, and it was already four o'clock when I awoke. I realized I had not even picked up any clothes for the kids yet. Four o'clock, and my teeny-tiny to do list had not even been achieved. Why was the day flashing by so fast when only yesterday every single minute seemed to move in slow motion? My mind was wandering again. I simply could not hold on to a single thought for any length of time. The theory of relativity ran through my head. Einstein must have messed up the theory of relativity when it came to measuring time on earth. He only got the time in space portion right. How ridiculous my thinking was. My head was rambling again. I had no control over where my mind was taking me. I'll drive over right now and get the kids clothing for the next couple of days. It shouldn't take too long. If I hurry, I can be back in time for supper.

    I decided to get up and deal with the rest of my list. I was still so tired. I did manage to give myself a pat on the back, however, for being so determined to accomplish all I had wanted to achieve today. So, I kissed the kids goodbye and hurried off for the drive to Randolph. Traffic this time of day would probably be rush hour, so I decided to take Route 2. It was just five minutes longer than the usual way, but at least I wouldn't be stuck in bumper to bumper traffic all the way down Route 128. That would be an endless ride. The drive went smoothly and before I realized it, I was already pulling up to Maple Drive, my beautiful home outside at last. I thought to myself, I hope Hank didn't chop down all the hedges. I don't believe I just thought that. Hank is a good man; he's just a little nuts right now. When we all get into court, things will calm down, I'm sure of it. Hank will realize there's no turning back and accept the prospects of the divorce. After all, it's not the end of the world. He can still see the kids, and he has more than enough money to resettle in a beautiful home somewhere else. This really is the best scenario for everyone. Why was I so afraid to go along with this simple scenario before? The last four years were hell on earth and yet, I was so stuck trying to hide the truth from the entire world, I suffered needlessly for all those years. I was thinking it all made sense to me now. I was confident things were going to turn out just fine for all of us, even Hank.

    As I drove up to the house, I noticed a strange car sitting in the driveway. Was someone visiting Hank? It couldn't be because Hank's truck was not in the driveway, only this strange white car sat there in its place. I proceeded to the front door and started to turn the lock, but my key wouldn't fit. Oh no, did he actually have all the locks in the house changed this morning while he was robbing the bank accounts. It seemed he was always one step ahead of me. He was thinking like a madman while I was still thinking our lives would be getting back to normal shortly once the anger passed. I was furious now. This was just one more battle he was winning. Damn it! I knocked on the door and immediately, a stranger opened the door. He asked who I was, and I answered, "Who are you?"

The man said, "Mr. Clark hired me to guard the house while he was away. He wanted to keep the house safe."

"You mean he wanted to keep me out of the house," I yelled. "Let me in," I said in my most demanding voice. "This is my house, and I need to get some clothes for my children." The hoodlum extended his arms out to prevent me from entering and demanded to see some identification.

How dare he, I thought. Then, I stated defiantly, "I am Mary Clark, Mrs. Mary Clark, and my husband is Hank Clark. If my husband were home, I am sure he would allow me to get some things for the kids."

The body guard said, "I'm sorry, lady, but it was your husband who hired me to keep you out, and I have to answer to him, not you."

I was outraged. How dare he, how dare Hank, I thought. Where was Hank's head? Did he think that if he punished me enough times that I would give into his insane lifestyle? He had to have realized that once we got to court, it would all be over, like it or not. I tried to push my way into the house, screaming in a high-pitched voice I was going to call the police if he didn't let me in immediately. Suddenly, there was a police car pulling up to my house and as the officers got out of their cruiser, they approached me, questioning what was going on here. I turned and said to the hoodlum, "How dare you call the police on me."

He retorted, "I have my orders, lady."

"My name is Mrs. Clark, and I live here. I can prove it, officer," and I went scavenging through my bag to pull out my ID to prove who I was and begged the officers to let me into my house. The officer was annoyed and questioned whether I had a court order or not.

"I don't need a court order to get into my own house, officer," I said. "I live here, and this thug won't let me in. I just need to get some clothes for my kids."

"I'm sorry, lady, but your husband stopped by the police station earlier today explaining that an episode such as this might be taking place and to be on the lookout should Mrs. Clark try to enter the marital home. He explained that you had destroyed the house the day before, and he was just trying to protect the home from getting any further damage. Unless you have a court order, I cannot let you enter."

"I don't believe this is happening. I didn't destroy the house, my husband did."

At this point, the officer said, "We only have a 'he said, she said' scenario to go on. If you want to get into this house, you will have to get a court order because at this point, we do not know who to believe."

"Believe me," I said. "I'm the good person here, not Mr. Clark."

"I'm going to have to ask you to leave now. Please don't make this anymore difficult than it has to be."

I was completely flabbergasted. My heart was pounding out of my chest, and I was sure I was blushing because I could feel the heat radiating from my face. I realized I was not going to win yet another battle on this playing field. Score one more for Hank. I left without saying another word, completely overpowered by the injustice. I was beginning to realize just how tough the real world really was out there. I was way too innocent to live in such a hostile environment, and I wanted out. As I sat in my car, putting my keys into the ignition, I found myself taking a huge deep breath to try to calm myself down before heading home. The drive home was endless. I couldn't shake off the events that had just transpired. Time had literally stopped. Once again, Einstein entered my confused mind. I instantly tried to put such nonsense out of my head and to switch to mind control; stay calm, Mary, stay calm. I would be home soon in the safety of my parents' home with the people I cherished most in the world. I couldn't wait to see my kids. As I opened the front door, I sang, "Hello, everyone, I'm h o m e. Come give Mommy a big hug."

• • •

The next morning, Mom and I decided to take the kids to a thrift store to let them choose some new clothes to wear. I called it our instant remake. Mom knew of a great shop just ten minutes down Governor's Avenue, so we all hopped into the car, and off we went.

Mom was right. The thrift store was a gold mind. The store had the nicest choice of clothing for the kids, and I was even able to pick up a couple of tops and skirts for myself. At checkout my card was denied. I tried a different card, and that, too, was denied. My mom could sense my humiliation and offered to use her card to pay for the articles of clothing.

Really, I said to myself, even my credit cards, Hank? I thought to myself, you bastard.

Underwear for all of us was next on the list, so we all hopped back into the car to take a quick ride to K-Mart. By now it was lunch time and since the kids were being so very good, Mom and I decided to treat them to hot dogs and chips at the local café. They all had ice cream sundaes for desert, and we began calling our little adventure a wonderful back to the future vacation. They liked that, and all began to laugh.

The ride home was light hearted. All the children were playing the ABC game where each one of them would call out the first time they saw something that began with that letter. The one who scored the most points at the end would be declared the winner. As they began looking for A words, Izzy cried out, "Art store." Then Becky cried out, "Bus," and Kenney saw a car and said, "C for car."

The kids continued playing, all laughing. It was so simple to make my kids happy. Such a silly game could bring smiles to their faces so easily. I silently thought, oh, to be that innocent again. Before we knew it, we were pulling into my mom's driveway.

As soon as we returned home, the phone rang, and it was Mr. Durkson. He said he was suggesting to the court a date one week away because of the extenuating circumstances and was quite hopeful that the date would be granted after speaking with the court clerk moderator. Mr. Durkson said, "Free your entire calendar for next week because when we get the date, we will have to move quickly."

I thanked him for being so thorough so quickly. Mr. Durkson continued, "If you could bring the retainer with you the next time we meet, it would be appreciated."

"Of course," I said, "of course." Where was I going to get $1,500 on such short notice? The thought of having to ask my parents for a loan was downright degrading, but I could not think of any other alternative. I decided I would broach the subject with Mom and Dad after the kids were bedded down for the night.

• • •

Well, at least one predicament was resolved. Mom and Dad came through for me again and immediately wrote a check out to Mr. Durkson for $1,500. How grateful I was while at the same time, feeling like a school girl living at home with Mom and Dad. If the truth be told, I was a thirty-year-old woman wishing I could be a child again.

• • •

Sure enough, we were in court in seven days, and Mr. Durkson asked me to meet him at the courthouse by 9 am Tuesday morning. I agreed and as I was making my way, borrowing Mom's car again, I was thinking how tough these last few weeks actually were. They wore heavily on my health, but today, no headache, thank goodness. Thank you, Lord, and please watch over me today, I prayed. I had never been to the Middlesex County Courthouse before, and I was always bad at following directions when driving alone. It was always so difficult to read the directions, look for signs, and drive at the same time. Women were supposed to be multi-tasked, which I was, but for some reason, this challenge always made me anxious. The directions turned out to be much simpler than I had imagined, and parking was easy to find as well. As I walked up the courthouse steps, I was whispering out loud, stay calm, Mary, stay calm. And with a final deep breath, I opened the door to the courthouse and entered the building.

I was surprised when I saw Mr. Durkson because there was Hank with his attorney as well. I had not imagined seeing Hank here. I'll have to be sure to ask more questions in the future of Mr. Durkson, I thought. He needs to explain all the details and not assume I would know Hank would be here. I was rattled, and I didn't like it. Here I'm trying to play mind control to stay calm, and instead I'm being bamboozled because my attorney wasn't clear with me. I'm more than annoyed now, I'm really fuming. I don't even know how to confront Hank. This was not in my plan. Is Hank going to approach me, because I'm sure as hell not going to approach him. I need to speak with Mr. Durkson in private right now before we enter the courtroom.

"Good morning, Mr. Durkson," I said. "I'm right on time as promised."

"Good," replied Mr. Durkson. "Let's go into this private anti-room. I want to explain how today's proceedings will go. There are some things I want to explain to you before we get into court."

I followed my attorney into the anti-room and closed the door. And I spoke before Mr. Durkson even had a chance to open his mouth.

"You never told me Hank was going to be here. You explained to me that this was a simple procedure to get me and my kids back into our house. You never told me Hank was going to be here, and with his attorney no less."

Mr. Durkson said "I'm sorry I was not clearer with you. I naturally assumed you would know that he would be here, and I do apologize for misleading you. In the future, I will be more explicit. I do realize that this is a first-time experience for you. The last few weeks have been rather unsettling for you, and I am sorry that this is all happening to you and your children."

Unsettling didn't even begin to tell the story, I thought.

"Thank you, Mr. Durkson."

"Mary, please call me Tom. We have to be comfortable with each other if we are going to work well together. What I need from you now, however, is for you to stay calm." He went on to explain what to expect once inside the courtroom, prepped me on some questions I might be asked, and told me these things never started on time and to please try to wait patiently.

"We don't want Hank to see you pacing up and down the corridor before our case has even begun. We need to look confident that we are in the right and that justice will prevail for you and your children today."

I agreed, and we sat quietly. He handed me a book and said, "Pretend you are reading while we are waiting to get inside." I agreed. We were still waiting a half hour later, and I was trying to be so strong and self-assured. I played drama when I was in high school, so I knew I could pull this off. I was proud of myself because not once did I glance Hank's way. It was difficult, but I did manage to maintain my composure. Just then the doors opened, and the bailiff ushered us into the courtroom. My attorney led the way, and I obediently followed. Just as we sat, the Judge entered the courtroom and proceeded to his bench. Then the bailiff said, "All rise for the honorable Justice Harry S. Ginsberg." After the judge was seated the bailiff said, "Please be seated."

Tom whispered in my ear, "Just follow my lead and when I want you to speak, I will let you know. Understand?"

I obediently nodded.

And so the case began. At first, it was a lot of humdrum legal mumbo jumbo, but then it became time for Hank to speak when the Judge asked him to explain himself.

Hank began a long tirade of accusing me of being a drug addict, saying, "If you put that woman in my house with my children, she will probably burn the house down. After all, she has already demolished everything inside the home as of last week, and I can't trust that she won't harm my children!"

I was stunned. I sat there numb. These lies were irreprehensible. My lawyer whispered, telling me what to say and how to say it when I was called upon by Judge Ginsberg. He then told me to cry if I could. Tears were always a strong defense. That may be so for someone else, I thought, but for me, it would send me spiraling off a cliff. I knew if I cried, I would lose it. Mind control Mary, stay calm. My lawyer continued to whisper a few last-minute instructions and then it was my turn to speak.

"Okay, Mrs. Clark," said Judge Ginsberg, "what have you got to say about these allegations your husband is accusing you of?"

I tried to explain that everything he just said was an outrageous lie and a deliberate attempt to smear my good name. In fact, he was the one who destroyed the house. "My children and I are presently living with my parents because he had locked us all out of our home. Please let me back into the house because my kids need to get back to school."

That's when all hell broke out. Hank was now defending himself with such despicable lies, and I was too thunderstruck to reply. I was speechless. The bogus fictitious lies he was telling were beyond the pale. I was thinking, Hank, what are you doing? Don't you realize you are hurting your kids? Suddenly, the Judge banged his gavel, bang, bang, bang, bang, bang, bang, and said, "Mr. Clark. That is quite enough. I am going to hold you in contempt of court if you do not get control of yourself." His attorney nudged his elbow and motioned for him to sit down and then leaned over and said something to him. I imagined it was 'shut up.'

Now the truth be told. Judge Ginsberg began to talk for quite a while, claiming he did not know who to believe. There was such disparage between testimonies that he was not quite sure how to rule. His concern at this point was for the children. They needed stability in their lives and being shuffled between home and grandparents, missing school, and being out of their normal routine had to be playing havoc on their lives. In view of this, I have no choice but to rule that the children become wards of the state and be removed from their grandmother's home immediately and placed in foster care."

"NO, NO," I cried. "Please don't do this. My children are so good, they do not deserve to be punished this way, especially so close to the holidays."

The judge glared at me, and I thought for a moment he would hold me in contempt, instead of Hank.

Then the Judge continued, "And furthermore, I order that psychological testing be done on the entire family, both separately and as a family unit, for a period not less than three months at which point the court will decide how to rule based on the psychological report. Further, the children shall have a guardian ad lebiam appointed so their best interests will be served. Finally, the court will appoint a state psychologist to conduct these evaluation sessions. This is my ruling. This is final."

He then banged his gavel, stood up, and left the courtroom.

I was annihilated. I was left an empty shell of a mother in despair as I fell onto the court bench. I turned to my attorney enraged and crying, "What just happened?" I was utterly and completely obliterated. Today, I walked into court, trusting my attorney. I walked into court with no house, no car, no clothes, no money, no bank accounts or credit cards. I walked into court with absolutely nothing, and now, I was walking out of court without my kids. This is beyond a nightmare. This is hell on earth, my kids, my precious kids.

"Do something," I said emphatically. "Do something, Tom. Go talk to the Judge in his chambers. The kids can't go into foster care. They can't live with complete strangers. Please do something, Tom. Do something."

He was not pleased with the Judge's ruling either and explained that this was not over. He told me he was going to speak with Hank's attorney immediately and between the two of them, hammer out some other kind of arrangement for the children. This had gotten completely out of hand now. My attorney wanted Hank's attorney to talk to his client, explain to him what he was doing to his children because the repercussions could be dreadful.

My attorney walked me out of the courtroom and asked me to wait while he met with Hank's attorney. They both disappeared and were gone for several hours. I was left in the hall with Hank. Here I was with Hank, the very person I loathed for sure now. How could he do this to our children? I was afraid to speak to him for fear I would punch him in the face I was so angry. I walked down the other end of the hall, trying to keep away from the bastard. I wanted to kill him. At that very moment, I wanted him dead. If looks could kill, Hank would be strung out horizontally on the courtroom floor totally and utterly and completely dead as a door nail. This was a side of Hank I never saw before, and I didn't know how to handle it. My husband had become perverse, and now he was truly despicable and vicious. I couldn't stand to be in the same room with him. I reached the end of the hallway and almost tripped over one of the benches because I was walking with my eyes filled with tears. I was fighting so hard to keep my eyes opened. This can't be happening; please tell me this is not happening. My mind couldn't handle this defeat. I started to cry and pulled some tissues from my pocketbook to blot my tears. I pressed my lips tight and sniffled and tried to stop crying, but my eyes continued to tear. I couldn't stay in the moment. I bit my lip, forcing myself to come to attention. All I could think of was that three months was an eternity for small children.

They would feel as though they had been abandoned after such a long time. What would this do emotionally to my children? It had to have a deleterious impact on them. It would ruin them. These happy go lucky kids would be so sad. I always saw a scene like this in the movies, but I never thought for one second that it would be happening to me in real life. My kids would be crying just like in the movies, only it would be hard cold reality front and center.

Suddenly I thought of an even worse situation. What if they were all placed separately? All of them would be alone with no one to comfort them. At least if they had each other to lean on, perhaps the unbearable would become bearable. Please don't let this be the case. Oh, Hank, I thought, for goodness sake, tell the judge you didn't mean what you said. Tell the judge you want me and the kids in our home. Tell the judge we will go to counseling, but please, let my kids live at home. Let my kids go, Hank, please!

I left the courtroom hoping the fresh air might do me some good. The whole truth and nothing but the truth was repeating and repeating in my head. I was beginning to learn that the whole world lies, even in court. I knew I should not have left him. I knew he would make our lives a catastrophic hell on earth. He was such a control freak. Between that and his dressing, what ever happened to that nice guy I married? Money, it was money. They say it's the root of all evil. It's far worse than that. It is Satan himself, living inside Hank's head telling him do this, do that, that a boy. If you listen to me, you will get your own way. Don't fret, Hank. Satan will take care of all your needs. Mary needs to be punished for leaving you. Keep up the good work, and follow my every desire, and you will break Mary. Victory will be yours.

Crying had swelled my eyes, and I had to blow my nose several times to clear my sinuses. No matter how many times I wiped my eyes, they continued to remain wet. I saw a bench just up ahead and knew I had to sit down or I'd fall down. It was covered with ice, but I didn't care. I wish I had my winter coat. After about five minutes, my legs began to become a bit more stable. I knew I had to return to the courthouse. By now my bum was stone cold from sitting on the ice, and I started to shiver. I silently said a prayer to St. Jude, Saint of the impossible. If ever there was an impossible situation, it certainly was now, right here, right now. I knew when I returned I would have to put up with Hank's face. Please let me be strong. I don't want to see Hank's face. I knew that if I saw his face, I would lose control of my calm, the very thing Mr. Durkson warned me about.

It was now 4 o'clock. The entire day had been spent in court and still here I sit. Actually, I was beginning to get scared because if a compromise had been reached, I surely would have heard of it by now. That's when the door finally squeaked open, and Mr. Durkson waved me into the courtroom. He told me he and Hank's attorney presented the Riley alternative to Judge Ginsberg, and he said he would take it under advisement. He is now ready to rule on his decision.

As the judge returned to the courtroom, I was told to approach his bench along with Hank. I was trembling, but Mr. Durkson assured me they had reached a resolve that he thought would be acceptable to me. Your friends, Mr. and Mrs. Riley, agreed to take care of the children for as long as needed. So Hank and I approached the bench and there we stood, waiting for the judge to render his verdict. I intentionally made the point to stand as far away from Hank as possible while still standing in front of the bench. The thought of Hank accidentally bumping into me should he sway my way was repulsive. I had to protect myself and not let him touch me, not now or ever again.

As Hank and I stood in front of the bench, the judge began to inform us that he was changing his original court order from foster care to having the Clark children stay with the Riley's while the family was in crisis. The judge then stated that his decision was in effect immediately and continued talking, but I didn't hear anything except that my kids would not be going into foster care, what a relief. The judge banged his gavel softly and disappeared into his chambers. No foster care, but the Riley's instead. Thank goodness. Hank and I stood there, still trying to digest all that the judge had just emphasized. I turned and left Hank standing there all by himself.

"Mary," Tom said. "I know this is unfair and very trying." Over the next three months, every one of the judge's requirements has to be met, regardless whether or not you get a flat tire, get sick with a bad headache or just can't get your parents' car to visit the kids."

I interrupted, "Why can't I at least get my car back?"

Tom replied, "Social Services doesn't care whether you own a car or not. They are only concerned about the welfare of the children. Take a bus if you have to."

Now I was really becoming agitated stating, "There is no bus service between Medford and Randolph."

"Then take a taxi," Tom said.

"Where am I going to get money for a taxi?"

"Borrow it from your parents," Tom retorted, "if you have to. Look, Mary, I know this is challenging and very complicated, but don't argue with me. I am already on your side."

I huffed, "I'm sorry. I know it sounded like I was scolding you. I'm just so worn out from this whole process. I know that the report presented by the psychologist to the judge will redeem my good graces. I will get my kids back once the court learns all about exactly how horrible Hank actually is. I promise I will be good. I will do whatever Social Services asks of me. I will get my kids back, right, Tom?"

"Yes," said Tom. He then went on to explain the court will be appointing a social worker for the kids who will meet with them once a week on Fridays. I thought, I can just imagine the drilling questions that will be asked of my children. How are they supposed to process questions when they are too small to begin to recognize feelings or understand their emotions? What a frustrating process Hank had forced me and the kids into. I never thought he could be so revengeful. My attorney continued to explain all that was required of me as I painfully listened to every exacting detail. As he continued on, I silently said a prayer in my head, 'please take this burden from me, please.'

• • •

As I drove home, I was trying to think of what I would tell the kids about their new living arrangements. I probably should say they would be moving for a short time, that they were going on a vacation while their house was being repaired and that as soon as the work was completed, they would be returning home. Luckily for them, they get to stay with the Riley family during this time.

All four of their children are friends of yours and you all go to the same school, so it makes perfect sense that this is the best solution for now. We certainly can't live in the house the way it is, so for now, this is best. Of course, Mommy and Daddy will be visiting you kids all the time you're staying with the Riley's. As I continued driving, I decided that this explanation might be all the kids could handle. No need to tell them they were wards of the state and that Mommy and Daddy had to obey everything that Social Services ordered of them. I was hoping Social Services would not be too rigid with their demands, but from what I heard from Tom, their standards were sometimes very difficult to meet. Enough thinking for one day, Mary, I thought. Just keep driving home.

Chapter VI

I first met Christine Riley at a parent teacher conference. Our girls were in kindergarten at the time. We were surprised to learn we lived just around the corner from each other. I liked Christine instantly. She was quite engaging, and conversation flowed from her quite effortlessly. She was so easy to talk with. As for me, I never did well with small talk. I always had to have a subject to discuss, or my chatter just wasn't free flowing. When talking with Christine, she always carried the bulk of the conversation, which made it easy for me to converse with her. We first got together with a quick lunch at her place, and I really enjoyed her hospitality. Little did I know then that this camaraderie would be the beginning of a very special friendship.

We both were practicing Catholics, and our value systems were quite similar. Pretty soon we began getting together more often to do various craft, sewing, or quilting projects, that sort of thing. We were both members of our church lady's guild and worked the holiday bizarre every year. Our booth sold all sizes of little and big dolls clothes. Everything from pajama wear to evening gowns. We worked together the entire fall season, getting ready for this huge event held downstairs at our church and always sold out our entire booth, what fun.

As the years moved along, our families became interwoven in our everyday lives. If we didn't see each other for a while, we would visit with a friendly phone call. We were just so much alike. How lucky for me. Christine was my constant companion.

It was at that time that Hank and I were fortunate to own a summer home in Maine, and the kids and I would spend our entire summers enjoying the beach and all the other activities this beautiful seacoast village had to offer. The Riley's were a big part of our summers in Maine. Sitting on our deck at high tide was breathtaking, and the channel was never the same color because of how it reflected off the sky. There were days when the water was navy blue and then sometimes it was steel grey, sky blue, or even pinkish pale blue. That was my favorite pale, pale blue. I tried to match that color in our bedroom. It made the room so serene, it had a calming effect.

As you looked out, you could see peaceful flowing waters with a backdrop of pure white sand dunes high as mountains and behind the dunes, a tip of the ocean could be seen beckoning. The twisting constant sound of the ocean was always present. That constant hum was calming and peacefully serene to our human psyche. But the most amazing was the smell of the ocean. The minute you stepped outside the cottage, you knew you were not in Kansas anymore, only Maine could smell that way. What a delicious perfume fragrance. It encompassed you permeating the entire air and if you were inside with a window open, the aroma filled the space with fresh sweet-smelling ocean breezes. Hank would always join us on weekends, and summers in Maine for the first seven years of our marriage were magical.

Our home was right on the water in a small gated community with a large recreational hall where all the kids would gather every night after supper after a long day at the beach. There was candy, ice cream, and sodas to be had, ping pong to play, a juke box for dancing, bingo, board games, talent shows, scavenger hunts, penny sales, and more. The activities were endless, and the kids always were all lined up at the hall, waiting for the doors to open every night at 7 o'clock sharp. Summers were enchanting and always slipped away much too fast.

We had many weekend guests, but our regulars were the Riley's. Their entire brood of four kids and our three really blended well. Christine and I were best friends, and our husbands got along so well, you could tell they thoroughly enjoyed each other's company. Hank and Dave could always be found enjoying a cold beer on our sun-filled deck where a lot of laughing could be heard. Both men enjoyed puttering, and they were always doing some little kind of enhancement to the summer cottage.

Whenever the Riley family came up, all the kids made it a point to dig for clams on the clam flats during low tide. The channel flats were loaded with hundreds and hundreds of clams with great big bellies. The kids always managed to bring home at least two or three gallons each time out, which was more than enough to serve the crew of seven kids. Digging was so easy. I would steam them all up and the kids downed those clams before you could say, who's hungry. There was always such laughter on those weekends. Life was good. Life was extraordinarily good.

So you see, rather than force Becky, Izzy, and Kenny into foster care, I knew the Riley's would come through for us. It was an enormous favor to ask of them, but I was desperate at the time, and I knew Christine would understand. I would have done the same for her had the situation been reversed. Our lives were truly interwoven from the start, and that's why it was easy to suggest their help with our children.

• • •

As soon as I got home from court, the first thing I did was call Christine. As I dialed the phone, I was thinking, there is no way I will ever be able to repay her for this tremendous act of kindness. The phone rang just once when Christine picked up.

"Christine," I said. "How can I ever thank you for what you are doing for my kids."

"Never mind that," Christine said. "What is going on? I couldn't believe the phone call I received from Judge Ginsberg asking for my help with your kids."

"Oh, my God, the judge actually called you at home?" I questioned.

"Yes," Christine said. "The judge called me at home asking for my help with your kids for the next three months. He explained that your family was in crisis and that the situation was desperate. Of course, I said yes, but to tell you the truth, I'm a bit stunned. What the heck happened?" It was then for the first time that I actually told Christine the true story.

I explained, "Hank dresses up like a woman. It's a compulsion that has gone perverse over the last four years, and I just can't live like this anymore. Our marriage has been sliding downhill for a while now. When I asked him for a divorce ten days ago, Hank became unglued and went completely ballistic. I never told you. I never told anyone. I was too embarrassed. I was so terribly ashamed and humiliated because I bore the disgrace of Hank's cross dressing for all these years. I always tried to hide the truth from the outside world, even you, Christine." I continued to explain what had been going on over the course of our marriage, and Christine simply could not grasp the full scope of the problem. She had no idea things were so dire.

"Oh, Christine," I said, "things went so terribly wrong in court today because of Hank. He told lies that I could not prove bogus without proof. The judge didn't know who to believe, so rather than put the kids in jeopardy, the judge took my kids away and ordered them into foster care. I'm desperate for help right now, Christine, because if you don't take them, the kids will all be placed in separate foster homes. I can't thank you enough. Words cannot express how grateful I am to you."

"Never mind all that. You know taking care of kids is easy for me, so don't fret about that. They are in good hands and will be well taken care of for as long as you need me." It was then that I realized beyond a shadow of a doubt what an invaluable wonderful friend Christine actually was. I then went on to explain that the judge won't allow the kids and me back into the house for fear of being harmed by Hank. I continued saying I would be allowed into the house tomorrow but only under police supervision with a social worker present as well. I would have only two hours to get the kids belongings and complete the transfer to your house, so I won't be able to get all their things. I will try to get as much as I can though. Right now Hank is extremely impulsive and unpredictable, and the judge is unbending when it comes to the house and vehemently refuses to let the kids and me back into our home. Hank is out of his mind right now and I don't know how to handle him, let alone manage through this situation. I don't know the time of the transfer, but it definitely will be tomorrow. The social worker will introduce herself to the children at that time before I bring them over to your house. As soon as I get the exact time, I'll let you know."

As Christine continued to talk, I thought it has already started. Social Services are now calling the shots. I have no say, but only to obey. Between the police escort and the social worker taking my kids tomorrow, I feel like a convicted criminal rather than the innocent victim. I'm being punished for Hank's outrageous misconduct. Why didn't the judge hold him in contempt when he was ranting and raving? At least then he would be spending a night under lock and key. He should have been punished for what he did; after all, he is breaking the law. Isn't stealing a car grand larceny? So why didn't the judge have him arrested? Instead the judge took my kids away from me. Where's the justice here? There is none. There is only the law and right now, the law isn't working for me. Hank just continues to win battle after battle, and I continue to keep losing my entire life. I'm beginning to wonder if I will be able to come out of this situation unscathed. I thought it would be a simple divorce. Instead it is turning out to be a domestic battle between the have's and the have not's.

As I hung up the phone, I decided it would be best to have an early supper tonight, so I could take the kids to the movies. I needed to do something special with the kids tonight since this would be their last night with me and their grandmother. Talk about the last supper! We could make the 6:30 show if we hustled. That way the kids would still get to bed at a reasonable hour. They always liked going to the movies, and the theatre right in Medford square was showing Bambi tonight. I'll fill them up with popcorn, and they will never know how sad their mother is. I don't know why Hank is doing this. He had a chance to renege everything he said in court and refused to recant his statements. He is such a bastard. It's one thing to punish me but to punish the children is beyond reprehensible, it's unforgiveable.

The night was a huge success and after the kids were asleep, I decided to turn into bed early myself. I couldn't stop worrying about tomorrow's events. How would Becky, Izzy, and Kenny react tomorrow? What if Kenny started to cry? And Becky, my sweet Becky, would undoubtedly cry knowing Mommy wouldn't be there after school. She was always so affectionate and looked forward to my hugs and kisses. How would no kisses from Mommy affect her? I wasn't really worried about Izzy. She was quite the independent young lady, even though she was only ten. Tomorrow will eventually come, like it or not. The inevitable is planned for 2 o'clock, and I have no say in it. How frustrating. This whole situation could have been avoided had it not been for Hank.

My mind was reenacting the day's events and being so restless, I felt I would never fall asleep. But I did sleep through the night. I was so relieved that for the first time in weeks, I was able to sleep without waking before dawn. I must have been more worn out from this whole ordeal than I realized. I awoke feeling well rested for the first time in months. I prayed, please, let this day go without incident.

The kids and I all had to be at the house by 2 o'clock where the police and social worker would be waiting for our arrival. If I could have run away, then I would have but with no money or car, I was doomed from the start of not being successful. Besides, where would I go? The silent voice in my head began to speak again, saying, start focusing on what is required of you today, Mary. Stay calm, Mary, stay calm. I was hoping that Hank would not be there, but with a police presence, I felt secure. What was I thinking? I didn't feel secure in front of the judge, and isn't he a higher authority than a police officer? Look what happened to me in court yesterday. Today could be even worse.

What was Hank planning? I must plan for the unexpected because up until now, Hank has always been one step ahead of me. I kept telling myself to settle down, settle down, Mary. So I crawled out of bed to begin my arduous day. I had to wrap my head around what was expected of me today and not get side tracked with needless worry and meaningless emotions. So I got up, got dressed, and went downstairs to start the coffee.

The transfer went easier than was expected and believe it or not, Hank never showed up. He caused all the havoc and wasn't present to see the result of his mayhem. I was grateful. I was surprised the kids didn't cry when I left them with Christine. I guess my story about an adventure at the Riley's paid off. Score one for me, finally!

The next few days seemed to drag on and drag on incessantly. I did manage to get all my belongings organized into my parents' home and was thankful I could hold my attention to the task. My first visiting day would be Tuesday, and I couldn't wait. Perhaps I should bring the kids a special treat. I know I can bring a dozen frosted cupcakes saying vacation time. That will solidify the lie of going on vacation. I can't remember the last time I was away from the children. I missed them dreadfully.

At last, Tuesday was finally here. It was unusually cold today, and winter was beginning to set in for the long cold frost. Living in New England meant living through four seasons, and the winter season was my least favorite, except for the holidays. The sky was completely dark gray with not a streak of sun shining through. What a drab, gloomy day, I thought. But my spirits would be picked up at 7 o'clock tonight when I get to see the children.

As I was driving over to see the kids, I thought they all would love to play the game Chutes and Ladders, so the game board was sitting in the backseat of my car. Damn it, I must be hitting every red light from Medford to Randolph. My timing is in perfect sync with every traffic light from here to Timbuktu. Once again, Einstein's theory of relativity shot through my head. My mind was playing tricks on me again. Get back to reality. Einstein has nothing to do with red lights, Mary. For heaven's sake, get it together, girl. Get a grip!

Finally, after driving an extra 20 minutes because of all the red lights, I finally pulled up to the Riley's driveway when all of a sudden, my head did a double take. I could have sworn I saw Hank's truck. No, it couldn't be. Your mind is really playing tricks on you now. I thought, I must really be tired. As soon as I get home tonight, I'm going to bed. While I was walking up the pathway to Christine's front door, I was thinking, I can't wait to see the kids. Then another bombshell hit. Christine was telling me it was Hank's truck I saw, only Kenny and Becky were in the truck as well.

"Whatever happened, Christine? Why on earth did you let Hank take Becky and Kenny out tonight when you knew it was my night to see the kids?"

"I had no choice," cried Christine. "He came into the house without knocking, and I never heard him enter. By the time I came back downstairs, Hank had already put Becky and Kenny's coats on and was saying goodbye.

He promised to have them back by 9 o'clock. I was so annoyed, I actually yelled at him saying he had no right to take the kids out because it was your night to visit and that you would be coming through the door any minute. Hank flipped, said that any minute was now and left the house. What should I have done, called the police?"

"Of course not, Christine, I'm sorry to put you through this. I will be reporting this to the social worker first thing in the morning, and she will advise how to handle this situation should it happen again in the future. I know there is no arguing with Hank. Once he gets his mind made up, it is unchangeable. Can I stay and wait for them to return? I would like to at least tuck them into bed tonight?"

"Of course," Christine said. "Let's sit down and have a real visit for a change. We haven't been able to do that for a while now. Explain to me everything because there are still some parts of this scenario I don't fully understand."

After filling Christine in with more details, two hours had passed more quickly than I had anticipated, and it was already 9 o'clock. Just then I could hear a car pull up the driveway and sure enough, it was Hank's truck with Becky and Kenny.

"You had no right," I reminded him.

Hank responded with an insolent bullish remark, "I have every right, they are my children."

"Your children," I said. "Where have you been for the last four years? You are never home, never make it home for supper, never make it home for the kids' bedtime, never make it home for my bedtime either. And you have the gall to call these kids your children."

I was so furious with him, I almost bit my tongue. All of a sudden, he was playing the doting father. I was fuming, but I didn't want to make a scene, so I let it ride, knowing that tomorrow I would deal with it when I spoke with the social worker. Tomorrow morning when the clock strikes 9 am, I will be on the phone with social services. They'll straighten you out once and for all, I thought.

The next morning, I was on the phone with social services but had to leave a message because the case worker was out of the office. As I hung up, I thought, I'll just follow up this phone call this afternoon. Unfortunately, when

I did follow up the morning phone call, the social worker had not yet returned to the office. I left my message again. The next day, the social worker never returned my phone call. I was beginning to wonder if this was how the next three months would play out. I knew social services was understaffed, but this was ridiculous. My kids were in trauma, and their case worker could not even be reached. If this continues, I will insist on speaking with the supervisor.

• • •

The days dragged on before the kids started their psychological testing. This incessant waiting was so difficult. By now I had obtained a part-time job which helped ease the waiting a bit. At last after waiting another week, the court finally scheduled the court ordered sessions. It was only five more days away, so I knew I could hang in there until then. Five days seems like an eternity, but I could do it if I put my mind to it. I was becoming stronger when it came to waiting now. I was doing a better job of staying in the moment, so waiting was not as painful as it was in previous days.

The day finally arrived, and it was pouring rain. What a dreadful day to be traveling. I always had trouble driving in the rain, but I knew I could do it when forced to. So, I loaded the kids into the car wearing their warmest clothing and used plastic garbage bags as their raincoats. Mom had a bunch of umbrellas, so I took all of them so each one would have their own. They could stay dryer that way instead of sharing. As I was parking the car Izzy said, "I'm not going in. That's all there is to it. I'm not going in."

"Izzy," I said, "Please don't be difficult today. I need everyone to behave themselves today. This is a very important day. The sooner we get this over with, the sooner we can all go back to our home. Please try to cooperate, Izzy."

"I'm not going in," said Izzy as she folded her arms and put a puss on her face. Becky and Kenny just sat there, not saying a word. At least they were cooperating. Izzy refused to get out of the car. It was still raining quite steadily. No matter how much I insisted Izzy get out of the car, she continued to refuse my request. I finally had to leave her in the car while I proceeded to the door with Kenny and Becky.

The appointment started on time, and the psychologist immediately observed that Izzy was not present. I couldn't believe it, but the psychologist got up and proceeded to dress for the weather, informing me that he would be going out to the car to try to coax her in and would I please accompany him while his assistant stayed with Kenny and Becky. I was surprised, but thankful that this doctor was so thorough in his practice. But then I thought it was probably required by the court order that he observe Izzy's behavior for a precise and detailed evaluation. He stayed out in the rain, talking through the car window with Izzy for ten minutes. She refused to let him in the car or roll down the window. What a little brat. I wanted to demand her obedience but decided not to interfere, so I silently stood with the good doctor out in the rain. By the time we returned to the office, we were both shivering and so his assistant brought us warm towels and hot coffee to warm us up. Warm towels I was thinking, this must be a regular occurrence, standing in the rain with patients. Why else would they have warm towels? I wasn't complaining and really appreciated the warmth on my cold skin.

The psychologist interviewed both Kenny and Becky separately, and I was not allowed in to observe either session. I had never been evaluated before and was wishing they would have scheduled me first. That way I would at least know what the kids were experiencing. I was trying hard not to imagine the worse, but it was hard. After all, those were my kids in there being questioned. The two hours dragged on but finally, the door opened and both Kenny and Becky emerged from the psychologist's office appearing to be okay. I was relieved because they seemed to have taken the episode in stride. Of course, they didn't realize what was going on. How could they? They were so young.

The psychologist informed me that the sessions went as was expected and that he would see them again next week. He then told me, "Mrs. Clark, I was not able to work with Izzy today and was very disappointed that I could not coax her out of the car. I am very concerned about her mental state. I feel she is so angry that having sessions with her at this time will be counterproductive. However, I do need to tell you that she will have to come to terms with this when she is 18 or 19-years-old because symptoms will begin to rear their ugly head. In a perfect world, it would be so much easier on Izzy if we could help her now at her young age. Unfortunately, that is not the case. I suggest you not press her into counseling at this time; it would only make matters worse. I look forward to seeing Kenny and Becky next week."

"Thank you, Mr. Nelson. I appreciate your extraordinary measures today in trying to help Izzy. In the meantime, I will try to make their lives as normal as possible. Thank you for your time today."

Over the next few weeks, the sessions went as expected. Individual sessions went well, but the family in group was troubling. Hank's true colors came out loud and clear, and the psychologist did not miss a trick. I can just image how revealing Hank's individual sessions were going given his performance during group sessions. He was only hurting himself with this macho approach. How stubborn he could be. Only this time, his stubbornness would only bring him misery. It was so obvious that he was not in his right mind. I was beginning to think that his cross dressing was only symptomatic of a much bigger problem. I hated these sessions. It always upset the children to see their father so agitated. After a session like this, I would always be forced to try to calm the children down. Sometimes finding the right words was difficult. How do you explain to the children that everything will be alright when in your heart you are wondering if it will turn out for the better? Oh, how I hate these sessions!

Chapter VII

It's been six weeks now since the family began our individual evaluation sessions and so far, things are going well, that is, for Kenny and Becky. Izzy never attends. She is still too angry and stubborn to cooperate, so going forward, only Kenny and Becky will be evaluated by the appointed court psychologist. I am hoping that the psychologist will list in his written remarks that it was important not to push Izzy into these sessions at this time for all the obvious reasons. As far as I can tell, there is no obvious impact on either Kenny or Becky attending their individual sessions. They never complain about going, and they seem to be unscathed after each session; so I am assuming that the psychologist is taking it slow with them considering their young ages. All three children seem to be adjusting to their new temporary home, and Hank is sticking to his schedule when it comes to visiting the kids after being scolded by social services for his bad behavior, as if scolding is going to prevent further incidents from occurring.

    I was right, scolding wasn't sufficient because two weeks later, Hank picked up the kids on my night of visitation. When I got to Christine's house, I was furious. Of course, there was nothing Christine could do to stop him except use her words. She had her marching orders from Social Services as well. She was only supposed to try to stop him verbally without causing a scene. Wasn't that a contradiction? Words can be incredibly confrontational, too, and Hank could retaliate with some pretty tough language when challenged. If this is the way Social Services is going to react every time Hank takes the children, when do I get to see them? Social Services still doesn't realize who they are dealing with if they think scolding would be enough to stop Hank. This was the most controlling man I ever knew. You can't hold back a control freak. He will win every time. Hank continued to rob me of my visitation six more times and social services continued to do nothing. I was disgusted with the situation. I was disgusted with the law. I was disgusted with the whole system. It seemed the only one who could win in this system was a bully, and Hank sure was a bully of the greatest magnitude. Maybe by the end of this grueling schedule of appointments and visitations, things will turn out for the better. No court in the land could possibly give custody of the kids to Hank after his psychological report reaches the court. His report has to be so damaging. His behavior during sessions continues to be erratic. The psychologist had to have seen right through this if he was any good and from where I sit, the psychologist was on top of his game.

The family group sessions are difficult for me and the kids. Hank continues to play mind games with us at these sessions. Some of his talk is so outlandish that even the psychologist takes issue with his statements. He doesn't let him get away with much.

Izzy did not attend the first session, and the psychologist insisted that she participate in future group sessions. I tried to explain how difficult it would be to get her to the sessions, but the psychologist insisted, saying, "Even if Izzy just sits in on the sessions and does not participate, it is important for me to observe her behavior. Sometimes body language can speak volumes. You can tell Izzy that she doesn't have to answer any questions if she so chooses. That should help get her out of the car and into the office."

That's when I insisted, "I know you understand how difficult Izzy can be, you have observed her stubbornness up close and personal. What if I still cannot get her into any sessions?"

"Then I will make a point to coax her out of the car. I need to observe her behavior. Without information about how she reacts with the family, I have no way of submitting a written report on Izzy; without the report, the judge could insist that until the report reaches the court, there will be no judgment in the case. That is extreme, I realize, but it is necessary that you understand the import of this situation."

"Believe me, I understand the import of this situation," I argued aggressively. "This entire ordeal has been extremely difficult on my entire family. It would be nice if you could acknowledge the difficulty I am experiencing here. Our entire lives have been turned upside down and all because of Hank. He is the bad actor here, not me, not the kids. It is because of his outrageous lies that we are in this terrible situation in the first place. Lies, all lies."

That's when Hank interrupted, "They are not lies, Mr. Nelson. The reason we are in this situation is because she is a drug addict and is always half-wacked out of her head. I cannot trust her with the kids anymore. The kids need to be with me at home. Mary has to move out of our lives, not me."

Mr. Nelson then took on a superior attitude and confronted Mr. Clark, saying, "Mr. Clark, please try to remember that your children are present. We are here not to accuse but to try to figure out how this family can move forward without harming the well-being of your children. There are five group family sessions required by the court. If all the sessions go like this one, my report will not be favorable. You could end up having your children placed in foster care. Do you understand what I am telling you?"

"I understand," Hank answered. "Just what makes you think you are so smart? Because you have a degree, well, so do I. I'm a hell of a lot smarter than you are when it comes to what is best for my kids. So, don't sit there with your high almighty attitude. Do you think it is easy living with this woman? Well, let me tell you, it isn't. I constantly have to take care of her, as well as the kids. She is not a well woman. She probably should be in a state ward under psychiatric observation. You'll see as these sessions continue; you'll see for yourself what a big cry baby she is. The least little thing upsets her. She is always picking fights in front of the children. I try not to participate, but she goes on and on until we both end up hollering at each other. That is not good for my kids. That's why I am here. I want my kids back at home with me and if you do not make that happen, you will be sorry."

"Are you threatening me, Mr. Clark?"

"No, I'm promising you; you better watch out, right kids, or he'll be really sorry."

Hank continued on with his tirade for what seemed an eternity. He was ranting and raving just the same way when he was in court and the judge told him to settle down or he would hold him in contempt of court. Obviously, Mr. Nelson couldn't hold him in contempt, but what he did do was end the session abruptly.

I was so disappointed. I never got a chance to retaliate, not that I wanted to. And the children, they had to sit through that obnoxious behavior. What was that teaching them? Hank was losing it. I only hoped that when all this was over, the psychologist would see right through him. All I wanted was my kids back. How could Hank continue down this path? He was so outraged about the divorce, I couldn't ever see him settling down. He seemed to be getting worse as each day passed. They say the truth will set you free. I can only hope that the truth will come out and that the court will give me back my kids. I miss them so much.

I'm convinced the kids don't understand why they're in attendance at these sessions. Family dynamics mean nothing to little kids. The kids just sit quietly at these sessions and try to answer the questions put to them as best they can. Mostly they're one-word answers, so I'm wondering how effective the kids can be at these sessions. I suppose it is more to see how they react rather than to hear what they have to say. I'm assuming that, but then again, I am not the psychologist. Most of the discussion is taken up with Hank and me. I just hope the therapist realizes Hank's outrageous statements are, in fact, shocking, ugly lies. I hate Hank. I hate what he is doing to our kids. Will this ever change? I don't see how it can. I'm desperate for answers and no matter where I look, I can't find any.

• • •

Another month went by, and it is now the end of February. Today is a beautiful winter day with bright sunshine and temperatures not too cold. The snow-covered roads are quiet when cars travel over them with that muffled sound that hard packed snow creates. I finally have a car, although it is not my thunderbird. My parents helped me get a car loan, which they had to cosign, and I am now driving a used Ford two-door car. It serves its purpose and allows me to visit the kids without inconveniencing my parents. I still have no money. All court proceedings are on hold during this three-month interlude. Today, I'll be grocery shopping and running some errands to help out my mother. It fills the day, and I don't have to worry about running into neighbors since I am now living out of town. As I grabbed my keys to begin my outing, the phone rang, and Mom called me back saying there was a phone call for me. I was hoping it wasn't social services making another one of their ultimate demands, which weren't requests at all, but orders.

As I grabbed the phone, I recognized the voice. It was Billy Marshall, our next-door neighbor in Maine. He was calling to tell me that I should be aware that Hank had sold our summer cottage to Jim and Sheila Sherman, a couple who also owned a cottage in our gated community.

"What," I said. "That cannot be because we are in the middle of a divorce, and Hank is not allowed to dispose of any marital assets at this time."

I thought, how can Hank get away with this? Isn't my lawyer supposed to protect me and prevent things like this from happening?

"I am sure," said Billy. "I spoke with the Sherman's, and they told me they had already signed papers at the passing that morning."

I was stunned. How could Hank sell our summer home? What about the kids? He was taking away their beautiful summers to get back at me. How vindictive can a person be just because his wife leaves him? I always knew he had the upper hand with me because of his controlling ways, but I never imagined he would take his pay back out on the kids. I was silent on the phone. I didn't know how to respond. My mind was thinking ahead to a summer of sadness for the kids, and all because I left their father. I thought, I've made such a mess of things. I can't imagine summers without Maine. It had become our way of life over the past seven years, and now it would leave a huge void in our lives. I knew my lifestyle would change once I left Hank, but I never for a moment gave thought to losing our summer home.

"Mary, are you still there?" said Billy.

"Yes, I am. I can't believe this is happening. Are you absolutely sure the cottage is sold?"

"Absolutely," said Billy, "because the Sherman's showed me the keys to the cottage and took a final walk through, making sure everything was locked up tight over the winter before departing. They had driven down from New Hampshire to complete the sale. It was a done deal."

A done deal, I thought. All I could do was sigh, exhale with a moan. There was dead silence between Billy and me, then for a few very long seconds before I finally found my voice and answered, "Thank you, Billy for letting me know. I will be calling my attorney to see if we can straighten this out. Thank you for the update."

As I hung up the phone, this was the first time I didn't have tears in my eyes when receiving bad news. I guess the last couple of months had made me tougher than I realized. Shocking news didn't seem to affect me the same way it had in previous days. I guess I was becoming used to the extraordinary pranks Hank was playing. Nothing seemed to surprise me anymore. Mom saw the distress on my face and when I told her what had happened, she was so angry with Hank, she said, "I'm going over to see Hank right now and give him a piece of my mind. He can't do this to my grandchildren. He simply can't."

I tried to contain her by saying, "Mom, what good would that do? It wouldn't resolve anything. I have to work this out with my attorney, not you. Think about it." I said. "Being so rash never achieved anything."

After our emotional debate about how to handle Hank, we looked at each other and decided to have a soothing cup of tea to help us both calm down before continuing on with our day. Score one more for Hank. He's won so many battles now, I've stopped counting.

• • •

It's been over three months now, and we still are waiting for the psychologist's reports. Until the court receives them, I have no case to discuss. Waiting is so hard, especially when it means that my kids have to wait as well. I just wanted us all back together again. That's when the phone rang. It was Mr. Durkson. I was hoping this phone call would be positive.

"Tom," I said, "what's up?"

"I just got notification from the court that the psychological reports are in and that the judge will be reviewing them shortly. Meanwhile, I'll be filing a motion requesting a court date as soon as possible."

"How long do you think it will be before we get into court?" I asked.

"It could be a couple of weeks. Please try to be patient, Mary. Once this is resolved, we will be able to move forward with our divorce case, and I'll be able to get you some money."

"That reminds me, Tom. I just got a phone call from my neighbor in Maine telling me that Hank sold our Maine summer home. Is there anything you can do?"

"He can't sell marital assets without a court order while there are divorce proceedings ongoing. To be on the safe side, I'll immediately have liens put on all the marital property to stop this rampage of selling off marital assets." He apologized for not issuing the liens sooner but didn't think that Hank would stoop that low given it was the children's summer vacation we were talking about. He was beginning to realize that Hank was capable of anything and to never under estimate his capability of outwitting the system. He continued to explain that Hank can't sell off marital assets without suffering any consequences. Just then I heard the tea pot whistle and looked up from the phone and saw Mom. I smiled a nod of assurance, so she would know this was not all bad news. Her worried face relaxed, and she began pouring the tea. When the phone call ended, I reiterated everything that Tom had just told me. It was good news about the reports and court date, but the summer home was on shaky ground, not such good news.

So, things are moving along. I've never been able to understand why it takes so long in court to address a simple proceeding. The law is way too complicated for the average individual to manipulate without a lawyer. But somehow Hank knows how to deal with the system. He has to have obtained this knowledge through his many business dealings over the years.

It was a Tuesday morning when we finally got a court date to hear the judge's ruling on the reports submitted to the court previously by the state appointed psychologist. I was told I would be able to read the reports on the day of the hearing and not before under court order. Court was set for tomorrow at 9 o'clock. Needless to say, I didn't sleep well that night. Once again my worrying mind would not let go of the day's events. I was hoping beyond hope that the forthcoming proceedings would rule in my favor, after all, Hank was a crazy lunatic, and I was sure the report would be detrimental for him. I finally fell asleep at 2:30 that night and lightly slept on and off for the rest of the night. I awoke at 7 o'clock startled and quickly jumped out of bed. Thank goodness I did not over sleep. I quickly got dressed, slurped down a quick cup of coffee, and went flying out the door to court. I knew how to drive to the Middlesex County Courthouse now, so at least driving would not make me nervously anxious. Everyone was there when I hooked up with Tom. Hank gave me a nod with a spiteful smile, and I just turned my head away in downright disgust. I couldn't believe how much I hated him now after these last trying months. I could never return to living with him again. The thought was abhorrent. Just the thought of it turned my stomach.

• • •

Tom, once again, whisked me away to a private anti-room. Once there, the reports were given over to me for reading. My lawyer said that Hank's report was so damming that his attorney had already submitted a motion to have the court impound them and sealed for no one to see.

"What about the judge," I said.

Tom replied, "Of course Judge Ginsberg has already read the report on Hank and allowed the motion to impound prevail. I knew the report would be revealing but never imagined that the report would be impounded by the court."

My lawyer told me that this was good news for our case and that today, he was petitioning the court to release the children into my care along with child support and a substantial check for first and last month rent and security deposit on an apartment. I had previously asked Tom to petition the court for the third time to please let me and the kids return to our home rather than live in an apartment.

"Of course," Tom said, "the first order of business will be to petition for returning to the marital home instead of living in an apartment."

I felt like I was finally getting my life back. The thought of getting my kids back today was heavenly bliss. I was exhilarated. The reports on Kenny and Becky were difficult to read because they clearly showed that the children were upset with their circumstances and wanted to return to their home in Randolph with their mother. The report on myself showed me to be a caring mother but very nervous about my circumstances and quite afraid of my husband as he continued to punish me with his unpredictable behavior and lack of impulse control. The reports took me thirty minutes to read through because all four were quite extensive. The report on Izzy was not very revealing because she was not attending individual sessions but only the family group sessions where she remained silent. The reports had a lot of information to digest, with some areas difficult to understand because of their wording in psychological terms. However, in the end, the reports were positive recommending that physical custody of the children be returned to the mother forthwith and that visitation rights of the father be allowed once a week under supervision with a social worker present. This would prevent Mr. Clark from cross dressing in front of the children. With the reports being read, Mr. Durkson and I entered the courtroom waiting for the judge to hear our case. All we could do now was wait.

"All rise," said the bailiff as the honorable Judge Ginsberg entered the courtroom. Once Judge Ginsberg was seated at his bench, the bailiff then stated, "Please be seated."

As we all sat, I had a nauseated stomach and was hoping that it would settle down. I have never been so scared of anything in my entire life. What if the kids remained in Christine's custody? Then all these past three months would have been in vain. I prayed, please don't let this happen, don't take my kids away again.

Judge Ginsberg wasted no time and got right to his decision. The hearing went as was to be expected and the verdict came down:

Mrs. Clark regaining custody of the children, and Mr. Clark being allowed visitation rights once a week under social services supervision. Child support was ordered of Mr. Clark, as well as a check to relocate Mrs. Clark and the children to a new place of residence. Mrs. Clark was ordered to collect the children immediately from the Riley family and was allowed to return the children to her mother's residence until such time as an apartment could be obtained for the family. As for returning to the house, our motion was denied without any further explanation.

I was disappointed about the house, but I was elated about the kids. The judgment went my way. I finally won my first battle. Or did I? Little did I know that events that followed would take a devastating toll on all our lives.

As I left the courtroom, I felt that the law finally prevailed and hoped that the future would now begin to calm down. Even with all of Hank's shenanigans, he still did not prevail. Maybe now he would begin to realize that divorce did not have to be as cruel as he was making it for the entire family. The heartbreak he caused over the last several months was so unnecessary. I said a silent prayer, thanking God that justice prevailed and asked him to please watch over us as we began our new lives in our new home.

I drove straight to the Riley's to collect my children. My heart was overjoyed as I entered Christine's kitchen saying, "Today is going to be the best day because today I get to bring the children home with me."

Becky and Izzy ran up to me with hugs, but Kenny stayed back. He had a solemn face, and I was beginning to realize that this entire ordeal was more than he could comprehend. It definitely was taking its toll on him. After all, he was only seven. How could he possibly understand his circumstances?

Christine invited us all for supper and that night, I packed up all the kids' belongings, anxious to start the journey home. Unfortunately, the thirty-minute car trip from Randolph to Medford was a catastrophic disaster. Kenny threw a temper tantrum the likes of which I have never seen before. The entire trip, he was kicking the back of the front seat and hitting the windows as he wailed inconsolably. I knew he no longer could cope and tried repeatedly asking him to please stop, but his wailing continued the entire ride home. What had happened to my beautiful, silly-faced little boy? He never had a temper and was always so giggly and cooperative. To see him like this was immensely heartbreaking. My heart was hurting so massively, I didn't think it was capable of healing. I knew this was Hank's doing. All those visitation days while the kids were with the Riley's he was insidiously poisoning Kenny's mind with trash talk. He was responsible for destroying the beautiful mind of an innocent child. I wanted to kill Hank for what he did to my precious son.

I was afraid to stop the car for fear that Kenny would run out of the car before I could calm him down. I couldn't stop the car. I had to continue on, even though the drive would take another twenty-minutes. I was praying that we all would make the trip without having an accident. It was so hard to concentrate on driving and talk to Kenny at the same time while he was screaming.

"Kenny, please calm down," I kept repeating, and Kenny kept kicking and crying. He was inconsolable. Nothing I said made any difference in his behavior. He just kept kicking and screaming and banging at the window. My heart was in my throat as I prayed, please let us make it safe to my mothers, please.

When I finally got to Governor's Avenue, just two blocks from my parents' house, I decided to drive directly to Medford Memorial Hospital rather than to Joyce Road where my parents' home was. I parked the car right in front of the emergency ward and took Kenny out of the car and threw him into my arms as I hurried him into the emergency room. Almost immediately, Kenny stopped crying, and I began to say, "Kenny, I am bringing you here to see the doctor so that he can help you calm down. It makes me very sad to see you like this, and I feel the doctor can really help you once he gets to talk with you. Please try to be a good boy." Kenny just listened without saying a word. His little face was all contorted, as was mine. The nurse realized we had a tense situation here and came running out to settle Kenny down. We did not have to wait long before a psychiatrist appeared and took Kenny immediately with him into one of the patient rooms. I was asked to wait outside while the doctor had a chance to talk to Kenny alone. As I was waiting, I wondered if I was doing the right thing or if perhaps I should have stopped the car along the way to better manage the situation. But then I realized I did the only thing I could do. Kenny had to be contained before we arrived at my parents' house. The doctor emerged after fifteen minutes, holding Kenny's hand. Kenny was walking with him calm as a cucumber. The doctor pulled me aside, explaining it would not be necessary to hospitalize him for overnight surveillance. He was successful at calming Kenny down without any medication and explained that his temper tantrum was sparked when he realized he would not be seeing his father. The doctor assured me it would be okay to bring Kenny home with me and that if the situation became tense again during the evening, to please bring him back to the hospital. What a relief. I was imagining that Kenny would have to undergo psychiatric therapy and spend the night in the hospital. By the time we finally arrived at Mom's house, we were all beat and we all went to bed as soon as we got settled in.

The next morning, I planned on taking the children to see the new apartment we would be moving into. But first, I had to cash the check Hank had given me for the deposit on the apartment. We were on our way out the door when the phone suddenly rang, and Kenny ran to grab it. Kenny listened very intently to everything that was being said to him, and then Kenny said, "Okay, good-bye."

"Who was that?" I asked.

"It was Daddy," Kenny answered.

"What did he want?"

Kenny slowly answered, "To say hi." He then ran off to get into the car with the girls. I should have realized then that something was not quite right. I should have been on my guard when it came to Hank's actions, but I was just so relieved that my kids were back, I didn't really put enough emphasis on the strange telephone call. Naively I thought, maybe he does miss the kids.

I drove to the bank in the square and quickly scooted into the bank with the children but was told unless I had an account in that bank, they could not cash my check. They explained if I went to the bank that issued the check, it could then be cashed. That's right, I thought. What was I thinking? We all got back into the car and took the thirty-minute trek to Watertown where the business was located, and Hank did all the business banking. The bank had huge windows from the floor to the ceiling, so you could see everyone in the bank. I parked right in front of the bank windows and explained that Mommy was going into the bank for just a moment and not to get out of the car. They could see me when I was in the bank, and I would wave to them once inside. "Be good," I said, "and then I'll bring you all back lollipops." I quickly scooted into the bank. I was the only one in the bank, so the kids could easily see me, and the transaction only took a minute to complete. However, a minute was too long because when I came out, to my horror, Kenny was gone. I only turned my back for a few seconds while I collected the cash. I was intently watching the kids the entire time while the teller was making the transaction.

"Where's Kenny?" I said in a high-pitched, frenzied voice to the girls.

"He got out of the car to see you," Izzy said.

"And you let him!" I said, raising my voice.

Izzy started to cry. I was so angry I said, "Why, why did you let him get out of the car?"

All Izzy could do was stare at me without saying a word. She could tell I was very upset and thought I was upset with her rather than the situation. I frantically circled the car and glanced at every angle of the parking lot but could not find Kenny. I started running across the street to the police station. I knew that Hank had something to do with this. Kenny would never have gotten out of the car by himself. He would have had to climb over the front seat in order to open the door. The car was a two-door sedan. I was hysterically frantic, so beside myself that I felt I was going to die. Not Kenny, Hank, I thought, not Kenny.

By now I was running so fast, I started to trip and went careening onto the pavement. Both my knees were bloodied. I was so upset, I didn't even feel the pain or realize that blood was dripping down both my legs. When I continued to run to the police station, I was breathing so hard, I was out of breath and started to get a side ache from running so fast. I finally reached the police station, screaming that my little boy had been kidnapped and immediately, the officer on duty came to my rescue. I tried to explain to him what had just happened but wasn't making as much sense as I wanted. My brain was working, but my mouth wasn't. I was crying and spitting out words, trying to make the officer understand what just happened.

"Go to Watertown Steel, my husband's business. It is just around the corner, and Kenny goes there all the time with his father. I know he is there, please hurry. I know Hank will drive away with him before you get there."

The officer left to investigate, and I rushed back to the car to get my girls. We all waited in the police station for almost a half hour before the officer returned and told me that Hank was not at Watertown Steel. The person he spoke to informed him that Mr. Clark was out on business and wouldn't be returning until noon. By this time, it was only ten thirty. I had calmed down somewhat by now and told the officer about the past three months and how difficult Hank had been about the divorce proceedings. The officer then took the girls and me to Watertown Steel to see if Hank had returned yet and to our good fortune, he was just pulling up in his green truck. Kenny was not with him. My heart sank. As the officer approached, Hank stopped in surprise.

"What's wrong?" Hank asked.

"Your son is missing, and your wife claims that you kidnapped him this morning," the officer said.

"That's ridiculous," Hank snapped. "Why would I do such a thing? It just goes to show this woman is crazy as a loon, and that's why I'm divorcing her."

I was aghast. I stood there screaming at Hank. My whole body was trembling so fiercely that I thought I would faint. I tried to gain control of myself, but all I wanted to do was throw myself on the ground and sob weeping acidic tears. I couldn't stop crying and was becoming hysterical at this point when the police officer asked me to calm down and not to worry. He would get to the bottom of this no matter how long it took. He already had officers circling the square looking for a little boy, and he was bound to show up.

"We live in a very safe town," the officer said, "and crime is very low here, so don't worry. We will find Kenny."

Then Hank callously said, "Then you better search the Charles River across the street because he probably fell in and drowned."

• • •

The girls were so upset when we returned home. They knew that Kenny was gone and kept telling me that Kenny was with Daddy.

"How do you know that Kenny is with Daddy? Did you see Daddy take him?"

"No," Becky said, "but Izzy told me Daddy took him."

"Is that right Izzy? Did you see Daddy take Kenny?"

"No, Mommy, but I didn't see anyone close to the car when Kenny got out. He wasn't kidnapped. He just walked away, and I thought he was with you. Kenny knows that Daddy's work is just around the corner, so he must have gone there. I think Daddy told him something."

"You do what?" I asked.

"I don't know. I just know that Daddy took him." Izzy said.

"Oh, Izzy, don't tell me you know Daddy took him if you didn't see Daddy take him," I said.

"Well, I just know," Izzy said, and she ran out of the room crying.

I turned around and saw Becky was about to start crying as well. I scooped her up in my arms and tried to assure her that everything would be alright. Kenny probably was with Daddy, and this was just a big mistake. But no matter how much I tried to console her, Becky cried out, "We'll never see him again, will we?"

"Of course we will. I'm sure Daddy knows where he is. You'll see. Why don't we all lay down for an afternoon nap? I bet we will all feel better when we get up. I'll take a nap right beside you. How does that sound?" Becky's face relaxed then, and the two of us snuggled up, and Izzy cuddled up with us, too. We all slept for two hours. When I woke up, I decided to call the police, hoping they would have some news, but Kenny was still missing. They were watching the plant where Hank works, and Hank was still there handling business as though nothing had happened. Obviously, he knew. Otherwise he would have been frantic looking for Kenny, and he wasn't. He didn't even try to pretend he was troubled. I knew Hank took him and that he arranged to have him hidden somewhere. Maybe he paid someone to keep Kenny hidden. I wouldn't put anything past him anymore.

Once again, I couldn't sleep that night. My eyes simply would not close. My worrying mind was envisioning the worse scenarios. But then I kept telling myself, of course Kenny was with Hank. Hank arranged this entire fiasco when he called Kenny this morning at my mother's house. I should have put two and two together then. How could I have been so stupid thinking for one second that maybe Hank really did miss the kids? Hank didn't miss the kids. He was hell-bent on taking his son, no matter what the consequences. I should have realized he was planning a new intrigue. Once again, Hank was one step ahead of me. But this time, he really crossed the line. I began thinking I didn't win anything in court yesterday. Hank must have known he would never be awarded custody of the kids, so he was planning this abduction right from the start. When was this nightmare going to end? Hank had been hoodwinking me now for four months, and he finally reached the pinnacle of his success; he had Kenny. My torture had just begun.

Hank continues to work as though nothing is wrong. He knows he has won, so why worry. Every day while the girls are in school, I drive by the plant to see if Hank is there. Some days I was lucky enough to be able to follow him, hoping he would lead me to Kenny, but no such luck. He is always doing banking or going to the post office or stopping for coffee.

When I followed Hank today, I thought he spotted me because he was stopped at a red light. Of course, I was two cars lengths behind him but still, I nervously tried to hide my face, hoping he would not notice I was following him. I was not sure whether he recognized my used car or not but couldn't be sure. I wouldn't put anything past him anymore. The red light was agonizingly long as I took in two deep breaths intentionally to stay unnerved while waiting for the light to turn from red to green. Finally, the light changed, and I continued to follow him but was afraid to follow him too closely, so I held back. That's when I lost him. Damn it! He was just driving too fast and was too far up the road for me to follow him. I can't even follow him to find my son. I always had trouble driving and trying to follow directions, so what made me think I would not have trouble driving when following Hank.

"Damn it," I said again as I drove home depleted. I had nothing left to give. By the time I returned home, I was exhausted. I took a nap and found myself being awakened by my girls when they came home from school. I woke up with a headache.

Today is Monday, and the cold winter air has a mean chill to it. I shivered as I went out to dump the trash. The sun disappeared for long periods of time behind a cluster of thick clouds, and the sky was that ominous color gray which winter loved to showcase. I hated days like this, so dreary. As I sipped my morning coffee, the phone rang, and it was Tom. He wanted me to meet him at the Randolph Town Court assessor's office that morning. He wanted to talk about the case, as well as assure me that all the liens had been placed on all of the marital property, so I very willingly wanted to see for myself that he was doing his job. I was still angry that he hadn't placed liens on all the property before Hank got away with selling our summer home, so I wanted to see for myself in black and white that all the liens were in place.

The assessor's office at the courthouse was upstairs and as I climbed up the old creaky flight of stairs, I thought, there had better not be any more surprises.

"Hello, Tom," I said.

Tom acknowledged my hello and said, "Come here, I want to show you something. As you can see, the liens have been placed on all the marital assets including the business, but do you know anything about this house in Plymouth?"

He turned to page 1276 and showed a one family house listed in Plymouth, MA. I had no idea what on earth this listing was about. Did this mean Hank owned a house I was not aware of? I immediately thought, that's where he goes to cross dress.

"I don't understand, Tom," I said.

"Did you know Hank owned a home in Plymouth?" Tom asked.

"Certainly not," I answered. "What else has he been hiding from me?"

"According to my appraisal sheet, there are still two more properties that are owned by Hank, which I haven't seen yet."

Tom proceeded to turn to the pages indicated on his assessor sheet and found two more properties. One was an apartment in New York City, and the other was a condo in Vermont. I was dumbfounded. I was beginning to grasp the totality of Hank's secret life. He was leading a secret life much more multifaceted than I was aware of. How perverted were his activities in these other locations? He talked about sex parties once, before he started therapy, but he never told me where they were held. I assumed they were somewhere else. I never thought for a second that perhaps these encounters were actually held at one of his properties. How hideous the thought. It made me sick and at that moment, I huffed a huge sigh. I couldn't manage my emotions right now with this new bombshell of information. Just how perverted was Hank, I was thinking. And how sick were these other people who attended these sex gatherings? Were they actually performing vile sex acts? I kept shaking my head in disbelief.

The attorney was surprised that he had so many holdings that I was not aware of. I kept telling him how wealthy Hank was and that the financial statement he had submitted to the court for child support was not true. He claimed to only bring a pay check home of $400 per week. That was ridiculous. How could he live in such an expensive, elaborate house for only $400 per week? My attorney told me that he was going to file a motion of perjury to the court and that Hank would be held accountable for his statements. Perjury is a federal offense that requires jail time if proven guilty. Tom then said, "In the meantime, Mary, try not to worry."

"How can I not?"

"I know this is difficult, but we just struck pay dirt, so let me do my job. I will get to the bottom of this rest assured."

"That's what the police officer told me when Kenny was abducted, and Kenny is still missing. What makes you think you will be any more successful than the police officer?"

"Because I can get a judgment, a police officer cannot. It has to go through legal channels," Tom explained.

I was worn out at this point and just wanted to go home. I started to yawn and became annoyed with myself. My body was revolting again, and I was having trouble keeping my eyes open. I didn't want any more surprises today but was bombarded, yet again, with a series of newly discovered information. It was too much for me to digest in one fell swoop. I kept yawning, so I knew I would have trouble driving home if I didn't leave quickly. I left and drove directly home to take a nap. This time I was awake before the girls got out of school. Thank goodness.

• • •

Since Kenny has been missing, I call the police station every day. They have assigned me my own detective, Paul Spilling, and he continues to keep me updated but usually it is nothing new to report.

"I'm sorry Mary, but I have nothing to report today. We are doing everything we can to find your son."

"It's been over two weeks now," I said. "I'm never going to get him back, am I?" The thought of never finding him was more than I could bear. Not knowing was way too frustrating for me to handle rationally. My days were doomed if something dreadful happened to Kenny. He was such a sweet boy. How could anyone hurt him? There was still no ransom being requested, so foul play was the theory being pursued at this point in time.

"To be perfectly honest with you," Mr. Spilling continued, "I believe that your husband has him stashed away somewhere because he is way too cool to be the father of a missing child. Is there anyone you can think of who may be caring for your son at this time?"

"The only one I can think of would be his godfather, Jimmy Muldoon. But he is in a wheel chair and can only walk with extensive braces and canes. I can't imagine he would be capable of caring for Kenny. However, I think you should check him out because my husband and Jimmy went to college together, and Jimmy is Kenny's godfather. Jimmy lives out in the Berkshires in the western part of the state, and I don't know his address."

"I'll get his address and check him out," Mr. Spilling said. "After I interview him, I'll get back to you."

"Thank you," I said in a monotone voice. I was very despondent at this point and knew that I had to do something rather than just sit at home and worry. I hadn't been sleeping well since Kenny went missing. They say sleep deprivation is used by the military as a torture technique. I was beginning to realize that without proper sleep, your body was not able to function well. I could now understand why sleep deprivation was so effective. At least if I was doing something, perhaps my exhaustion would finally let me find sleep.

By now I had a steady part time job because my child support was so little, and I found that I could hardly make ends meet on such a small amount of money. My attorney has to do something about this because I'm falling into bankruptcy. I decided to take the matter up with my attorney and then go and find Kenny myself.

My attorney immediately issued a charge of perjury of a Financial Statement:

The Endless Pursuit | 79

Whereby Hank Clark signed under pains and penalties of perjury dated 5/29/80 his financial statement not declaring $1,000,000 of unclaimed assets. With this motion filed in the Commonwealth of Massachusetts Trial Court on charges of PERJURY so be it.

Now, I'm going to search for Kenny. My next-door neighbor, Mike Pearl, was single and very fond of my children. Mike also had a license to carry a fire arm and agreed to take a two-day trip with me to the northern part of Maine in search of Kenny.

Hank summered during his youth in a summer homestead up in the northern part of the state and had taken me to this area with the kids for a hunting trip once. The kids and I played all day, taking hikes, swinging on swings, and swimming in the pond while Hank went off hunting every day. It was so quiet there, you could hear a pin drop. It was an extremely remote area of Maine with only dirt paths to drive on and very few people lived in the region. It would have been the perfect place for Hank to hide Kenny. He certainly had enough money to pay someone to hide Kenny while the divorce was ongoing. After all, he hired a thug to keep me out of the marital home months before. So, exploring this region of the country made perfect sense to me. I was pretty sure I would be able to find the hideaway that Hank had taken me to when we went on the family hunting trip. I was pretty good at remembering driving landmarks and signs. I just was bad at following driving directions. So the plan was for me and Mike to leave first thing Saturday morning and return late Sunday night. That would give us enough time to search the region, staple up some posters, talk to some townspeople, and meet with the sheriff in that area.

Now that this plan was in place, I needed to talk with my girls. With my mother agreeing to take the girls for the weekend, all that was left was to print out some missing child posters and let the girls know they were having a fun weekend with their grandmother.

"Girls," I called after supper Wednesday night, "come into the kitchen and sit with Mommy." The girls came running in saying, "Why do you want us to sit down, Mommy?"

"Because I have something fun to tell you," I said.

"I love surprises," Becky said. "What is it?"

"How would you girls like to spend the entire weekend with Memere. She would like to take you girls to the zoo on Saturday, stay overnight Friday and Saturday, and take you both ice skating on Sunday. How does that sound?"

"Yeah!" yelled the girls.

"Okay, then it is settled. We will leave after school on Friday."

"Goodie," said Izzy. "I'm bringing my favorite game."

"Me, too," said Becky. "I'm bringing my ice skates."

"Sounds like a plan to me," I said in my most upbeat voice. "Now let's get ready for bed."

PART II
LOOKING FOR KENNY

Chapter VIII

It was Saturday morning and only 5 o'clock when I awoke from a sound sleep. I had been sleeping better these days, but this morning, for some reason, I woke up early, too early to start the day. I couldn't go back to sleep. Even though I was yawning, and my eyes were heavy, I knew my mind was wide awake, thinking about what the day might discover. So, I decided to get up and watch the sunrise.

They say you are your mother's daughter. Growing up, I can remember she watched the sun rise more times than not. She was always an early riser and often just liked to sip a cup of coffee watching the sun come up over the hill. Unlike me, Mom never needed a lot of sleep. If she got six hours of sleep, she could roll through her day easily without slowing down. She was full of vitality and always on the go. Growing up, I can't count how many times Mom would share with us kids how beautiful the sunrise was that morning. I can hear her voice now, talking about how gorgeous the sunrise was, even more exquisite than when the sun sets because everything was so clean and fresh, the beginning of a new day with nothing to interfere with its beauty, just the beauty of God shining through. So here I lay, my mind wondering. So I decided to get up and watch one of those sunrises Mom's always talked about.

As I sipped my coffee, I began thinking about how long a drive it was to the northern part of Maine, a good eight or nine hours from Randolph. It was late March, and the winter was still hanging on, so I knew it would be cold way up in Maine. Better dress warm, I reminded Mike, because the snow doesn't melt up north until late April early May. Sure enough, here comes that sunrise Mom always bragged about, gorgeous!

The weather report today says it's going to be in the low forties with some clouds and lots of sun, so it should be a good traveling day. I decided to eat a big breakfast, hoping it would carry me for a good five or six hours before we had to stop for lunch. I promised Mike I would pack one of my world-famous picnic baskets with fried chicken, potato salad, seafood chowder, chips, and some of my mom's homemade pickles. I had baked a pound cake and some chocolate chip cookies. I packed those up, as well as a jug of fruit punch, a thermos of hot coffee, and half a dozen water bottles. That should do it, I thought. The least I could do was feed Mike a decent meal since he had volunteered to pay for the entire trip. That was so generous of him. But then, he knew how broke I was and how life had treated me so badly. He felt sorry for me, but that was okay because I felt sorry for me as well.

It was now 7 o'clock and just as promised, Mike was right on time as I heard his car parking in front of my apartment housing. I was on the first floor, so I heard all the traffic.

"Good morning, Mike," I said, as I opened the door.

"Good morning to you," Mike said with a big smile.

Mike was a tall man. He had very long legs and looked really good in a pair of jeans. He had a rough complexion, fabulous blonde mustache, and big blue eyes. His best feature, however, was his voice. He had one of those voices that belonged on the radio, the kind of voice that women swooned over. So, there he stood, wearing a spring jacket.

"Mike," I said, "I hope you're planning on dressing warmer than just a spring jacket?"

"Don't worry, I have plenty of warm clothes in the car including a winter coat and a couple of blankets."

"Blankets?" I said. "We're not going to the North Pole."

"No, but I was a boy scout, and I always come prepared," he laughed. "Don't forget to bring that picnic lunch you promised."

"It's right here as promised," I happily stated. "It's the least I can do for you since you are doing so much for me."

"Oh, this is no big deal," Mike said. "I am happy to do it, and you already know that, so stop feeling guilty. I want to do this for you."

How could I ever thank him enough? And there certainly were no words that could express my gratitude. To give up a whole weekend for me was so generous. So, with it being 7 o'clock, it was time to load up the car and start the long trek to Maine. Mike was easy to talk to and had a good sense of humor, making the trip a comfortable one with plenty of chatter back and forth.

So as we began our journey to find Kenny, my heart was hopeful that this just might be the place that Hank was hiding my precious little boy. Hank always felt comfortable when he was in Maine, and Northern Maine was his favorite because of the wonderful hunting season that Maine had to offer. Moose, deer, and black bear were the commodity of the day, and Hank always got his buck. If it had a rack, he'd always bring it home but as for the venison, he always had the local butcher carve it up and donate it to the church. The people in Northern Maine were mostly poor with very little opportunity for good work. Most of their work was seasonal, and that made it tough to make ends meet. Feeding these families was a nice way of giving back. What a shame that Hank's good ways were falling by the wayside. All the goodness in him was being sucked up by the ugly perversion he was practicing, and now the rage he was experiencing made him seem wicked and unscrupulous. All the good was gone. I still was so ashamed and did not want people to know that I was married to such a monster. You are judged by the company you keep, after all. People must think that I am as bad as Hank is. Only I am too good. I was raised Catholic and went to Catholic schools for thirteen years. There is no doubt that my upbringing had a tremendous influence on my way of life and the way I thought. I was so good and yet so naïve. Lately I noticed that I was washing my hands all the time even though they were not dirty. What was that all about? The counselor said it was about shame, not guilt. Once things calmed down and my life got back to normal, this habit most likely would go away. But what if it didn't? What if it lasted a lifetime? For goodness sake, Mary, try to stay in the moment. Stop feeling sorry for yourself and start focusing on the trip ahead. After all, this just might turn out to be a glorious day. I had already planned out what I would do if I found Kenny. Of course, the police were part of that scenario.

It was now 10 o'clock, and Mike needed a pit stop which was just as well because I needed to stretch my legs. I walked around the parking lot a couple of times, trying to get my energy pumping again, and it seemed to work. By now, we were in the state of Maine just past Biddeford and still had a way to go. The Maine Interstate 95 was a two-lane highway, straight as an arrow, so the drive could become monotonous, straight road for miles and miles with only wilderness to see in between the big cities, like Lewiston and Farmington and Presque Isle. There were no signs or billboards of any kind because they were outlawed in Maine. Keeping the highways pristine was the thinking of this state. The state motto was, "Life the way it should be." You knew when you were on this highway, you were driving into the wilderness. No wonder there was so much wild life up in this region. It truly was a vacationland paradise.

So, Mike and I continued our journey to Coplin Plantation, that small remote village close to the Canadian border. We were looking at another good five hours of driving, and Mike said he wasn't tired. Mike enjoyed road trips. It was one of his hobbies, so driving long distances didn't tend to tire him. As for me, it made me logy.

Our next pit stop would be the Rangley Lakes. It was a huge body of water and was known for its moose population. What an ugly animal a moose was. Because of the size of its long, lanky, skinny legs, a moose was so much bigger than a horse. And it had the biggest head, most of it being all nose. It moved slowly, just meandering along, but when aroused, it could sure take off. You didn't want to be in its path when it decided to book it through the bush.

We now had been driving for over six hours, and it was time to stop for a quick lunch. We ate in the car because it was now in the mid thirties and too cold for a tailgate lunch. Mike enjoyed every morsel. He had a good appetite, and I was pleased I had put up the basket, even though it was a bit of work. Only two more hours of driving, and we would be there. I was thinking of the landmarks now of how to get to this remote part of Maine where Hank used to hunt. It was beginning to take shape in my mind, and I was confident I would be able to find that old house on the top of the mountain.

As we got closer to Coplin Plantation, I began seeing landmarks that were familiar, and I knew I would be able to find the dirt path road that took us up to the old camp lodge with its crooked floors and squeaky stairs. Sure enough, it was just up ahead when we found the road, and Mike turned right into the deep forest woods. It was a good two-mile drive before we came to the first house showing any signs of life. All of a sudden, the front door of the house opened and out stepped a man in overalls covered in paint. I turned my head and stared so hard at this man, hoping I would recognize him, but I did not. So, Mike continued to drive along the bumpy snowy road. There was still quite a bit of snow in the forest, and some parts of the road were still covered in snow as well. However, we were able to keep on tracking along with no delays and before I realized it, we had reached the old log cabin. We were on the top of the mountain.

We hid the car in the forest and decided to approach the cabin by staying out of sight and making our way through the forest very quietly. I was afraid if anyone saw us, they might start yelling, or worse, shooting to scare us away. I didn't know what to expect. Up this high in the mountain, the forest floor was still covered with snow and the ground was still frozen, making it easier to remain quiet while treading along. There were a lot of thick pine trees and blue spruce, so hiding from view was easy.

"We're here," I whispered. We both were breathing heavy by now and took our time to settle down before laying out a plan.

Mike said, "Let's circle the cabin from the back to see if anyone is at home." As we trodded to the back of the house, suddenly, a thrashing sound howled through the woods. It scared us half to death. We both stood tall to see what the noise was, fearing it might be the owner, but it was only a deer. Thank goodness, I thought. We were thinking we had been found out and were ready for a challenging confrontation. Obviously, we were not supposed to be there. It was posted property. Once the deer passed, we continued on toward the back of the house, and it turned out to be locked up tight for the winter season. There was no sign of inhabitance. Disappointment didn't express how I felt. I was so sure that Kenny would have been there. I was angry, and I pounded my feet into the snow. Mike could sense my frustration and gave me a hug. I began to cry. The thought of losing Kenny, again, hit home, and I was beyond consoling.

Mike walked me back to the car and started to pull some old cans out of his trunk.

"What are you doing?" I asked as he continued to grab half a dozen of the old rusty cans.

"We are going to play pistol practice for a while," Mike said.

"What are you talking about?" I said all confused, thinking the last thing we needed here was a gun. Mike started to line up the cans on an old log and then proceeded to get his pistol out.

As he was loading in the bullets Mike said, "I'm going to show you how to shoot. It will help you get some of your frustration out." So he gave me a quick lesson, cocked the pistol, put it in my hands, and told me to aim for one of the cans and just squeeze the trigger. I was so angry then at Hank, I felt like I could have killed him right then and there, so I took aim and with all my concentration, shot the pistol, shooting the can dead center off the log. I then took another shot and hit that can as well.

"You are one heck of a gun woman," Mike said. "What a good shot you are."

"Only because it was Hank I was shooting at, not the can. If only life was so simple." I couldn't believe I said such a statement out loud, but I did, and it was hanging out there for the entire world to hear. I would have killed Hank at that moment if he was the can.

"Feel better now?" asked Mike

"For sure," I said. "Let's get off this mountain and go into town. We can post some flyers and talk to some townspeople. Maybe someone will know something," I said.

So Mike collected his old cans, unloaded his pistol, and we started to drive back down the mountain when all of a sudden, we came upon another truck on the road. This was unusual because no one lived up here that I remembered. Only this truck had a little boy sitting in the cab, and he had blonde hair. Where had this truck come from? I gasped.

"Mike, that looks like Kenny!" I blurted out. "Please, just follow this truck until we get off the mountain. You can pass him then because I can't tell whether or not it's Kenny. I need to get a better look." It was five minutes more driving before we got to the main road. Mike started to pass the truck as I strained to see. By now I was gagging with fear. What if it is Kenny? How can Mike stop his truck? Oh, please God, have it be Kenny. As I strained my eyes so hard, they hurt, trying to see my little boy. Sadly, it was not. I moaned. "It isn't Kenny," I said. What a disappointment. "Let's just keep driving into town."

We made town by 4 o'clock, parked the car, and went inside the local grocery country store. There we had a chance to meet with some locals, as well as the store owner. We told them why we were searching for my little boy, showed everyone a picture and a poster, and asked if anyone knew anything or saw something out of the ordinary. No luck. There were only three other stores in town, a bar, a laundromat and a Maine State Rangers office. We made contact at all of them but with no luck. The Forest Ranger suggested we meet with the police chief and gave us his home address because he was out on the road and usually headed home around 5 o'clock. He gave us driving directions and twenty minutes later, we were pulling up to a lovely little cape with a big front yard and three little boys running and playing, so full of energy. There was no police car, but his wife and three young boys were all at home, waiting for Daddy to come home from work.

Alice King was a very understanding woman and made us feel right at home. She offered us some hot coffee while we waited for the sheriff and offered condolences for the loss of my son. She could not imagine what I must be going through because she had a little boy just seven-years-old like Kenny. Sure enough, the sheriff made it home by 5 o'clock on the dot.

"Honey, there are some people I would like you to meet," Alice called out as the sheriff pulled open the back kitchen door.

"Hello," he said as he entered the living room. "What can I do for you?"

"My son is missing, and I was hoping that perhaps you could help shed some light on the situation," I said as calmly as I could.

"Tell me more," the sheriff answered back.

As I explained the situation, I could see the sheriff's concern for my child and was touched by his compassion. He explained he would be happy to make some inquiries and notify the local police in the next few towns over, but other than that, there really wasn't much else he could do. He offered to call the Watertown police and was happy to work with them to help solve the case if we preferred. Of course we agreed to such an offer, thanked him for his concern, said our goodbyes, and went on our way.

We stayed at a little motel on the highway that night. All I wanted to do was have some supper, take a shower, and hit the sack. Emotionally I was drained, and Mike understood. We decided to finish whatever was left in the picnic basket since the nearest eating place was fifteen miles down the road. The nearest drug store was a thirty-minute ride. I thought to myself, how do people live like this up here. Why don't they move to a more settled community where their lives could be so much easier? I just couldn't imagine living a life up here. It seemed like there was more wild life than people life up here. After finishing all that was left of our afternoon lunch, we decided to turn in for the night and agreed we would get an early start tomorrow because the drive was long, and I wanted to pick up the girls from my mother's because they had school in the morning. The drive home was quiet. We both were reconciled that the trip was disappointing, but at least we could scratch this lead off the list and put it to rest.

• • •

With the girls in school, I decided to do some more investigating. This time it would be in Plymouth at the house that Hank bought and I never knew about. But first I would need a hammer and a screw driver if I had to break into the house to try to find some clues about Kenny. I needed a babysitter, too, so I called the church to see if they could help me out and thank goodness, they could. As I went about my day, I was thinking about the other properties Tom had found that Hank owned. Perhaps I should take a trip to Vermont to explore that location as well. As for New York City, maybe the Watertown police could help investigate that site. Of course, they could have investigated all the properties Hank owned. I wondered if they were doing just that. I decided to call Paul Spilling at the Watertown police station. Luckily, he was in when I called, which was a first. We usually always ended up playing telephone tag, so to find him in was a real treat. We discussed the case, and I gave him the new property locations I had discovered but so had he, and he was already on top of it. I thought to myself, he actually is doing his job. Why was I so untrusting? I didn't trust Social Services or the court or my lawyer and now Mr. Spilling. I thought, I've made such a mess of things. None of this would be happening if I had not left Hank. But how could I have stayed. It would have killed me. And what if he ever dressed in front of the children? When he was in drag, he called himself Joanna Carr. Joanna, Joanna, Joanna. It sickened me. Everything about him sickened me. The days of having a wonderful life and a wonderful husband were over. Time to face the music, Mary, and try to stay in the moment. So I went on with my usual day, went to my part-time job at the library, and was back at home when the girls came home from school.

I couldn't wait to drive to Plymouth. It was a thirty-minute drive from Randolph, and I had called a real estate broker for the driving directions. Pretty clever, Mary, getting driving directions from a real estate agent, I told myself. I was beginning to understand why suspense movies were so popular. They certainly gave you a rise of excitement watching them, trying to figure out what would happen next. I was literally living a Hollywood movie. They say the truth is stranger than fiction, and I sure can attest to that, I thought. The babysitter arrived, and I left to begin my what, adventure, expedition, outing, investigation? What should I call this little rendezvous to Plymouth? What does it matter, I told myself, just keep driving.

I arrived at the Plymouth home around 8 o'clock. It was in a nice lower-income neighborhood, so I had to be careful with fear someone would see me snooping around. How do burglars do it without getting caught? The street was lined with street lights all up and down the street, so I was thankful a street light wasn't in front of the house I wanted to enter. I pulled into the driveway rather than park on the street. I didn't want to cause suspicion of a strange car parked on the street that a neighbor might not recognize. Before I got out, I looked all around to make sure no one was out walking their dog or something.

It was pitch black tonight, no moon, which was a blessing for me. All the better not to see you with, my dear. I thought, sounds like the big bad wolf story. Guess I still can laugh sometimes. I quietly got out of the car and scooted around to the back of the house. It really was pitch black. I had a teeny tiny flashlight and would only use it if absolutely necessary. I managed to find the back door and stood there breathless. I was actually afraid. This was a marital asset, and I was actually afraid. How stupid! I had never broken into a house before and had no idea how to do it. The door had six panes of glass, so my hammer would come in handy. As I went to smash the glass, so I could undo the lock, I stopped short. I couldn't do it. I couldn't believe I was so scared. I went to hit the glass again with my hammer and still couldn't. I thought, what is wrong with you, girl? I had to do it. There might be something inside worth seeing. I raised the hammer and held it in mid air for about ten seconds until finally, I had the guts to break the glass.

It made more noise than I thought it would. What if one of the neighbors heard it? Thank goodness it is not daylight savings time yet. That isn't until next month. Well, if Hank can steal my car under the cover of darkness, then I certainly can get inside this house under the cover of darkness. I reached inside to unlock the door and opened the door very slowly, making sure it didn't squeak. So far, no one had seen me. I quickly went inside and used my little flashlight and shined it only on the floor from my knees down. No spooky flashlight shining through the windows for me, I thought. I was in the kitchen, and there wasn't anything out of the ordinary here. I walked into the other room and was utterly shocked. The room was filled with dozens of mannequin heads with wigs in every style and color you could fathom: long hair, short hair, ponytails, blonde, brunette, red heads, even gray. One even had pink tails. There was a complete wardrobe hung up on a clothes rack. There were gowns and fake furs and sexy lingerie. I couldn't believe what I was looking at. Obviously, Hank's cross dressing was much more lewd, insidious, and menacingly vulgar than I could ever have envisioned. Once again, I was sickened by the sight of this. The thought of him parading around the house in these outfits was too much to even dream up. I thought, who am I married to? I was so ashamed. I wouldn't even want Christine to see this. I left the room and went upstairs. Shock number two. I was horrified. The room was filled with cameras, lighting equipment, tripods, and even large lenses of every kind and size. There was even an umbrella used for lighting. Hank's perversion was completely out of control. He can spend all this money on this junk and not give enough child support to even take care of his kids, the bastard. I was incensed with outrage. The therapist told me I had a tough time displaying anger. Well, not tonight. I was unequivocally angry; I was fuming.

All this time, he was doing this and never told me. He said he wanted to quit when he first confessed, but he never told me it was this obnoxiously ugly. It's obvious he has no intention of quitting, ever. No wonder he can only have supervised visits with the children. Just what did his psychological report say that was so damming that the court impounded the report. Seeing this has to be just as damming as reading the report. No wonder it was impounded! I wish Hank was impounded. If the police think Hank stashed Kenny somewhere, why don't they lock him up until he tells us where to find him? What's wrong with the law? Every time I mention it to my attorney, he tells me to let the police handle it. It is their job.

I decided to check out the entire house including the attic, if there was one, and the cellar, which there was. There was no Kenny anywhere to be found, only the ugly truth, the painstakingly ugly truth. I took the only picture of Hank in drag that was there and grabbed a wig and left. I drove home, numb.

• • •

The judge allowed me to move the kids' bedrooms, a sofa, and a kitchen table and chairs into the apartment on May 2nd. Hank was to let us in and let the movers do their job. I rented a U-HAUL and asked my cousin Ronny and Mike to help with the move. They came to my aid, and we all drove over to the house to get the kids' beds. But when I got there, the house was locked up tighter than a drum with no Hank and no body guard anywhere to be found. I thought, how am I ever going to get in. If I don't move today, I still have to pay for the U-HAUL. Why are you doing this to me, Hank? Even the kids' beds you won't let us have. What kind of a father does that? I called my lawyer and explained the situation and he told me, "Break into the house. Don't tell anyone I told you to, just break into the house. Break a window and get into the house. But be quick and don't delay because if Hank returns, it might insight riot in him."

I agreed and Mike broke the glass at the back door. We were instantly in, Mike and my cousin went straight to work, wasted no time, and before I knew it, everything was loaded into the truck. I wanted to take more but once again, the fear factor came front and center. I wasn't allowed to take my bed under court order, which meant that I would have to buy a mattress at least. Hank was supposed to be there, which he was not. I felt safe with two men by my side, and I knew that if Hank did appear and was confrontational, at least they would come to my rescue, but Hank never showed up, so the situation never materialized. We sped away with the U-HAUL loaded up and never looked back.

My mother popped in for a quick visit a few days later, loaded up with her finds from a yard sale. She brought silverware, pots and pans, and some dishes, even a salt and pepper shaker. I was thrilled. We had so little in the apartment. This was the first time my mother was able to see the apartment, and she liked it. It was small but nice. It had a small kitchen, living room, and three bedrooms upstairs. The kids' beds were all set up, and I had purchased a mattress for myself. My mother noticed there was no TV and offered to bring one of hers over. I was grateful for the yard sale finds and resided myself to shopping only at thrift stores to stock up my kitchen and the apartment. I told Mom that it couldn't happen too quickly because I had no money.

"Nonsense," my mother said in a very determined voice. "I've already stopped by the bank and have brought you $500 to help you get by over the next month. And don't say no. You know you need it. Now, let's have a cup of tea. I can boil up water in one of these pans I brought you."

"Thanks, Mom," as I gave her a big hug.

It wasn't until we were drinking our tea that the idea came over me.

"Mom, how would you like to follow Hank around town? He might just lead us to Kenny. I tried to the other day but was afraid he would recognize me because I was only two car lengths behind him. However, look what I have."

I left the kitchen and ran upstairs to get the wig I brought home from Plymouth the other night and clopped back down the stairs as quickly as I could with the new treasure found in my hands.

"Look what I have, Mom. I got this out of the Plymouth house where Hank goes to cross dress. We can use it as a disguise. You've always been good at following cars, not like me. Do you want to do it? Do you want to wear this wig and follow Hank in your car? He won't recognize it's your car because a woman with long dark brown hair will be driving. He'll never guess it is you. You have short, grey hair, Mom. He can't possibly recognize you and then you could follow him for as long as it takes."

"Well, I don't know," Mom said. "I suppose I could. But what if he leads me to Kenny, what should I do?"

"Call me immediately and stay put. If he comes out of the building with Kenny, follow him. And whatever you do, don't lose him, especially if he has Kenny in the truck with him. Now, let's get this wig on you," I said hopefully.

It was then that I started to laugh and laugh and laugh. My mother looked absolutely ridiculous. My mother looked into her pocketbook to grab a mirror and when she saw how ridiculous she looked, she began to laugh as well. We both had a good belly laugh for ourselves, something that we desperately needed. It was catharsis for the soul.

"So, this is what it feels like to be a private eye," I said teasingly.

"Honestly, Mary, the things you have me do."

Mom took off, dressed to kill or shall we say, dressed to follow. She was gone for about two hours when she returned to my apartment.

"Why are you back so early, Mom?" I asked her as she came through the door.

"Oh, now don't get angry, but I lost him," she said so disappointedly.

"How could you lose him? You were supposed to be right behind him because he wouldn't recognize you in the wig," I said.

"Well, he stopped to go into the bank and so I parked way down the road, so he couldn't see me and when he came out, I was so far behind, I was never able to keep up with him. I lost him," Mom said.

"Why did you park so far behind?" I asked.

"Because I was afraid he might recognize me," she said.

"Recognize you. For goodness sake, Mom, I'm standing right in front of you, and I don't know who you are," I shouted.

That's when we both started to laugh again.

"Some detectives we turned out to be," I said as I took the wig off my mother to finally recognize who I was actually speaking to. Low and behold, it was my mother after all.

Chapter IX

It's been several more weeks now, and the police still have not found Kenny. At this point, I am absolutely certain that Hank has him stashed someplace. I was praying so fervently that someone decent would be caring for him, but how decent could anyone be who would agree to take Kenny away from his family. I was sure that Hank was paying him well, the sleaze bucket. I thought how bad Hank had become since I asked him for a divorce. Here he was, paying someone to take our son rather than pay child support for his own children. How did he expect us to live on $200 a week? The court system definitely was not working for me. Hank clearly stated on his financial statement that he only brought home $400 per week. How was splitting his pay check in half fair. $200 for Hank, and $200 for the kids and me. Where's the logic. I decided I would call my lawyer and ask that we see another judge when filing future motions. Obviously, this judge didn't like women. Just then the phone rang, and it was Paul Spilling from the police.

"I have some news I want to report to you," he said.

"Really," I said.

"Do you know anything about a passport for Kenny?" Paul asked.

"A passport," I questioned. "Kenny doesn't have a passport."

"Well, he does now," said Paul. "It was issued on March 30th."

"Is it in his real name, Kenneth Clark?" I asked.

"Yes, it has to be because you need a birth certificate to get a passport. There was no visa issued yet, not from the state of Massachusetts," Tom stated matter of fact. Is there any country you can think of that Hank would have sent Kenny?"

"No," I said. "I can't imagine Hank sending Kenny out of the country, although nothing would surprise me anymore."

"Well, I will be checking back with the immigration office weekly to see if any visa has been issued on Kenny. Does Hank know anyone in Europe or South America?"

"I don't know."

"What about Mexico?"

"I don't know."

"What about his business? Is there anyone from out of the country that you know of that your husband does business with?"

"I'm sorry, Paul. I just don't know. To my knowledge, Hank has not begun any international business. All his business is in the states as far as I know. At least Hank never mentioned it to me," I said.

"Very well, Mrs. Clark. I will keep you informed if I acquire any new information. In the meantime, please know that we are still trying to find your son. Your husband has been reporting to work every day since the kidnapping, so I just want you to know that we are keeping a close watch on him."

"Are you watching him on the weekends because if he was going to see Kenny, it would most likely be on the weekend," I said.

"Unfortunately, Mrs. Clark, we do not have the man power to watch Hank 24/7. I wish we did, but we don't. As it is, we check on him once a day, each day of the week, and then only once, sometimes twice if we have the chance. He knows we're watching him, so I'm sure he's very guarded."

"I don't understand why you can't arrest him and hold him until he tells you where Kenny is," I said.

"I wish we could, but we have no proof, no grounds to hold him. He would be out of jail within hours if we held him. What you need is a bench warrant, and I don't think you could get one without proper evidence."

"I understand. Thank you for calling." We said our goodbyes and then I hung up the phone very saddened by what I had just learned. As I was mulling it all over in my head, it occurred to me that Paul had mentioned no visa being issued out of Massachusetts. What if a visa had been applied for in another state? The Boston office wouldn't know about it. I could call all the U.S. Consulates along the eastern seaboard looking for a visa on Kenny. I can't afford to call from home, but I can call from work during lunch. So, I have a plan now. I breathed a sigh of relief. I finally can do something that might pan out. This was a very good lead. First thing Monday, I'll start calling the Consulates for immigration information. I have a plan now, thank goodness.

It took almost three weeks to research all the immigration offices in each state along the eastern seaboard, including Maine, but no visa was ever issued on Kenny. I even asked the Florida U.S. Consulate to check on visas to South America between the times Kenny was missing. They volunteered to check all the ships and planes flying into South America, explaining it would take three days to search through their databases, and they would get back to me. But even they were unsuccessful in finding any visa being issued on Kenny. After three weeks of hoping, this turned up to be a dead end. By that time, the other properties owned by Hank in Vermont and New York City had been checked out by the Watertown police, and nothing came out of it. I was so very disappointed at this point that I started to cry. I decided to let my tears come out full stream until I got everything out of my system. The girls were in school, so I would have time to pull myself together before they got home. I cried for twenty minutes. I guess all that had transpired over the last six months finally caught up with me. I did feel better after my cry but was so tired, I ended up taking a nap. Again, thank goodness I woke up before the girls got home from school. I was trying to be strong for them, so it was important that they never see me in bed in the middle of the day again. It upset them too much.

A few days later, it was Paul Spilling on the phone again, only this time, he asked about a phone number to Bogotá Columbia and did I know of such a telephone number. Paul had obtained a warrant for Hank's telephone records from both the house and the business, and this was the only suspicious number they couldn't check out without an interpreter. He went on to say he was calling just to keep me in the loop of information. I thanked him and as I hung up the phone, I thought to myself, I can get a translator to help place a call to Bogota faster than they can and decided to call the high school Spanish department. After explaining my story, I was offered a translator but had to travel to her home because she was incapable of placing an international call from school. I was excited with the prospects of calling Bogotá. Because her schedule was jammed packed, she couldn't hook up with me until next week though. As I hung up the phone, I sighed, another wait.

The day to meet the translator finally arrived, and I was anxious to start the drive over to Stoughton, the next town over where Helen Beckett lived. It was a beautiful spring day, and everything took on that beautiful shade of green that spring has to offer. The cherry trees were blooming; the apple trees were beginning to pop as well as the azalea bushes in their shades of red pink and white. There wasn't a cloud in the sky today. It was the perfect spring day and as I drove along, I was thinking that perhaps this would be the perfect spring day for me, too. The traffic was very heavy in Stoughton, and I had to pay close attention to my driving and my directions. I always got nervous when driving to a new location, but I was driving carefully and slower than usual, so I could recognize street signs. I was looking for Timber Lane and was sure I must have passed it because I was told if you see a Dunkin Donuts, then you've passed the street. There it was, Dunkin Donuts, so I had to turn around. Now I had to look for the street from the other side of the road, which was always difficult for me. I thought I saw it but not in time to make the turn, so again, I had to turn around before I could turn onto Timber Lane. It was a very long street, about a half mile long, and the house I was looking for was supposedly on the right. As I drove slowly, looking for number 213, a little boy suddenly came running out on to the street. I slammed on my brakes, and my heart was in my throat. His mother came running into the street, yelling for him to stop, and quickly scooped him up into her arms. She smiled at me as she shook her head, mouthing thank you. I was really rattled now, and it took quite a few moments before I could begin to move along. There it is, 213. I parked in the driveway, took a deep breath, climbed up the front stairs, and rang the front door bell. It took a while for Helen to answer the door but when she opened the door, I realized she had to descend a flight of stairs before she could come to the front door. I didn't realize she lived on the second floor. She welcomed me into her home as I introduced myself, and we both climbed up the stairs and into her kitchen. She offered me a drink and I asked for water, I was so parched. I wanted to get right to the phone call, so I handed Helen the telephone number and offered to pay for the call, but she wouldn't hear of it. I watched intently as she dialed the phone. She had to work with the operator because she didn't have the country code to Columbia and within a few seconds, she nodded to me as the phone began ringing. She began her conversation in Spanish and from there on, it was a matter of just waiting because everything she said was a mystery. I couldn't understand one word of Spanish.

"She has a daughter who lives in Watertown," Helen said as she held her hand over the mouth piece.

"Get her name and address," I whispered.

"Un memento," Helen said as she grabbed a piece of paper and pen to write down the information. The conversation continued for another two minutes and then Helen said to me, "She is very nervous about her daughter. She wants to know if she is in some kind of trouble. Do you know a Margareta Cortez?"

I shook my head no and was wondering who this person could be. What if the woman on the phone wouldn't give us her address, I thought. I could search the phone book, but what if she had an unlisted number? How would I find her? I kept searching my mind with the name Margareta Cortez, repeating it over and over in my head, hoping it would spark a memory, but it didn't. By then the phone call was ending and as Helen hung up the phone, she was nodding her head in disappointment.

"I am sorry, but this mother I was talking to was very concerned about what was going on with her daughter. She said her daughter had just met a man in Watertown that she was dating who seemed to be very nice. Mrs. Cortez had no information about a little boy gone missing and again began anxiously asking about her daughter. She was only concerned about her daughter and not about a missing child. It sounds like this is a dead end."

"Not entirely," I said. "I have a name to follow up on. Perhaps she will be able to help me." I then thanked Helen for her time and kindness and departed. All the way home, I kept thinking about this girl and if perhaps the man she had met was Hank. God help her if it was, I thought. According to the translator, the mother sounded so innocent on the phone. I bet her daughter was innocent, too. And if Hank wasn't seeing her, then why was her mother's phone number on his telephone bill. What was the connection? I found myself playing detective again and began to realize why investigations took so much time to come to a conclusion. I had to stop thinking about this for now and concentrate on getting back home because the girls would be getting out of school shortly. So, as I hurried along, I thought Margareta Cortez would have to wait for another day.

The next three days, I was working, so I couldn't go to see Margareta while the girls were in school. Then it dawned on me, she probably works anyway and wouldn't be home during the day. I need to see her at night. She probably wouldn't see me if I called, so perhaps I should just go over without announcing myself. So, I called the church, asking for help with a babysitter, and couldn't get one until Thursday, three days away. Waiting for me was becoming much easier by now. Anything worth pursuing always takes time. If it is worth pursuing, then it's worth waiting for.

It was finally 7 o'clock Thursday and after the babysitter settled in with the girls, I took a drive to Watertown. Margareta lived on Palfrey Street, which I was familiar with, so at least getting lost at night was not a worry. It was a pleasant night with temperatures a little chilly but then again, it was early spring in New England, so the weather was right on track. As I pulled up to Margareta's house, I saw that the lights in the living room were on, so I was thinking she must be home. I had the picture of Hank with me that I stole from the Plymouth house. It was so vile. I knew once I showed this picture of Hank in drag with a surprised look on his face because he was captured with both hands tied to the bed post, that Margareta would be shocked and horrified. I knew that once I confronted her with this ugly truth, she would probably be deeply hurt as well, which I felt badly about. But I had to remind myself why I was here; first, to get information about Kenny, and second, to warn this innocent victim that she was playing with fire. I knew it would be a difficult conversation, but I knew I had to be brave and continue on with my plan to find Kenny. I approached the house carefully but intentionally hesitated before

I rang the bell. My hands were actually shaking. There was always the possibility that once I introduced myself that Margareta wouldn't let me in. I was hoping that would not be the case. They say curiosity killed the cat. I was hoping she would want to talk. I didn't want to hurt Margareta. I just felt she needed to know who she was dealing with. I finally rang the doorbell, and a very pretty, young girl who must have been no older than 20 answered the door. I was surprised she was so young. I introduced myself.

"Hello, are you Margareta? I am Mrs. Clark, Hank's wife. I would like to talk with you. May I come in?" She was surprised by my visit and at first, just stared at me. After a very long pause in the conversation, Margareta said, "What do you want?"

"I want to talk to you only for a few minutes, if I may. I would like to talk to you about Hank," I said.

"What about Hank?" she asked.

"Please, may I come in?" I said.

She was reluctant, but she did step aside and waved me in. She lived in a cute little bungalow, which was smartly stylish and very tidy. She seemed very shy and quite hesitant to start the conversation as I took a seat in her living room. I introduced myself again and began to explain why I left Hank. She learned that Hank was a cross dresser and that he had kidnapped our son and sent him away and that it was almost seven months now since Kenny was last seen. She just stared at me in disbelief. She was astonished that this wonderful man she had just met a month ago could be so depraved. She challenged me and said, "I don't believe you. Hank could not possibly do those things." Just then, her aunt appeared in the living room, and she introduced herself as being Margareta's guardian. Now I knew she was young, perhaps even younger than I had originally guessed she might be. Margareta told her aunt what I had told her about Hank, and her aunt was very concerned.

"I have met Hank," she said, "and he seemed very nice."

"He can be quite charming when he wants to be," I explained.

"Why do you say such things about this man?" she asked.

"I don't want to see Margareta get hurt. If she continues on with this relationship, it can only end in tragedy. To tell you the truth, I was hoping she could tell me something about Kenny. I love him very much and want to bring him home. I have searched relentlessly for the last seven months, and my heart still aches for him. He is a very sweet boy and only seven-years-old. Is there anything you can tell me about Kenny that Hank may have told you?" I asked Margareta.

"The only thing he told me was that he was staying with his uncle for a little while until the divorce could get settled. I had no idea he was missing for so long. The way Hank explained it to me, I thought he had been with his uncle for only a couple of weeks," Margareta said.

"I'm sure he has not been telling you the truth right from the beginning," I said.

"I don't know if I believe you," Margareta said. It was then that I introduced the disgusting picture of Hank and handed it over to Margareta's aunt. She gasped when she saw it, and Margareta grabbed it hastily out of her hands.

"Oh no," she cried. "This cannot be true." She was now wailing loudly in disbelief. Her aunt tried to console her but couldn't, as Margareta ran out of the room. I was very distraught, too. I hated to see her like that. I wanted more information about Kenny, but I knew the visit was over and there would be no more conversation between Margareta and myself. I talked with the aunt, asking her to call me if she leaned anything about Kenny and left her my phone number. The visit was over, and I wasn't even there more than five minutes. It took only five minutes to dash my hopes. But I did have a lead, Hank's three uncles. We rarely heard from them. It was the typical family, only see them at funerals and weddings. I would be surprised if they even knew that Hank and I were in the process of getting a divorce. However, it was a lead, and I knew I had to contact each one of them just in case they knew anything about Kenny. The visits would have to be a surprise, however, could not take the chance of giving them any warning of my coming just in case Kenny was actually in their care. I had to catch them off guard, so a surprise visit would have to suffice.

The evening went as I had expected. I knew Margareta would be devastated by the news about Hank, but I had to do what I had to do. I was so hoping that Margareta, although innocent, would shed more light about where Kenny might be. As I drove home, I fought back my tears and kept rubbing the wet tears from my eyes. I felt like I was at the end of the investigation because I doubted that any one of the three uncles would be part of this hoax. And I knew I would be hearing from Hank about my visit with Margareta. I am sure he would be outraged and was prepared for yet another one of his retaliations against me. But it was done, and all I could do now was wait for the aftermath to come hurtling down on me. I managed to get myself under control and continued to drive home. The evening was over, and I only had a shadow of a clue from Margareta. I knew once I was home, I would be calling it an early night.

It's been six weeks since I last spoke with Margareta, and I have not received any child support since. I was right thinking that Hank would retaliate. He was so furious with me because Margareta broke off their relationship. When he had to appear in court to answer the charges of non-child support, he was infuriated, and my attorney had to step in front of me to protect me from Hank's charging. Mr. Durkson immediately called the court officer to our attention, and Hank was reprimanded and told he would be held on charges if he didn't settle down. My lawyer whisked me away to a private anti-room, and we talked about the proceeding that was ahead of us. Hank was going to be forced to come up with all six weeks of child support or be hauled off to jail, so my lawyer said. I didn't believe him. Up until now, every time I went to court, I always lost. After seven months of anguish, being perpetrated by Hank against me, I was not hopeful that today's court hearing would end in my favor. The hearing was ex-parte, and Judge Ginsberg was not in court today. I breathed a sigh of relief. Today, Judge Sherman would be hearing our complaint.

"All rise," The bailiff said as Judge Sherman entered the courtroom. "Please be seated," he continued.

The lawyers stated their case, with Hank's lawyer claiming that all the child support checks were mailed and that Mrs. Clark was trying to get paid twice by issuing this false complaint. The judge asked to see both Hank's and my checkbooks. The judge examined both with great consternation and then asked to see both our licenses. The judge then asked for any cancelled checks of paid child support that Hank had in order to prove that he in fact did pay his child support. It was then that Hank's lawyer presented the court with all six cancelled checks.

"I never received any checks," I whispered to Mr. Durkson.

"I know," he said. "Let me handle this."

Finally, Judge Sherman spoke and asked me to come to his bench and sign my name on a piece of paper he presented me. I looked at my lawyer and he nodded consent, so I approached the bench with great trepidation. It was then it occurred to me that Hank must have been signing my name and cashing the checks himself. He knew he would be challenged in court and that he would need to produce the cancelled checks as proof of payment. I signed my name, and the judge studied my signature. The judge then compared my signature to the cancelled checks and then made a determination.

"It is obvious that these cancelled checks were not signed by Mrs. Clark. The signatures on all these checks, which appear to be all the same, are not remotely close to Mrs. Clark's signature. I order you, Mr. Clark, to write a check in the amount of $1,200 immediately. If you cannot make the payment here and now, you will be jailed until such time as payment is made in full. Do you understand, Mr. Clark?"

I couldn't belief my ears. A judgment actually was going my way. Thank goodness Judge Ginsberg was not in court today. Lucky for me, I thought. Hank was fuming as he wrote the check and when finished, he threw the check in my face with contempt. The judge banged his gavel and threatened Hank with a contempt charge, and Hank was forced to pick up the check and hand it over to me. I didn't say a word, and neither did Hank. We all left the courtroom in silence. Hank continued to walk out of the courthouse, and Mr. Durkson held me back. He told me his motion to have Hank present a revised financial statement had been delayed, yet again, because he changed lawyers again, and the lawyer needed time to bring himself up to speed on the case. I thought, another delay. Seven months of stall tactics, when does it end? Hank had now gone through three lawyers. The lawyer he had in court today was Mr. Olsen. Little did I know then that this lawyer would turn out to be a charlatan who was in it only for the money. Another day in court, thank goodness it was over.

• • •

It's been seven months now and still no Kenny. He'll be turning eight in just a few days, and I won't be there for his birthday. I wonder if the people he is with even know it's his birthday. I personally went to each uncle's house and found them at home. They all were surprised to see me without Hank, and they had no idea that we were in the process of a divorce, let alone that Kenny had been missing now for almost seven months. They were horrified to be perfectly honest. This lead was indeed a dead end.

It was then I felt Hank and I had to talk and that this horrific situation had to end. He was now on lawyer number four and perjury charges and an increase in child support still hung in the balance. I knew what he was doing. He was dragging out every single motion to its ultimate limit to bleed me dry, and it was working. I felt I just couldn't continue on like this. Something had to give. All I wanted was for my kids to be safe and well taken care of. I wasn't even asking for the house. He can keep the house. All I wanted was a decent place to live and raise my kids. I know I'll have to work a full-time job eventually because I simply cannot continue to borrow money from my parents. I had been out of the work force for fourteen years now and had only a high school education, so I knew starting pay for me with any job would be low. These are Hank's kids, not my parents, and the court has to make him pay a more reasonable child support payment. I have no more money even to pay my lawyer. I am flat broke. I decided to call Hank and try to reason with him. I was sure he didn't like the situation anymore than I did. I had tried to call him in the past, and it was always futile. You simply couldn't reason with him. What made me think I could reason with him now? I dialed the phone anyway, and Hank picked up on the second ring.

"Hello," he answered.

"Hank, it's me, Mary," I said. "We have to talk."

"No, we don't. I have nothing to say to you," Hank snapped back.

"Please, Hank," I begged. "Don't hang up the phone."

"So, what do you want?" he snapped back angrily.

"I want Kenny to come home and the divorce to be over."

"You did this to yourself, Mary. You ruined everything. I begged you to come back after you first left. I told you I couldn't live without you and the kids. Do you remember? But you wouldn't," he continued, "So reap what you sow."

"I couldn't stay with you because you never said you would change. You never said you would do anything different. All you said was you couldn't live without us. You had your chance to change but didn't. If anything, you've gotten even worse now."

"If you don't get the courts off my back," said Hank, "you will never see Kenny again for as long as you live." That was the first time ever that Hank admitted he had taken Kenny. I was relieved but afraid for Kenny's sake. I said, "Where is he? Don't you realize you are hurting him by keeping him away? He will probably need psychiatric care when he comes home, and all because of you."

"So, what are you going to do, Mary? It's your choice. I'm not bringing him home until you get the courts off my back," he argued. By this time, he was becoming unreasonable, and I knew that he was going to hang up if I didn't give in. I absolutely believed every single word he just told me about never seeing Kenny again. I knew that with all his money, this situation could go on endlessly. I knew he could take Kenny out of the country along with all his money, and I would never see Kenny or Hank ever again. I explained to him that all I wanted was a small decent house somewhere with adequate child support to raise the kids, nothing more.

"Just please bring Kenny home," I begged.

"Talk to your lawyer," Hank said. "It's up to you, Mary." And then he hung up. I started to cry and couldn't stop myself. Why didn't Hank tell me before that he had Kenny? He always told me that he probably drowned in the Charles River because I was not taking good care of him. How cruel he had been for seven long months. He loved torturing me. Finally, he admitted that he took Kenny. I didn't know what to do. Should I call the police or my lawyer? The police would question me. Hank would deny everything. My lawyer would believe me. So I wiped my eyes and decided to call my lawyer.

Tom Durkson was not surprised to learn that Hank had Kenny stashed away somewhere. He advised me not to notify the police just yet. It would only drive Kenny further and further away. Hank was beyond reason and was capable at this point of doing anything. If Hank could have been watched 24/7, there might have been a chance that he would eventually lead us to Kenny. He had to have been seeing Kenny over these last seven months. I had reached the point of saturation. I couldn't handle one more anything in my life. No more court motions, no more police investigations, no more work, no more mothering, no more anything. I thought to myself, what am I going to do? I am going mad. I have to get by this some way. Reasoning with Hank was out of the question. It was obvious unless Hank got his own way, this situation would go on forever. I had to do something but what?

"Mary, are you there?" Tom called out. I suddenly came back to attention and out of the daze I was in. "Why don't you meet me in my office, and we'll go over some possible alternatives for the case. It's better if we spend a full hour with each other so we get this right." I agreed, and we made arrangements to get together the next morning.

Meanwhile, I decided to hire a private detective to follow Hank 24/7 with the hope that Hank would eventually lead us to Kenny. So, I called Paul Spilling and asked him if he knew of a good detective who could follow Hank. Paul was skeptical because even with the police watching him, Hank was very careful in covering his tracks. He felt I could be wasting my money, but I insisted this was my last ditch effort to find Kenny. So, Paul put me in touch with Lawrence Hopkins, supposedly a very good private eye.

My plan was beginning to take place but with no money, the chance of that happening was pretty slim. How was I going to get a big wad of cash? By this time, my parents were tapped out, so I couldn't go to them for help. Then I had an idea. I'll call my aunt. Her husband is my godfather, and they had always been generous with me when it came to birthdays and Christmas. They were very wealthy, so tapping into them wouldn't set them back. So, I called them immediately, and they agreed to help me. They were very sorry to hear of all the difficulty I had been going through. The entire family was aware of the situation, and everyone was praying for me. But after seven months, all their prayers had not made any difference. Kenny was still missing, and I was still broke.

To my good fortune, my aunt mailed me a $3,000 check, and it was in the mail within two days. With this payment, I could have a private detective follow Hank for three weeks. After that, the investigation would have to end because I would have run out of money.

So I contacted the private detective, and he started my case immediately. Mr. Hopkins kept me updated daily, but the information was always the same, no news. The three-week clock was ticking, and I was praying that something good would come out of this escapade. But after three very long weeks, nothing new was discovered, and I was out $3,000. That's when I called my attorney.

"Tom," I said, "I can't go on like this anymore. Hank has broken me, and I have to move on. So I've decided to drop all the motions on perjury and his financial statement. If you can just get me enough money to buy a little house somewhere and some decent child support, Hank will settle the case and bring Kenny home."

"Mary, you don't want to do this. There is way too much money at stake. We are talking about at least one million dollars due you. Do you realize how that would change your life?" Tom stated.

"I do, Tom, but it is only money. Money can't bring me happiness. I am willing to work full-time to support my kids if you can get me some decent child support; I just want all my kids home. I want Kenny home and after seven months, I have reached the point of no return," I said, determined to end this insane situation once and for all.

"Mary," Tom said. "I still cannot advise you to go forward with such a small settlement. You could regret this for the rest of your life. Think of what kind of a life you could give the kids with that kind of money."

"What kind of life am I giving them now? Between work and mothering, I feel like I'm slipping away. I cry myself to sleep every night. I am exhausted all the time, I continue to borrow money from my parents, and I can't even afford to buy the girls an ice cream cone. This is no way to live, and you know this could continue on for at least another year, if not longer. You understand the law, Tom, so you know it's true. I have been trying so hard to stay strong for the girls, but I know there have been days when my girls could see how sad I was;

and they have actually caught me crying on a couple of occasions. They need to have a happy mother again, and I need to get on with my life. If it wasn't for my parents, I don't know what I would do. I can't live like this anymore. I'm on poverty row. If I went on welfare, I would be better off than what I have now."

"Alright, Mary," said Tom. "I'll start the paper work, but I want you to know that we can always go back to the court for a modification in the future, so this case is not necessarily over. I can protect you in the future with a modification, Mary."

"I understand, Tom," I said. And with that, I hung up the phone.

• • •

Two months have now passed and the Judgment of Divorce Nisi after hearing all persons interested is adjudged nisi that a divorce from the bond of matrimony be granted for said plaintiff, for the cause of cruel and abusive treatment as provided by Chapter 208 ss 1-2 and that upon and after the expiration of six months from the entry of this judgment it shall become and be absolute unless, upon the application of any person within such period, the Court shall otherwise order. It is further ordered that the parties are ordered to comply with the terms of an agreement filed, incorporated, and merged in this judgment but shall survive with independent legal significance.

Defendant shall convey to plaintiff approximately 14 acres of undeveloped land located in Stow, Massachusetts recorded in Middlesex Registry of Deeds, Book 780, Page 115 Certificate #126141 and a one story house located in Plymouth, Massachusetts recorded in Middlesex Registry of Deeds in Book 13107, Page 402 on or before October 17, 1981.

Defendant shall pay to plaintiff the sum of $10,000 by August 27, 1981. Said money shall be made payable to Attorney Tom Durkson, attorney for the plaintiff for services rendered.

Defendant shall transfer title of 1977 Ford Thunderbird to the plaintiff for sum of $100.00 the receipt of which is hereby acknowledged.

Defendant shall pay to plaintiff the sum of $250 per week for support of wife and minor children until all children reach the age of 18 years.

Defendant shall provide financial support for college education for said children. The children shall consult with their parents concerning said education and any decision concerning same shall be made jointly.

Defendant shall maintain major medical health insurance on said minor children and the plaintiff, to be paid through Watertown Steel Company as that plan is presently in force.

This agreement shall be merged in the divorce judgment however it shall have independent legal significance between said parties.

Needless to say, my attorney was not happy with this settlement. It afforded me only the purchase of a small home after selling land and a 100-year-old house. It provided minimal child support and health insurance, a poor man's settlement considering the assets were worth well over two million. However, the court never heard that information because the perjury charges on the financial statement were dropped allowing the original financial statement to stand. I signed this agreement with the understanding that Hank would bring Kenny home. He promised he would and even though I did not trust him, I was praying that he would keep his word. The court knew nothing about this side private agreement between me and Hank. What made me nervous about this arrangement with Hank was that it was not put in writing and was only agreed upon by word of mouth. Once again, Hank had all the power. And I still didn't trust anyone. I got the court off Hank's back. Now it was time for Hank to bring Kenny home. But why wouldn't he? He certainly didn't want the status quo to continue, otherwise he would never have settled. I had to believe that he would keep his word. I simply had to believe, I had to. And so I wait.

• • •

Chapter X

It was a Wednesday afternoon when the girls got off the school bus, all excited to tell me something.

"Mommy, Mommy, guess what, Mommy?" Becky was yelling out.

"What's so exciting that you have to tell me?" I said.

"Mommy, Kenny is home. Daddy had him at school today, and I saw Kenny. He was at the bus stop when I got out of school, and I saw him," Izzy said.

"What did you do when you saw your brother?"

Izzy said, "I said hi, but I didn't say anything to Daddy."

"Is Daddy bringing Kenny home to our house; do you know?" I questioned Izzy.

"I don't know," Becky said.

Izzy said, "Yes, Mommy. Daddy said Kenny was living with him now at home."

"Oh my God, I don't believe it. Kenny is finally home. Let's go see him right now."

"Girls, get in the car," I said. "We are driving over to the house right now."

My mind was racing, and I thought, I wonder what Kenny will be like. Will he be the same or will he be very sad? I couldn't bear it if he was sad. I kept driving, not saying a word to the girls. They continued to chatter like little girls do, but I still didn't respond. I just kept driving and thinking only of

Kenny. The ride seemed endless. Why is it taking so long to get there? It is only a fifteen-minute drive from the apartment. Why aren't we there yet? My heart was pounding out of my chest. Now I knew what a panic attack must feel like. I couldn't catch my breath and thought I would have to pull over to the side of the road before continuing on. Please, dear God, help me get there safely. I kept driving. Driving was slow because rush hour traffic was just beginning. I knew I had to calm down if I was going to get me and the girls safely to Maple Drive. I started to take deep, deep breaths to help catch my breath. I continued to do this for a full minute until I could get hold of myself. The girls were getting scared that I was breathing so hard, and I don't know where I found the strength to pull it all together, but I explained to the girls that mommy was just very excited, that's all.

"Don't worry, girls," I said. "There is nothing to worry about. Mommy is just fine."

"But you are still breathing so hard, Mommy," Becky said.

"I know," I said. "I am trying not to breathe so hard, but I guess I am just too excited to see Kenny. Are you getting excited?" I asked the girls. They were, and they kept jibber jabbering until we reached home.

As I pulled into the driveway, Hank's green truck was parked in front of the house. He didn't know I was coming to see Kenny. I had never called him before leaving with the girls. Please, Hank, be good, I kept on whispering to myself. Please, be good, be good, be good. Let me see Kenny. There was always the chance that he wouldn't let me see him. He didn't have to bring Kenny to school so the girls would be shocked. He could have made better arrangements rather than have the girls have to tell their mother that Kenny was home. The girls seemed to only be excited to see their brother though. They didn't appear to be anxious in any way, just excited to see their brother.

We all got out of the car and as soon as I knocked on the front door, Hank opened the door and just glared at me. He said not a word about Kenny being home. Why was Kenny not running to the door to see who it was? Wouldn't that have been the normal thing to do? I managed to spit out, "The girls told me that you brought Kenny home and that he is living with you here. Can I please see him? The girls would like to see him, too."

"All right, come in," Hank said. Then he called Kenny, and he came from the den to the front hall to see us. He was so beautiful. What a beautiful little boy, I thought. He seems to be okay. Or is he? Why is he walking toward us so slowly? Shouldn't he be running? Does he even remember me, I thought. As he slowly approached us, he began to hug me in slow motion. Everything he did was deliberate and in slow motion. He didn't say anything. I told him how glad I was that he was now home and that I missed him very much while he was away. But Kenny still did not say anything. I asked him where Daddy had brought him, and he didn't know. All he could say was that he lived on a farm with twin boys, and everybody spoke French. I was numb. Canada, I thought. Was he in Canada? Why, oh, why did Hank do this to Kenny. It was obvious that Kenny was glad to be home but that he was profoundly sad. He had no energy in him, and he kept shrugging his shoulders every time one of us spoke to him. The girls hugged him and said they loved him.

"Kenny, would you like us to stay for a little while and visit with you?" I asked.

Kenny just shrugged his shoulders with just the slightest remark.

"I don't know," Kenny said.

"Well, we would like to stay for a little while if you want us to," I said.

Again, all Kenny could do was shrug his shoulders. It was obvious that he was deeply depressed, and I wondered how I was going to get him well if he continued to live with Hank. Hank would never allow me to take him to a psychologist. Hank behaved poorly during our family sessions, so why would I think he would allow me to take Kenny to therapy sessions. Hank hated them. I was thinking, I can't leave Kenny here to live with Hank. What if he dressed up in front of him? How would that impact Kenny? He was now eight-years-old and should be going to school. Was I supposed to allow Hank to raise him in this house? What about visitation rights? I didn't know what to do. I decided to talk with Hank for a few minutes to try to work out some kind of arrangement where the girls and I would be able to spend time with Kenny. Hank agreed and said, "You can see him whenever you want, but you have to call first. And if you do anything to get me in trouble with the courts again, you will never see him again for as long as you live." I was hoping that the girls didn't hear Hank say that. Thank goodness, they were in the next room with Kenny. So, I agreed and quietly said our good-byes to Kenny. It broke my heart to leave him. I wanted so much to have supper with him and to read him a story and tuck him in for the night. But Hank wouldn't allow that, maybe someday, but not now.

I was quiet the whole ride home, thinking seriously about how I was going to fix this predicament. The thought of Kenny living with Hank was unacceptable; and I knew that if the courts got wind of this, there would be hell to pay. After all, Hank's visits were supposed to be supervised with a social worker present. So, to have Kenny actually live with Hank was really pushing the boundaries. Since the divorce several weeks ago, Hank had made no attempt to visit with the girls. I was wondering if he ever would. All his concerns were only about Kenny, his son. He did have daughters, too, but apparently girls didn't matter, only boys did.

I remember when our first two babies were girls, how disappointed Hank was, he so wanted a boy. He had made some pretty tough statements about a girl baby; so much so that his father actually had to have a private conversation with him. He should have been so grateful that our babies were born healthy, but he wasn't. Hank had two friends from college that we kept in touch with over the years, and both couples had buried babies six months and one month old. These babies died before our babies were born, so Hank clearly understood the tragedy of burying babies. Both funerals were very hard to attend and even brought a tear to Hank's eye. So, to have him treat our girls with such indifference was a disgrace.

As I was driving home, I thought about discussing Kenny with my attorney. Right now, I was thinking that it was better to leave Kenny where he was rather than upset Hank to the point that he might send him away again. Hank's thinking was very fragile at this point, and I believe he truly did want Kenny home with us. But given Hank's state of mind, hoping that he would behave rationally was probably too much to hope for. So, for now, it would be a very guarded setback. Perhaps my attorney could give me some better advice than letting things lie as they were. I needed advice and guidance as to how to proceed but was afraid to ask social services. They had a myriad of health professionals that probably could have offered some sound advice but giving them even more authority over our lives would have been almost unbearable. I finally had legal and physical custody of my children and giving that status up to have social services step in would have been a giant step backwards. I couldn't live with their rules of authority again. It was too demanding and difficult.

It's been a full week now, and Hank still won't let me take Kenny out of the house when we visit. He still doesn't trust me, and I certainly don't trust him. After speaking with my attorney, we both agreed to not upset the apple cart right now, as long as things seemed to be palatably acceptable. Social Services still didn't know that Kenny was home. I was afraid to inform them, and Hank certainly was not going to contact the agency. So, for now, the status quo would have to reign supreme. That is until I received a phone call from the Superintendant of Schools in Randolph.

Kenny had been home for only eight days now and already, Hank was refusing to send Kenny to school. He had tried to enroll him in a private school for boys in Newton, but they were filled up, and he refused to send him to public school because he was afraid that kids would ridicule him about his father's dressing. During the divorce, Hank had gone public with his cross dressing. He actually paraded around the neighborhood in full drag for the whole world to see. In his sick demented mind, he would tell everyone he saw that he had to dress up like this because he missed his wife so much. Of course, no one bought into that insane logic. Once a neighbor actually called the police about disorderly conduct, and it was written up in all the town's newspapers. So sending Kenny to public school was out of the question in Hank's mind.

The phone rang and when I picked up, it was the Superintendant of Schools.

"Mrs. Clarke, I am the Superintendant of Schools in Randolph, and I need to tell you that your husband refuses to send your son Kenny to public school. He is insisting that he home-school Kenny and that is absolutely out of the question giving his background and circumstances. The reason I am calling you is to inform you that if Kenny is not in school within one week, that the state will step in and remove Kenny from the home. At that point, he will become a state ward, and both parents will be under the authority of Social Services. If there is anything you can do to encourage your husband to do the right thing and send Kenny to school, it would help to avoid this misfortune."

"Sir, I had no idea that Kenny was not in school. My husband never told me that Kenny was not attending school. In fact, he led me to believe that Kenny was attending school and that all was going well with his transition into public school."

"Mrs. Clark, I am sorry to inform you that that is simply not the case."

"I can assure you that I will make every effort to get my son to school," I said. "Please," I begged, "don't press charges until I have had a chance to try to intercede. I know that my husband wants the best for his son. How much time will you give me before the state steps in?"

"One week, Mrs. Clark, starting today. If this matter is not resolved by next Friday, charges will be brought against your husband, and Kenny will be removed from the home and turned over to the state."

"Yes," I answered. "I understand completely the gravity of this situation and will be contacting my husband today to try to resolve this unfortunate state of affairs."

"Let me give you my private number, Mrs. Clark, so you can keep me in the loop as to how things are progressing. I am hoping for your sake and Kenny's that your husband can be brought around. Feel free to call me with any questions. Thank you for your cooperation."

As I hung up the phone, I thought, nothing is ever simple when it comes to Hank. Is this how the rest of my life was going to be? Getting a divorce didn't fix the situation, it only made matters worse. What I didn't realize then was that divorce doesn't end the relationship, it only changes the relationship when children are involved, and trying to reason with Hank, now that we were divorced, would continue to be a monumental problem for the rest of my life. Once again, my thoughts returned to the same resolve; I should never have left Hank. But of course, that was ridiculous. I couldn't stay with him either. So, what was I to do? I could stay or leave, but both scenarios were problematic to say the least.

I decided to call Hank to talk about Kenny. I dialed the phone and when

Hank answered, I said, "Hank, the Superintendant of Schools just called me about Kenny not attending school. What's going on?"

"I'm not sending him to public school because all the kids will make fun of him because his father dresses in drag. I want him to go to Fesseden School for Boys in Newton, but they are already full for the year. I signed him up for next year but this year, I want to home-school him. The superintendant told me I can't do that, and I don't agree, so I have my attorney working on a solution."

"You're not qualified to home-school Kenny, Hank. Please be reasonable here." I begged Hank to listen to my logic of home schooling versus public school just for this year. Next year he could send Kenny to Fesseden School for Boys but for this year, he simply had to obey the law and send Kenny to public school, or the state would step in and take Kenny away from him and make Kenny a ward of the state. But Hank wouldn't hear of it. He had all the right alternatives, not the Superintendant of Schools, and who was he to dictate how to raise his child. I knew I faced an uphill battle and asked to meet with Hank in person, so we might be able to work out a solution that would satisfy both the Superintendant and Hank. Hank refused. He had already made up his mind, and his attorney would be filing a motion to allow Hank to home school Kenny. I knew that once the court realized who Hank was that his motion would ultimately be denied. Meanwhile, Hank was putting Kenny in jeopardy if he continued on in this vane.

Hank, as was expected, was unreasonable. Nobody was going to tell him what to do when it came to his son. My worst fears were beginning to be realized. Having the state step in and have Kenny put in foster care would be more than I could handle. I knew I had to call my attorney for direction and was hoping that he would have the right answer to resolve this problem.

I was very distraught when I hung up the phone with Hank. This was never going to end, is what I was thinking. I knew my attorney had to be reached today and hoped that he wasn't tied up in court all day. So, I immediately called him. Thank goodness, he answered the phone.

"Tom," I said. "I have a situation that is quite drastic right now and need your advice. Hank refuses to send Kenny to public school, and the Superintendant of Schools in Randolph just called me informing me that Kenny would become a ward of the state next Friday if Hank did not comply with the law. I don't know what to do."

"Mary, Hank can't do that. He will be arrested, and Kenny will be taken out of the home. Unfortunately, I am tied up in court all week and won't be able to get to court to file a Writ of Habeas Corpus. What I am suggesting you do, Mary, is go to court right now today and get a Writ of Habeas Corpus issued immediately. That way you can give the order to the police, and they can take Kenny away from Hank."

"How can I do that, Tom, I am not an attorney."

"You can do this, Mary. You are a smart woman. All you have to do is meet with a court moderator and explain the situation. She can get you in front of the judge today. You can leave the court with the Writ and bring it directly to the Randolph police. They will handle it from there.

"Are you sure I can do this?"

"Absolutely, Mary, you have no choice. If you delay, Kenny may be sent away again before next Friday and then this whole nightmare starts all over again."

"All right, Tom. I'll do it, but can I invoke your name if I need to?"

"Of course, Mary," Tom said.

Our conversation ended, and my head was swimming with information that Tom had tried to coach me on. What if I forgot some of what he had told me? No, I had to remember everything, absolutely everything, so I grabbed a piece of paper and wrote, as fast as I could, all the steps he had outlined me to take. I just hope I didn't forget anything.

It was now eleven o'clock, and I knew that court ended at four o'clock, which didn't leave me with much time. So, I called my mother, asking her to come over to babysit the girls when they got home from school and then I hurriedly drove to the Middlesex County Courthouse, hoping that all would go well. I knew what I had to do, and I felt I could do it. After all, this was my little boy I was rescuing. If this all turned out well, I thought, tomorrow I might actually have Kenny living with me. That would probably outrage Hank, but I had to be brave and move forward with my plan to save Kenny. Having him gone for another year would destroy my little boy. As it was, he needed to be under doctor's care, so we could get him some help if he was living with me. Kenny needed to have a normal life. He deserved to have a normal life, and Hank was so determined to have everything his way, he was destroying our little boy. Why he couldn't see that, I thought.

I couldn't find a parking space at the courthouse and had to circle the courthouse four times before a parking space opened up. I rushed into the courthouse and asked one of the bailiffs where I could find a court moderator, that it was an emergency, and could he help me. He motioned with his left arm in that direction, saying I should ask for a Maureen Taylor in the clerk's office just down the hall. So I briskly walked to the clerk's office and put in my request. Unfortunately, I was told I would have to wait because she was with another client and to take a seat. So I sat.

The courthouse smelled of coffee, and I was wishing I could have a cup, so I let my nose lead me to the snack counter out at the far end of the hall and slowly sipped a cup. I was mulling over how I would start the conversation with Ms. Taylor and hoped that she could get me into see the judge today. The chances of that happening were slim, but at least I was in the right place. If I didn't get to see the judge today, there was always Monday or Tuesday. But would that be enough time? What if Hank decided to move Kenny this weekend before I could have him served with the Writ of Habeas Corpus? I started to pray that I would be able to see the judge today in spite of the time of day. I realized I would be last on the list if I was able to meet with the judge, and I was hoping that it would not be Judge Ginsberg. I truly believed that he didn't like women, and that made me very nervous. But I was already nervous, so what difference did it make.

As I waited, I watched all the people walking up and down the courtroom hall and wondered where they all came from. There had to be at least a hundred people, if not more, in court today. I was thinking that all these people had such grievous problems that the only way to resolve them would be to take the matter to court. What a shame, I thought, that so many people were so stressed with their lives. I was still somewhat naïve but over the last nine months, I did become more familiar with the outside world. The world could really beat you up if you let it. You had to fight for every single morsel. You had to be tenacious and relentlessly pursue justice for the right causes, or you were doomed to live a life of misery. I kept telling myself to be strong and to patiently wait. It was two o'clock before I could meet with Ms. Maureen Taylor, and I was thinking as I entered her office that the chance of anything happening today given the time of day were next to nil. Ms. Taylor was a young woman, probably in her early thirties and was very attractive. She wore a dark colored suit with heels and looked very serious. She introduced herself without even a smile and asked me to please be seated.

"How can I help you, Mrs. Clark," as she looked at her pink note to see my name.

"My attorney, Tom Durkson, has advised me to come to court today to request a Writ of Habeas Corpus."

"That is a pretty serious writ, Mrs. Clark. Can you explain why you need such a writ?"

I then began to tell her the whole story of how Kenny was missing for almost nine months and continued to tell her everything, trying not to leave anything out. I had to remember in chronological order all the points that were relevant to my story. Ms. Taylor listened intently to everything I had to say and never once interrupted me until I was finished. She then asked me some questions about the urgency of the matter and a question about my attorney as well. She explained that she would try to meet with the judge today but could not promise me anything because it was already 2:30 pm. She further explained that if she wasn't successful at getting me in to see the judge today, that I would have to return to court on Monday.

"I understand," I said, "but Monday may be too late. Today is Friday, and I am afraid that my husband will take Kenny away this weekend."

"I realize that, Mrs. Clark, and I am earnestly going to try to get you into see the judge this afternoon. You may have to wait a couple of hours though, if I am successful, is that alright?"

"Absolutely, I'll wait for as long as it takes. Thank you, Ms. Taylor."

As she left, I was thinking that the most important part of the process had already been accomplished and that the next step would be meeting with the judge. Ms. Taylor did tell me that she would introduce the matter to the court and then the judge would ask to speak with me.

I had to get some fresh air, so I decided to take a brisk walk around the courthouse. As I breathed in the cool, fresh air, I began to relax and realized that whatever would happen today would be; there was nothing more that I could have done to try to save my son from harm. I had done all I could do. I finished my walk and returned to the courthouse and noticed that it was now three o'clock. I saw Ms. Taylor was in one of the four courtrooms off the main hallway. So my case had not come up yet, and I had time to grab a sandwich at the snack bar. I must have been hungrier than I realized because I gobbled down my tuna fish sandwich quickly as though I were starved. I looked around the hallway for a pay phone but could not find one and decided to ask one of the bailiffs where I could find a pay phone. He told me that public phones were only outside down the block as there were none allowed in the courthouse. I had wanted to call home to let Mom know that I would be home later than anticipated but that I was hoping for the best and not to worry. However, I didn't want to take the chance of missing Ms. Taylor while I left the courthouse, so I decided not to phone home.

I continued to wait and wait and wait. There were still so many people in the hallway, even as late as 3:30 on a Friday afternoon. I was beginning to get worried because I knew that court ended at four o'clock, and my hopes of getting in to see the judge might not happen this afternoon. Finally at four o'clock, the courtroom door opened, and Ms. Taylor motioned me into the courtroom to meet with the judge. Thank goodness, I thought. She introduced the case, and the judge requested she come to the bench. After several minutes of conversation, the judge looked up at me and said, "Mrs. Clark, if I were you, I would do the very same thing. It is for that reason that I am issuing you a Writ of Habeas Corpus. I will have my clerk prepare the Writ for you while you wait. You should bring the Writ directly to the Randolph police, and they will handle the matter from there. Do you understand?"

"Yes, your honor, I understand."

"Please approach the bench so that I may obtain your signature on this required document." So I approached the bench and signed the document. I was thinking that I was signing my life away. Little did I realize what the result of such a Writ would cause. But I was so innocent then, I felt I had done the right thing. I was convinced that since the judge would have done the same, that I had in fact made the right decision. So court ended, and I patiently waited for the typed Writ before starting home.

I drove straight to the police station with the Writ and was told that Social Services had to be present when presenting the order. I didn't understand why Social Services had to be present until the police chief explained that it was part of the written order.

"I'll contact them tonight so that we can plan on serving the Writ first thing Saturday morning." I tried to explain the urgency of serving the Writ tonight, and the police chief assured me that they would monitor the house during the evening to assure that Mr. Clark was still at home.

"We will call you when the Writ is being served, Mrs. Clark. The best thing for you to do right now is to go home and try to get some rest. Tomorrow will be an emotional day for everyone concerned."

"Thank you. Let me give you my phone number," I said.

We said good night to each other, and I finally was on my way home after a very long day. I was pretty worn out but was feeling kind of relieved now, thinking that everything would be alright now and that Kenny soon would be home with me. I didn't want to get my hopes up, but I couldn't imagine anything going wrong since both the police and Social Services were involved in serving the Writ. It should be a simple procedure. The police present the Writ and Social Services escort Kenny out of the house. He will be home with me before noon, I was thinking. But nothing could have prepared me for what was about to happen Saturday morning.

• • •

I was so obstinately restless with my sleep that night. I kept fading in and out of sleep and never really did completely fall asleep Friday night. I awoke with a headache. Damn it, I thought. Of all days to get a headache. I wanted to be at my best for Kenny, and a nagging headache would certainly hold me back a bit. I called my mother and asked her to stay with the girls that morning. That would allow me plenty of time to collect Kenny and finally bring him home. I didn't want the girls at the scene, thinking that it would be too emotional for them. So, I waited for Mom and a phone call from the police before leaving the house. Mom was at the house at nine o'clock but by 10 o'clock, I was still waiting for a phone call from the police. I waited patiently until eleven o'clock and then decided to drive down to the police station to see what the delay was. But when I got there, the police chief informed me that all hell had broken out at the house when the police tried to serve the Writ.

"What are you talking about? You were supposed to call me when you were serving the Writ so that I could be at the house with the police. Why didn't anyone call me?"

"I apologize, Mrs. Clark. Our desk clerk was supposed to make that call. Apparently, something went wrong."

"So, where is Kenny? I want to bring him home with me now," I said.

"Mrs. Clark, I'm sorry to say, but there was quite a scene at the house this morning."

"What kind of scene?" I asked.

"Why don't you come into my office so that we can talk in private."

"Now you *are* scaring me. Please tell me where Kenny is."

"Please, Mrs. Clark, let's go to my office." As he escorted me to his office, I was petrified to learn anything about what had happened that morning. I couldn't understand why Kenny was not here. Oh my God. What if Kenny was hurt? That would be why he wasn't at the police station. How could the police botch this up? After all, they are trained to handle all kinds of domestic issues. Surely collecting a little boy should not have been that difficult. Or was it?

"Mrs. Clark, when we got to the house to serve the Writ, Mr. Clark opened the door and was dressed as a woman. As soon as we had explained we were removing Kenny from the home, Mr. Clark went ballistic. He threatened us verbally and then picked up a rifle that was fully loaded and told Kenny to run to his bedroom. Mr. Clark then held the gun on the officer as he proceeded up the stairs. When he reached the top of the staircase, he fired a shot in the air to startle everyone. He then told Kenny to run to his room and proceeded to give the shot gun to Kenny and told him to lock himself in his room with the gun and if the police tried to break into his room, to shoot the police officer. The police charged Mr. Clark after he released the gun and held him at bay. However, the entire time that Kenny was locked in his room, your husband kept yelling out for Kenny to shoot the officer and kill him. He continually said, 'shoot the policeman' over and over again. We could hear Kenny in his room crying. We tried to talk to him through the bedroom door, but it was a good fifteen minutes before we were able to push through the door and apprehend Kenny. He never shot the rifle but just stayed sitting on his bed when he saw the police officer. No one was hurt, but we had to escort both Kenny and Mr. Clark out of the house in handcuffs. Unfortunately, that is the law. Even Kenny had to be handcuffed. Mr. Clark is now in jail awaiting arraignment Monday morning, and Kenny has been taken away by Social Services. I can put you in touch with their department if you would like."

"Of course I want to talk to Social Services. I want to take Kenny home."

"I'm afraid that is impossible, Mrs. Clark. Kenny is now under the control of Social Services and has now been deemed a ward of the state. You no longer have physical custody of your son; the Department of Social Services does."

I sat there in shock, stunned beyond belief. My poor little boy must be so traumatized. What a horrific scene to put a little boy through. I couldn't even begin to imagine what Kenny must be experiencing. He probably thinks he was being arrested along with his father because they put handcuffs on him. How could the police put handcuffs on a little boy? I hated Hank with everything that was in me for putting Kenny through such trauma. At that moment, I wanted Hank dead. What was wrong with this man? It was more than just cross dressing. It had to be more. What normal person would be acting out the way Hank had been over these last nine months? What could he possibly be thinking when he gave Kenny a fully loaded rifle and told him to kill the policeman. What kind of father does that? It was now obvious to me that Hank was suffering a mental breakdown. Even after the arraignment, the court probably would commit him to a state hospital for psychiatric observation rather than sentence him to jail time.

"I would like to see Kenny now. Where has Social Services taken him?" I asked.

"I believe they have placed him at the Nazareth Childhood Boarding School in Jamaica Plain. I'm sure once they hear from you, they will want to meet with you privately to explain all that they are doing for Kenny. I know this must be hard. I am sorry you and your son have been put through such a bad set of circumstances."

"I don't know whether to be angry with you or to thank you for protecting Kenny from getting hurt. I can't even think anymore."

It was then that I broke down and started to cry. The police chief recommended I go home and get some much-needed rest and assured me that everything would work out okay. "Once you've had a chance to speak with Social Services, I am sure they will be able to answer all your questions. In the meanwhile, you may want to call your lawyer, Mrs. Clark."

"My lawyer," I snapped.

"It's for your own good, Mrs. Clark," the sheriff stated.

As I drove home, I had to pull over to the side of the road. I was having trouble focusing on driving. I think I was in shock. At least I felt like I was ill. I didn't really know what shock felt like, but if I couldn't even drive myself home, perhaps I was actually in shock. I decided to sit there until I could collect my wits, calm down, and stop crying. I knew I would be sitting there for a while, and that was okay. It was then that a police officer pulled up and inquired if I was alright. I wasn't, and I asked the officer to please drive me home. I was too ill to drive.

• • •

When my mother saw me being escorted by a policeman and no Kenny, a look of terror filled her face. The officer told my mother I was not well and that I had asked him to drive me home saying, "You might want to call a doctor," he told my mother before departing. My mother listened intently and thanked the officer for bringing me home. After he left, I told my mother the entire failing fiasco.

She was struck with horror and began to cry, saying, "Why is Hank doing these awful things? I don't understand what has come over him."

"To tell you the truth, Mom, I don't know either. He has become completely deranged and is clearly out of control. Now he is under arrest and is being arraigned Monday, so for now, he is behind locked doors." I went on to say that I believed once he was arraigned on Monday that he would not be leaving on his own free volition. "He's in a lot of trouble now, and I don't see how he is going to be set free. The charges are pretty severe, contributing to the delinquency of a minor, threatening to kill a policeman, resisting arrest, attempted murder with an assault weapon, lewd and insidious behavior with a minor, and disturbing the peace."

My mother sat in silence as I told her the entire story, and she could not believe what she was hearing. It was indeed a nightmare of profound proportion, and she had trouble digesting much of the story. She continued to ask questions about what she had just heard, and I tried to answer as best I could, but after a while, I just couldn't cope anymore and asked for a break. That's when I went upstairs to lie down, and I didn't wake up until 6 o'clock. When I went downstairs, my mother had made supper for me and the girls and was happy to see me get some much-needed nourishment into my body. She offered to spend the night if I needed her, but I sent her home. I just wanted to be alone. I didn't want to talk to anyone anymore. I just wanted to be left alone.

My mind would not rest, and I was constantly reminded of Kenny and what he must be experiencing. Away from home for nine months with strangers, and now this horrific, terrifying nightmare. I didn't know how I was going to get through this crisis or how I was going to protect Kenny. I was so drained from the last nine months, the thought of having to muster up strength to get through this next fiasco was beyond my ability. I prayed for strength and perseverance, asking God to please help me through this dreadful hardship. I felt I was being tested and that I would fail this state of affairs, losing both my son and my sanity. I knew God was listening, but he just wasn't answering me right now. He was asking me to wait, but to wait for what. All hell had already broken out, so what was left? Me, I was left, and I was a wretched wreck. Mom put the girls to bed and then left, and I followed shortly after hoping for a new day, a new beginning, a new resolve. What would tomorrow bring? Only tomorrow would tell.

I couldn't wait to call social services Sunday morning and awoke at 6:30 am. Their office didn't open until nine o'clock, so it would be two and a half more hours before I could place the call. Was I even capable of waiting so long? I was shaky, had a headache, and was sick to my stomach. My nerves were playing havoc with me, and I knew I had to find a way to settle down, or I would never make it through the day. Not knowing what it would bring only made me more unsettled. How could I turn my mind off? It was then that I found myself on my knees, praying so desperately to God that I felt a calm rush through my body. I felt as though God had put his hand on my shoulder, and I knew he would be right by my side today watching over me and Kenny. Thank, God; I thanked God for listening and for bringing me peace.

Nine o'clock came quicker than I had imagined, and social services requested I meet with them at the Nazareth Childhood Boarding School where Kenny was being held. I had an 11 o'clock appointment and left way ahead of time because I knew I would have trouble finding that school in Jamaica Plain. I had never been to Jamaica Plain or driven the Alwifebrook Parkway in my life. This road was curve after winding curve after curve, so watching for directions would be more difficult than normal. I had all I could do to just keep my mind on driving, so many curves with traffic bumper to bumper, only a two-lane highway, and cars on the other side of the road driving just as fast and oh, so close to the divided line. I didn't get lost but by the time I got there, my nerves were shattered. I sat in the parking lot for a good twenty minutes, trying to collect my thoughts and calm down. If this social worker saw an overwrought mother, I felt that would put my seeing Kenny in jeopardy.

The doors were locked, so I rang the door bell as I took a good hard long breath. I was ushered inside. The social worker didn't keep me waiting, and our meeting lasted about a half hour. She explained what the school would be doing for Kenny and that he would be meeting with the resident psychiatrist daily for as long as needed. She also told me that Kenny was facing charges of assault to murder and assault by means of a dangerous weapon. He was turned over to the Massachusetts Department of Social Services where we have full legal and physical custody of Kenny. She then told me I would not be allowed to see him for at least a month. Kenny had been through a life altering experience, and he was quite shaken by the entire episode. He actually asked the question, am I in jail, when the police escorted social services and Kenny to the facility last night.

What Hank had done to my precious son would never be forgiven. Hank was loathsomely despicable as far as I was concerned. All I wanted was for Kenny to be okay. But would he ever be okay again? I can't even imagine an adult recovering after being put through what Kenny was forced to face. How was a little boy so innocent supposed to heal himself from such a shockingly horrific occurrence? The thought of not even being allowed to see him was so hurtful to me. Did this social worker think that holding my son in my arms and telling him how much I loved him would bring him harm? Social Services were actually trying to protect him from not only his father, but from me as well. I was not the perpetrator. I was the victim, as was Kenny. How could they keep us apart? I questioned the department's logic, and she insisted that it had to be that way. But I was more persistent, and she finally agreed I could see Kenny. She brought me out to the main hallway and asked me to wait there while she collected Kenny but when she returned, she informed me that he had said he didn't want to see me. My heart wept. All I wanted was to hold him in my arms, but Kenny said no.

But wait. Just then I heard footsteps being shuffled down the corridor around the corner and when Kenny appeared, he couldn't even hold his head up. His head was down, his shoulders were drooped, and his feet were dragging on the floor. He was in a deep depression, and it broke my heart. He made his way over to me so slowly and then laid his head on my lap. I lost it and cried out and held him so lovingly, all I could say was, "I love you, Kenny," over and over again. After a minute, the social worker interrupted and took Kenny away saying that was all Kenny could handle today. But truly, that was all I could handle as well. I drove home depressed beyond intellectual capacity.

The next day was Monday, and I drove myself to the courthouse to see Kenny being arraigned. Hank was being arraigned, but supposedly, Kenny was being arraigned as well on charges of attempted murder and unlawful use of a fire arm. Social Services had appointed an attorney ad lebiam for Kenny and that attorney was present as well. We waited all morning for the case to be heard but then were told that court was taking a lunch break and that court would not be reconvening until one o'clock.

Just then I saw Hank walk by me, saying I'm going to lunch. He never returned to court to be arraigned. When court convened, all charges on Kenny were dropped, and the attorney and social services left to return Kenny to Nazareth Childhood Boarding School. I was numb. Hank skipped out on $5,000 bail, and Kenny was taken away from me for at least a month, an entire month. How was I supposed to get through thirty more days before I could see Kenny again? He would think that I abandoned him. He surely could not comprehend why his mother was not seeing him, or his father for that matter. Would he assume that he would be away somewhere new this time for a very long time again? What could possibly be going through this special little boy's head, alone again with strangers? I didn't trust Social Services before, and I certainly didn't trust them now. Would they be doing the right thing by him? I was told Kenny would be meeting with the psychiatrist every day and yet, I wouldn't be there to offer a hug after any one of those sessions, my precious little Kenny. My heart was busting in agony. Tears came yet again. I thought I was over crying when catastrophes struck. But this was the greatest abuse of all. Kenny was home, and now he was taken away.

Two days later the papers reported:

- A 40-year-old local father who allegedly left his 8-year-old son with a shotgun Saturday and told him to kill police and thereafter to commit suicide, disappeared from District Court Monday before he could be arraigned.
- A warrant was issued for his arrest. Police were still looking for the suspect today.
- Hank Clark of 36 Maple Drive appeared at District Court Monday morning allegedly with a knife and $50,000 cash on his person, according to a court officer. A court officer confiscated the knife. But Clark left the courthouse before he could be arraigned on charges of assault to commit murder, assault by means of a dangerous weapon (the shotgun), contributing to the delinquency of a minor, and dis-

turbing the peace, according to an assistant clerk of courts.
- After Clark's failure to appear for his arraignment on those charges Monday, the court revoked Clark's firearms identification (FID) card that had been issued in Watertown in 1968. An FID card allows the bearer to own firearms but not to carry them. Last year, Clark's permit to carry a handgun was seized by Watertown Police.
- On Saturday afternoon, Randolph Police seized 26 firearms and thousands of rounds of ammunition for those guns from Clark's Randolph home after the alleged incident involving him, his son, and the shotgun. Clark had been released from jail Saturday afternoon after he posted $5,000 cash bail.
- The alleged incident began about 10 o'clock Saturday morning when police went to Clark's home to serve a Writ from Cambridge Probate Court ordering him to surrender his son to the court in a custody suit brought by his wife, police said. After police arrived at Clark's Maple Drive home, the 40-year-old father allegedly answered the door dressed as a woman.
- When Clark learned what police wanted, he grabbed his son and locked himself and the 8-year-old in a bedroom, police said. He warned the police he would "waste you" if the police did not leave, police said. Police radioed for additional officers.

  After repeatedly asking Clark to come out, the 40-year-old father reportedly said he would. But when he did, police continued, Clark slammed the door shut with his son still in the bedroom and allegedly told him to kill the police if they tried to enter the room and then to commit suicide.
- Police said the boy eventually opened the door but jumped back and held a loaded single-barrel shotgun on Det. Charles Ryan for 10 to 15 minutes before Ryan was able to talk him into disarming it. Shortly thereafter, Ryan grabbed the shotgun, ending the tense incident.

  As a result of the alleged incident, the 8-year-old boy also faced a hearing in the Juvenile Division of District Court on charges of assault to murder and assault by means of a dangerous weapon. He has been

- turned over to the Massachusetts Department of Social Services, according to police.
- After Clark and his son were arrested Saturday, Police returned to the Clark home about 2:30 P.M. with a court order to search it. In the presence of his attorney, the 40-year-old Clark opened a safe in the house that contained ammunition and many of the 26 firearms police found in the house. Among the 26 firearms were 10 handguns, a number of shotguns, .22 caliber rifles, other rifles, and a Colt AR-7 Semi-automatic weapon. Police said Monday, the semi-automatic weapon had not been converted to an automatic weapon as had been their concern.
- According to sources, a safe in Clark's home also contained an estimated $50,000 cash.
- Clark will forfeit the $5,000 bail he posted Saturday since he failed to stay for his arraignment Monday.
- Court officials said Clark also faces a show cause hearing today on a charge of failure to send a child (the 8-year-old boy) to school.
- About a year ago, the 8-year-old boy had been the object of an intense search by law enforcement officials and private detectives after he disappeared during a court suit by his parents over the boy's custody, police said. After a divorce was granted, the boy reappeared, police said.
- The 40-year-old Clark is a native of Watertown. The fugitive father owns Watertown Steel Company, Inc. at 385 Pleasant St., Watertown, police said.

When I read the papers, I realized that the police chief had not told me the entire story. The story in the papers was even worse than the story I was told by the police chief. No wonder Kenny was depressed. It is amazing that he didn't actually have a mental breakdown. My mind couldn't rest. Over and over again, all I could think of was my poor Kenny. How much he had been through over these last nine months because of Hank. It had to have damaged Kenny beyond repair. Yet he laid his head on my lap at Nazareth. He wanted to be loved. He was a good boy, but did he believe he was good or did he feel he was bad and deserved to be in jail. I couldn't reason, think one more thought, or understand one additional thread of logic. My mind was empty, and my heart was broken-shattered to a thousand pieces. I felt it was beyond repair.

• • •

Part III
Healing Kenny

Chapter XI

As each day goes by, I try to give the girls as normal a life as I can. It's hard because the girls keep asking about Kenny. All I can say is that he is away getting well because he is very sad. The girls don't understand saying, "But wouldn't he be sad being all alone, Mommy?"

"I'm sure he probably is, but he is under a doctor's care, which is a good thing."

"Will the doctor make him better?" asked Becky.

"I hope so with all my heart," I answered.

"But I don't understand, Mommy. You could make him happy like you make us happy, so why does he have to be away from all of us?" Izzy stubbornly argued. "Why can't you make him better? You make us better when we are sick, so why can't you make Kenny better when he is sad?"

"I don't know how to take care of Kenny right now, not in a way that would make him well. You see, Kenny is not only sad, but he is sick, and he needs to be under a doctor's care right now. The doctor needs to have Kenny all to himself for just a little while so that Kenny can get well. Do you understand that this is for the best?" I tried to convince my girls of this big fat lie. I didn't believe a word I was saying and yet, there was a little piece of me that did believe that the psychiatrist must know what he was doing. Kenny was so profoundly sad that I didn't have a clue how to pull him out of this dreadful place he had fallen into. I had to start trusting again. I had to trust the psychiatrist. Right now, this doctor is a complete and total stranger to me, so I decided to call his office first thing in the morning to introduce myself and to request a private meeting with him to discuss Kenny's case. Surely, the doctor couldn't deny a mother a small meeting after expressing such genuine concern for her little boy. That is unless he too is under court order to work on Kenny's case. If he is, his guidelines would be very guarded, and perhaps I would be denied a meeting. I hope this isn't the case, I thought.

Ever since Kenny was taken into legal and physical custody by Social Services on that dreadful Saturday morning, my girls were also required to meet with a social worker weekly. It didn't seem fair but because the entire family would be impacted by Kenny's circumstances, the Department of Social Services stepped in and obtained legal custody of my girls, once again, with me having physical custody. Hank no longer had legal or physical custody of any of the children. Their rationale was that the family, once again, was in crisis and with Mr. Clark now being charged with a felony and at large, the Department ordered they obtain legal custody of my girls until the family was no longer in crisis. Living with Hank meant the family would always be in crisis, so did that mean that Social Services would be in my life forever? I had to wonder. I was so worn out from being under the Department's scrutiny. I remember when Hank demanded I get the courts off his back, or I would never see Kenny again. This set of circumstances was just as difficult for me. Would I ever get the system off my back? This was all because of Hank. Once again, the kids and I were being punished because of Hank's corrupt appallingly shocking behavior. I felt my life was doomed because Hank was in it. I prayed that the FBI would get their man and that finally Hank would be put in jail where he belonged. Then maybe, just maybe, the kids and I could get our lives back again.

The girls' social worker was Carol Daily. She was just 26-years-old, and I was not impressed with her as our case worker. She was young and single and had no idea of what life with Hank, a cross dresser, could be like. Even with Hank being on the run, Ms. Daily was pushing for some kind of family resolve where we all could live in harmony. After all, that way the kids would have both parents to raise and love them. Harmony wasn't in Hank's vocabulary. I fought this with the department's director, stating that Ms. Daily was too young and way too idealistic to take on such a difficult case, but I got nowhere. The department was understaffed, and the kids and I would have to make the best of it. I'm a 35-year-old woman being forced to take orders from a 26-year-old social worker. The system just wasn't working for me or the kids. It seemed Hank got away with murder, and we got punished for it. When is enough enough? So for now, this is the way it has to be.

• • •

The days went slowly by and every night, before I put the girls to bed, we all said a prayer for Kenny's quick recovery. That way the girls were little by little becoming convinced that Kenny would be getting well and would be returning home to us in a short while. At least that was the plan. We had to wait and so we prayed.

Finally, the long month away from Kenny had passed. Carol Daily approved my taking the girls along for the visit, so we all drove together with anxious anticipation. When we saw Kenny, he was still very depressed and walked slowly and had drooped shoulders. He did hold his head up, and he was not shuffling his feet, so that was an improvement, but I was hoping for a better rehab than what I saw. It was then that I realized how deeply Kenny had been damaged by the ordeal he had been put through. My poor baby; my beautiful little boy was no longer smiling. Would he ever smile again? My heart drifted downwards to utter despair. If hearts could cry, you would have heard mine wailing. I knew this journey had just begun for me and Kenny and that I had to find the courage to see this through. I had to learn to say the right things and behave a certain way so that his progress could continue to improve. It was then that I decided to request another meeting with Kenny's psychiatrist. This time, I was hoping to meet with him personally and not just talk about Kenny's progress over the phone. That phone call a month ago was not very enlightening. In fact, it practically told me nothing. The doctor kept repeating that Kenny was still quite sad but was progressing and that was all he had to report at that time. He did ask me to be patient and let him do his job and that right now, not seeing Kenny was truly the best thing for Kenny. I didn't understand his logic then, and I still don't. I truly believed that if I were allowed to see him between some of his sessions that Kenny's spirits would be lifted, however, the psychiatrist did not agree with my concept; and he had the final word. So this time when I called the psychiatrist, Dr. Benjamin MacHaskell, I would be all the more insistent on meeting with him personally. After all, that way he would get to meet me. Didn't he need to know what I was like? How could he eventually return Kenny to my custody without having ever known me? It only made sense. I had to know from a medical point of view if Kenny was progressing as well as could be expected. But more importantly, I had to learn how to behave and react to my son's behavior in a way that would be beneficial with his recovery. I had to take the lead here. I had to insist on a personal meeting with Dr. MacHaskell. So I decided to make the call when I returned home after visiting Kenny.

We were allowed to see Kenny without any supervision. The girls had suggested bringing his favorite board game to play with him during the visit, which I thought was a wonderful idea. So, we all played Chutes and Ladders for the half hour we were allowed to spend with Kenny. The visit did go smoothly without any outbursts or temper tantrums. Kenny was subdued, but a couple of times he did show a slight smile while playing the game with me and his sisters. The visit was much too short. I wanted to stay longer, but the Director of the Nazareth facility was emphatic that the visit be held to the half hour standard. So, we all made the best of it. We all had a chance to hug him and kiss him and tell him how much we loved him; and I held his hand every chance I got. So, we all drove home that day, excited to see that Kenny was getting a little bit better. The girls so innocently chatted about Kenny all the way home. It was fun to listen to them. How simple children made everything seem possible. If only it were so.

The next day after the girls went off to school, I called Dr. MacHaskell's office. I was determined to arrange a meeting between the two of us to discuss Kenny's progress at Nazareth. As the phone rang, I hoped for a positive conversation. It was only 8 o'clock in the morning, so I was hoping to find the doctor in before he began his appointments for the day. I was well pleased that his nurse put me right through to the doctor.

"Good morning, Mrs. Clark. How can I help you?" the good doctor said.

"Thank you for taking my call, Dr. MacHaskell. I was wondering if we might be able to arrange a meeting between the two of us to discuss Kenny's progress and to get a chance to finally meet each other. I am anxious to hear about Kenny's progress and want to ask your advice about how I can help with Kenny's recovery," I said.

"Certainly, Mrs. Clark," answered Dr. MacHaskell. "I am glad you called because I was planning on meeting with you shortly anyway. I apologize for the delay, but it was important for me to deal with only Kenny without being influenced by any outside interferences. Not that you were an interference but so that I could dedicate all my efforts to only exploring Kenny and his circumstances."

"I understand completely, doctor. I can meet with you at your convenience," I said.

"Very well, Mrs. Clark, I will have my nurse arrange for our conference as quickly as my schedule will allow. Thank you for calling." He then transferred the call to his nurse who scheduled an appointment for me the following week.

As I hung up the phone, I was pleased that the call went so well and that finally Dr. MacHaskell wanted to meet with me. I was sure that once he saw who I was and how I behaved, versus Kenny's father's behavior, that the doctor would be encouraged that Kenny could someday return home to a sensible home with a loving mother and family.

At this point, Hank was still at large, and the FBI had still not located Hank. My attorney said that it was simply a matter of time before Hank was apprehended and handed over to the authorities. Tom said the FBI always gets their man. I had heard that phrase but assumed it was simply a slogan of the department and not necessarily a reality. But, rest assured, it was a reality, and my attorney was confident that Hank would eventually end up behind bars.

• • •

Today, I awoke a little apprehensive because my appointment to meet with Dr. MacHaskell was scheduled for 10 o'clock at his office at the Nazareth School. I was anxious but excited. I lay in bed with a smile on my face. I couldn't believe it, but I was actually happy for the first time in a long while. I felt safe knowing that Hank was on the run, so he would not be interfering with me, the girls, or Kenny in any way, shape, or form, and that was a very good feeling indeed. And I was excited to be meeting with the good doctor because I was hopeful that Kenny would be making progress in his therapy. The sun was streaming full throttle through my bedroom window, which always made for a happy start to the day. As I waved goodbye to the girls as they boarded the school bus, I was thinking that this was going to be a good day. I get to hear all about Kenny and his progress. I wanted to know if he had settled into his new school and whether he had made friends. Kenny didn't volunteer much information when we visited with him. I always had to coax him into having a conversation with me. Sometimes I felt as though I was asking him question after question because he just wouldn't open up and start to talk on his own, but he still was not the little boy I knew that was always giggling and saying silly things like 'jumping for joy' or 'what is your forte?' That piece of him was missing, and I guess I was looking for some assurance that that piece of Kenny would eventually be found.

It was a thirty-minute drive from Randolph to Nazareth, and I drove with no radio playing. I was turning over in my mind all the questions I wanted to ask Dr. MacHaskell, making sure I wouldn't forget any of my concerns. When I arrived at the school and parked the car, I quickly wrote down all my views and questions, so I wouldn't become distracted when I was in conference with the doctor. It would be my cheat sheet, so I felt confident that I would be leaving with all my concerns addressed.

"Good morning, Mrs. Clark," said Dr. MacHaskell as he welcomed me into his office.

It was a small office with only a desk, a small table for two, and one couch. As I looked around, I noticed that he had pictures of his family on his desk, which was endearing. Perhaps he used these pictures as talking points in his therapy sessions, I thought.

Dr. MacHaskell motioned for me to take a seat on the couch and then said, "I have a written report that you may take home with you, Mrs. Clark. It is what we will be discussing in detail this morning, so feel free to ask questions as we go along. I'll try to answer them as best I can."

"Thank you," I said.

"I'd like to begin by saying that I like your son very much. He is a sweet boy who has experienced some hard times and is trying to deal with this trauma as best he can. Right now, while he is still quite sad, he is experiencing post traumatic stress syndrome."

"Oh dear, that is not what I was expecting to hear," I said, showing great concern for such a grave illness. "This is the first time I have ever heard that terminology used to describe my son. Why was I not informed of this before by Social Services?" I asked.

"Because he hadn't been diagnosed before, only assessed by social services psychologists. Let me stress that I don't want you to worry about this term. We are working on this problem with him every day that we meet and are hopeful that this syndrome will eventually be put to rest." Dr. MacHaskell went on to explain that Kenny enjoys reading animal stories. However, he continues to remain withdrawn when it comes to his ability to relate to adults. He seldom initiates a conversation with adults. As for Kenny's ability to relate to other children, Kenny continues to be uninvolved with peers. He seldom participates in any group activity. He usually sits by himself, reading. Kenny does not voluntarily participate in group activities. He prefers to work and play by himself. He is a multi-sensory learner, which is good, and his attitude toward most things is fair. As for self-concept, Kenny continues to appear extremely depressed. He has continued to exhibit certain stereotyped behavior and sounds.

This was not what I was expecting to hear. I knew he was still depressed and rarely smiled, but his ability to relate to adults and peers was upsetting to hear. It was then that I asked what I could do to help Kenny progress. The doctor explained that I should continue to show love and patience, not to correct but to encourage and to share fun and happy family happenings, not specific events which he missed because he was away from the family. The doctor further went on to explain that on average, Kenny was doing as well as could be expected. "Kenny is making progress, but it is very slow. He has been through a horrific set of events and is performing better than I would have imagined, given his set of circumstances," Dr. MacHaskell said. "I don't want you to worry, Mrs. Clark. This is a lot of information to digest in one fell swoop."

"It is a lot to digest," I said. "I was hoping for a more positive report. I understand all the school issues, and those can definitely be addressed with some special educational intervention. It is Kenny's state of mind that troubles me. I have recognized that he does have difficulty talking with adults, me specifically. I always feel I have to coax him to open up to me and so far, I have not succeeded in this area. Please tell me that Kenny will eventually be able to be brought around."

"I am very hopeful that Kenny will eventually be lifted out of his depression and the more he is exposed to positive experiences, the more he will progress with his ability to participate in a more normal way. Again, Mrs. Clark, I must stress that I don't want you to worry."

"That's easier said than done. It is obvious that his father has done great harm to Kenny. There are times when I blame myself for leaving his father, which started a series of irrational events and even worse, the horrific episode which transpired prior to Kenny's coming to Nazareth a month ago. All of this insanity started when I left the marriage, and I sometimes feel had I not left Hank, none of this misery would have taken place."

"Obviously you could not have stayed in the marriage. Your husband is a transvestite. Staying in such a marriage would eventually have been detrimental to all your children. As it stands now, only one child has been seriously impacted. The social worker reports to me weekly about her sessions with your girls as going well and that they are progressing quite nicely. Remember, they have not experienced what Kenny was forced to accept in his daily life for almost a full year. Such events do not simply disappear from one's mind. Kenny is exhibiting symptoms that correlate with what he has experienced. We are doing everything we can to help Kenny work through this maze of issues and are hopeful that Kenny will heal. It will take a great deal of time though, and

Kenny may have to be here at Nazareth for quite sometime. I know that's not what you want to hear, but I don't want to sugar coat Kenny's condition either. What I would like to suggest is that Kenny start making home visits, perhaps for an occasional weekend. Let's start slowly and see how those visits go. Would you like that, Mrs. Clark?"

"Very much, but I do have a question. What if Kenny doesn't want to return to Nazareth after such a weekend at home?"

"I have a pamphlet I want to give you to help you react and phrase things appropriately if that situation should arise. The pamphlet is extensive, and I want you to study the conversation portions of the pamphlet so that you can commit them to memory. Any conversation should role off your tongue and not be forced. This pamphlet will help you achieve that." Doctor MacHaskell then wound up the meeting, and we said our goodbyes.

All the way home, I was dumbfounded. I was so taken aback by everything I had learned that I found myself bowled over. I had no idea that Hank could have destroyed such a beautiful mind. I wanted Hank dead. Maybe the FBI would locate Hank, and there would be a shoot-out, and that would be the end of all my problems. What a horrible thought. I had to stop whining and was determined to learn all I could to help my son get well. I could go to the library and do research on Kenny's condition, post-traumatic stress syndrome. The more I learned, the better I would be able to help Kenny. I loved him so much. My heart ached for Kenny. It wasn't easy being a mother, but no one ever told me it would be this hard.

• • •

The months passed and little by little, we were allowed to see Kenny more often and for longer periods of time. It became a normal part of our daily lives now. At first, it was once every two weeks, then weekend visits once a month, then after two months, it was once every week. All this time, Kenny was attending school and participating in extra curriculum activities and slowly, he began to come out of his depression. His home visits were for the most part happy family get-togethers. However, there had been moments when there were tears and sometimes even acting out. Once he even shouted out at the girls with clenched fists, ready to fight. That was disturbing. It hurt to think of Kenny being angry. I so wanted him to be a happy little boy again. But wishing can't make things come true.

We were still under the Department's authority. I was told that Kenny could not be taken out of state by Social Services. I had requested permission to bring him to my parents' cottage in Maine for the weekend and was denied. So, the girls went with Mom and Dad, and Kenny and I spent the weekend at the beach, just the two of us. My parents' cottage was in the same complex as our former summer home was, so the kids had lots of friends and oodles of activities to enjoy. Of course, Kenny wanted to go. He so loved it there; and he especially loved the beach where he would ride the waves with his little surf board all day long. It was summertime now, and my parents wanted all of us to join them at their cottage. Visits there were always fun, and I hated to have to deprive Kenny of the adventure, but the department was persistent that Kenny not be taken out of the state. Hank was still at large, it had now been four months and still, the FBI was not able to locate him. I didn't have a clue where Hank could be hiding, and apparently neither did the FBI. I couldn't understand the department's logic about not allowing Kenny out of the state. Kenny would be just as safe there as he would be with me at home. Weekends were always planned family activities, so we were out and about. I truly believed Kenny was not in danger. After all, Hank was still on the run and would never attempt to do anything foolish concerning the children because it would place him in jeopardy with the FBI. I wondered if Hank even knew that the FBI was looking for him and that he was a wanted man. But then again, how would he know if it wasn't on the news or in the papers. It wasn't public knowledge and of course, the FBI investigation was undercover. All the same, Hank had to know that there would be a warrant out for his arrest, thus the hiding out from the law. So with Hank in hiding, why did the department insist that Kenny not be allowed to travel to Maine to spend time with his grandparents?

This order prevailed for the entire summer, and I finally had had enough. I felt as though I was saving one child and losing my two girls. The department's logic was to bring the family together. This order was achieving just the opposite, keeping our family separated. Carol Daily was still our case worker, and her recommendation to the department was always to keep Kenny in Massachusetts no matter what. I lost all respect for this case worker, so I finally wrote a letter to the Director of the Department of Social Services explaining I was losing two to save one and would they please reconsider letting Kenny travel out of state.

It wasn't a week later when I received a phone call from the Director of the department requesting a meeting with me. Finally, I thought, I am getting a response to this stupid policy. The meeting went well and after I explained how special Maine was, I was given permission to bring Kenny to his grandparents' cottage. Hallelujah!

The next weekend was Labor Day, and I was finally allowed to take all three of my children to my parents' cottage in Maine. We were so looking forward to the weekend, especially Kenny. It would be his first visit to Maine this summer, and he was so excited.

"Mommy, I can go to Maine with you?" he yelled out with joy.

"Absolutely, we all can go together. Won't this be just the best fun," I said.

At last I felt as though I was getting my life back. We all couldn't wait for the weekend to come. As I drove from Randolph to Nazareth to pick up Kenny for the long holiday weekend, I couldn't believe how wonderful I felt. I was finally given permission to enjoy all three of my children together in Maine. I felt like I was just let out of prison. Social Services had been extremely difficult to deal with over the entire summer, and I finally won my first argument with them. I couldn't believe it. When Kenny saw me, he started to run to me with a big happy smile on his face, and he said, "I can go to Maine with you now, can't I?"

"Yes, you can," I said happily and loaded him into the car for our quick drive home. The girls were waiting in the driveway for us, jumping up and down and yelling out yeah as we drove in. What a wonderful weekend we were going to have.

I already had packed and bought some groceries for the weekend trip. The kids helped load everything in the car, including their pails and shovels and Kenny's surf board. The drive was only an hour and a half, and we sang songs and told spooky ghost stories the whole way. The kids were so happy. There was no way you were going to wipe off those smiles from their little faces. We all were overjoyed and absolutely delighted to be driving to Maine. Kenny had not seen his grandparents all summer long, and my parents were so looking forward to a weekend with the entire family. The weather was perfect: sunny skies, 80 degrees, and no humidity. It was going to be a perfect weekend.

My parents were sitting in their front yard when we pulled up to their cottage. As soon as the kids saw them, they all ran with glee to say hello to Memere and Pepere. It was just about supper time, and Dad already had the grill going. We were all having hotdogs and steaks with baked potatoes, green salad, and of course, a yummy dessert Mom baked fresh that afternoon. After supper, the kids went to the hall where all their little friends were lined up waiting for the hall doors to open at 7 o'clock sharp. As soon as Kenny saw his favorite cousin, Sherwood, they ran into each other's arms. How wonderful, I thought. Kenny is so happy. I'm so glad he could make the trip with us. We were going to have three glorious days and wouldn't be returning home until Monday night after supper.

The hall doors opened, and the older kids went right in to start the juke box, and all the little ones went right to the penny candy counter. Penny bingo was the activity of the night, and Kenny always won every time he played. Go figure. I stayed the whole time in the hall with the kids. I didn't want to leave Kenny for one second. I wanted to watch him enjoy playing bingo with all the other kids in the complex. There were a good fifty younger kids all playing, so the winner would be collecting a lot of pennies. After bingo, the kids played ping pong, or at least they tried to. Kenny was not very good, but that was okay. Every time Sherwood or Kenny would miss the ball, they both started giggling. Oh, the thrill to see Kenny so happy and giggling again.

Four months had already passed since Kenny went to live at Nazareth, and the doctor told me that it would still be a little longer before he would be released into my custody. Kenny was progressing well and to see him here and now, one never would have guessed that this little boy was even remotely sad. He had come so far in his healing and was doing well in school, too. He loved reading stories. I bought a brand-new story book for Kenny to read tonight; a story about a messy moose who lived in the woods in Maine. I knew he would love it.

The sun was still high in the sky, and it was a perfect summer evening. It stayed light until 9 o'clock, so the kids would be turning in late for their bedtime tonight. 9 o'clock came so quickly. It was time to walk back to the cottage. Sherwood and Kenny had their arms around each other's shoulder as they walked ahead of me and the girls. They were so cute together. The girls were jibber jabbering with each other, and I was humming a silly song as we meandered toward the cottage when suddenly, a car drove by and slammed on its brakes. The door opened, and Kenny was grabbed and thrown into the car. The car then sped off. It was Hank. I saw Hank driving with a woman. It was Judy Costello. I couldn't believe it. I had a feeling she was living with Hank because I knew she left her husband just around the time I left the marriage. Her little boy, Guy, and Kenny used to play together often. To see her with Hank was disturbing. To see Kenny taken was shocking. Where did Hank come from? He must have been awfully good at covering his tracks because where was the FBI now when I needed them. I was horror stricken, and the girls were crying and yelling. I immediately grabbed the girls' hands and started running toward the cottage. When Dad saw me running with the girls, I started to yell out, "Hank took Kenny. Did you see his car?"

"No," Dad said. "I didn't see Hank's green truck."

"He wasn't in his green truck. He was in a grey car with a woman. Did you see a grey car pass by here?"

"As a matter of fact, I just saw a grey car drive up the road. I didn't pay much attention to it though. I don't remember seeing Hank driving the car."

"He went that way?" I asked

"Yes, that way," Dad said.

I ran into the house and started to dial 911. I was frantic and operating at full velocity. I was so close to having a panic attack it scared me. I had all I could do to explain what had just happened to the operator. I told 911 that my ex-husband had kidnapped my son and that he was headed up north on Route 1 and that he was with a woman. I explained that he was a wanted felon and that the FBI was involved in hunting him down. To verify any of this, you can contact the attorney general, a Mr. Dellahunt in Massachusetts, who is involved in the case as well. The dispatcher asked me some questions about what Kenny was wearing, and I tried to answer her questions as best I could. She then put the call through to the Maine State troopers as she explained that they would be in pursuit of Hank and my son. They asked me to stay close to the phone, so they could keep me informed.

Just then, a neighbor came in hearing all the commotion, and he reported that he had witnessed the entire kidnapping. I asked him if he would be willing to talk to the police and tell them exactly what he had observed. Maybe he could shed some light on the hijacking. I handed him the phone, and he immediately began a conversation with the dispatcher. My mother then gave me a hug and said, "I'm so sorry. The police will find Kenny. Hank could not have driven too far and if he turns onto the interstate, the State Police will definitely catch up with him because it is a straight road, and you can see ahead for over a mile. They will bring Kenny back. I just know it."

"And what if they don't, Ma," I said. "This whole fiasco starts all over again. Carol Daily was right. I should never have brought Kenny out of state."

"That's ridiculous," my dad said emphatically. "Hank could just as well have taken Kenny when he was staying for a weekend at your house. So, don't go blaming yourself, blame Hank. He's the bad ass here, not you."

"Oh, Dad," I cried as I threw my arms around him and began to sob. Dad tried to console me, but I couldn't stop crying. Now the girls started to cry when they saw the state I was in. I grabbed both of them, and we all cried together. Becky cried out, "Why is Daddy doing this, Mommy?"

"I don't know. I guess he just wants to be with Kenny," I said

"I hate him," Izzy screamed and ran into the bedroom wailing. She kept repeating "I hate him, I hate him," screaming at the top of her lungs.

By then, the neighbor, Roy Harris, who had witnessed the entire episode, volunteered to let me use his radio police scanner.

"That way you can hear what's going on. There are all kinds of communication between troopers when they are pursuing a felon," Roy said.

I wanted to go, but I was supposed to stay close to the phone. I didn't want to leave the girls either, but I wanted to go with Roy. I had to know what was happening. Just then, Dad said, "Go with Roy, honey. We'll stay close to the phone and if we need you, we'll come get you. We'll take care of the girls. Go, honey, go now."

I left without even saying goodbye to the girls. I was only focused on the police radio.

Roy quickly walked me over to his cottage and immediately went to the police scanner and began to punch in some codes and before I knew it, I was listening to the State Troopers in pursuit of Hank. They were radioing back and forth and were in hot pursuit of Hank's car. They had already caught up to his car when, all of a sudden, all hell broke loose. Hank pulled the car over to the side of the road, and he and Kenny started running into the woods. Hank kept yelling out to Kenny, "Run as fast as you can and keep running. Don't stop, just keep running."

As the trooper was reporting this, the other trooper jumped out of the car and started chasing Hank through the woods. When he reached Hank, there was a scuffle, and the two men began wrestling on the forest floor. As they rolled and kicked at each other, Hank managed to punch the State Trooper in his face and instantly, the trooper's nose began to bleed. They continued the brawl as they struggled with each other, rolling around on the ground when Hank let out another punch. This time his punch hit the trooper's jaw, and Hank heard the trooper yell out in pain. Hank's adrenaline was pumping hard by now. They continued to wrestle on the ground with each other when all of a sudden, Hank grabbed the trooper's gun right out of his holster and proceeded to put the gun to the trooper's head yelling, "I'll kill you if you don't let me run. I'm going to get my son and if you follow me, I'll kill you."

The officer knew that this emotional encounter had to be scaled back and started to try to talk Hank out of the gun saying, "You don't want to do this. You don't want to shoot a State Trooper; if you kill me, you will go to prison for the rest of your life. Don't do it, man, don't do it. You don't want to shoot a trooper. Think of your son."

The trooper kept trying to talk Hank out of the gun as Hank continued to yell to let him run. Hank kicked the trooper in the leg and kept yelling to let him run. Finally, after a very long, five minutes, Hank surrendered the gun, and the State Trooper handcuffed Hank and led him back to the cruiser. The State Trooper then radioed for a helicopter on the scene ASAP so that Kenny could be found. When the helicopter reached the scene, radio contact between the cruiser and the helicopter was ongoing, and I could actually hear the motor of the helicopter as it circled the woods looking for Kenny.

"Oh my, God, I can't stand this. What if they can't find Kenny? What if he tripped or broke a leg or worse, hit his head and is lying in the woods unconscious?"

"I'm so sorry this is happening to you. They'll find Kenny. The Maine State Troopers are well trained, and they will find Kenny," Roy said.

I stayed for another hour listening so intently, I thought I would go deaf. Roy suggested I get home to the girls, get them settled into bed, and try to calm down. "Ask your mom to make you a cup of tea and hold the cup with both hands, feeling its warmth. It will be soothing, trust me." That was just like Roy. He was always kind and thoughtful. I left and returned home completely exhausted without one ounce of energy left in my body. I kept repeating in my mind, why, why, Hank, why?

When I got home, the girls were still up, sipping on some homemade hot chocolate that Mom had made for them. Both Becky and Izzy's eyes were still red from crying. What a horrid mess this was. At least Hank was arrested. I had to trust that the police would find Kenny. The Maine woods can go on and on forever. During the summer months, the news always reports several times about someone getting lost in the woods. Most times, the tragedy ends up positive; however, once the tragedy was indeed a tragedy. The little boy that was found had died all alone in the woods. I prayed to God that would not be the case here. I couldn't bear it if Kenny was never found or worse, dead. It is then I went into the bedroom and got on my knees and started talking out loud to God pleading my case while weeping non stop. My expression of grief was heartfelt as I prayed fervently to God. I had never prayed so desperately before. I knew God was listening as I kept praying, "Please God, keep Kenny safe." I continued to pray for a good ten minutes until I could cry no more. That's when the phone rang, and it was the Maine state police saying that they found Kenny, he was safe, and I could pick him up at the State Troopers office on Interstate 95.

"Thank God," I said.

I told Mom and Dad about the phone call and that Kenny was safe and sound. They both hugged me and said thank God as well.

Dad told me how to get to the Maine State Troopers building on the interstate, but I just couldn't follow his directions. My mind was too convoluted. As a result, Dad decided to drive me himself. That probably was for the best; that way neither Mom nor Dad would worry whether I found the building or arrived safely.

It was a twenty-five-minute drive to the State Trooper's building and when we arrived, Dad offered to stay behind while I collected Kenny. When I entered the building, I could see Kenny sitting on a bench all by himself. There was an officer on site as well. Otherwise there was no business going on. When I walked up to Kenny, I noticed he had no shoes on.

"Where are your shoes, Kenny?" I asked.

"They fell off my feet when I was running," Kenny said.

"Did you hurt your feet?" I asked very concerned.

"No," Kenny answered.

"Were you afraid that you were lost?" I asked.

"Yes, Ma," Kenny quietly answered.

I then asked the officer where my ex-husband was, and he informed me that he was being held in jail for arraignment on Tuesday for attempted murder of a Maine State Trooper, assault with a deadly weapon, kidnapping, and child endangerment. I couldn't say anything. I was speechless. I just looked at the officer and nodded my head and said to Kenny, "Let's go home, honey," as I picked him up and hugged him in my arms so tightly. I never wanted to let go of him again. I hugged him all the way to the car. I told Dad when we got into the car about all the trouble Hank had gotten himself into and that he was in jail now, my poor little boy. What a harrowing experience. He was so scared, he actually ran right out of his shoes. It was a miracle that Kenny wasn't hurt. God did hear my prayer after all.

Chapter XII

The ride home from Maine that weekend was a sad one. The kids were not talking, and I was expressionless. What a long arduous ride home. What started out to be a glorious weekend with my three children turned out to be an outlandish nightmare. When would this nightmarish life I was living ever end? Hank was finally in jail, so for now, we got a slight reprieve. But what if Hank was let out on bail again? This whole sad situation could start all over again. Just the thought of it made me shiver.

We all arrived home safe, and it was time to bring Kenny back to Nazareth. I knew I had to tell the Director about the kidnapping and was dreading the thought of it. I also knew once Carol Daily got wind of this, she would be even more encroaching. I could feel my freedom slipping away. I was so completely worn out from the last year of episode after episode. I didn't know how much more I could bear alone. My parents had been so supportive over this past year, but I couldn't continue to lean on them for my own self-reliance. It was time for me to seek out a counselor for myself, if for nothing else but to vent.

The Director already heard the truth about the weekend, and she was extremely upset and deeply concerned about Kenny's mental state of mind. Delahunt's office of the attorney general's office notified her Monday morning. This was just one more harrowing experience that now had to be added on to the already long list of episodes that had impacted Kenny's state of mind. This definitely was a setback and as a result, weekend home visits were curtailed indefinitely. Further, all future visits with Kenny would be required to take place at Nazareth. There would be no more home visits. So all the progress we had made with Kenny, trying to matriculate him back into family life, was suddenly halted until further notice. I felt as though I would be living with Social Services for the rest of my life. I definitely was going to seek out a counselor for myself. I had to talk to someone, anyone, to vent.

• • •

Barbara Kovar came highly recommended by my family doctor as a counselor who might be helpful for me to engage with. So, I contacted her office the next morning, seeking an appointment. I was a little disappointed to learn that I would have to wait over two weeks but was hopeful that she might be able to help me. Meanwhile, I would just have to chug along as best I could. But more importantly, I was anxious to meet with Kenny's psychiatrist to find out exactly how badly this past weekend impacted Kenny's progress to date. So, after I had completed my phone call with Ms. Kovar's office, I dialed Dr. MacHaskell's office to arrange an appointment. The doctor was anxious to meet with me as well. It was important that he be briefed with all the details of this past weekend, so he knew what he was dealing with. Dr. MacHaskell asked me to see him the next day. He felt it was imminent that we meet quickly so he cleared his schedule to accommodate our meeting. I knew that Kenny must be in crisis again and was willing to do whatever was asked of me to get Kenny well. The fact that the doctor was willing to clear his calendar for me gave rise to concern. Tomorrow was already here, and I knew it was going to be a difficult morning reliving the entire episode with Dr. MacHaskell. I didn't sleep at all the night before, not for a minute, so I knew remembering in chronological order would be a challenge.

"Good morning, Mrs. Clark. Please be seated," as Dr. MacHaskell motioned me into his office. "Please make yourself comfortable."

"Good morning, Dr. MacHaskell," I said as I took a seat on the sofa. I planted myself firmly into the cushions of the sofa, waiting for the conversation to begin, expecting to be blasted for this incident. I didn't know whether I was going to be chastised or consoled and was quite anxious to just get it over with. I thought I was well prepared for this meeting but with lack of sleep, I definitely was not at my best.

Dr. MacHaskell started by saying, "Mrs. Clark, first let me say how sorry I am that you and Kenny had to endure such an ordeal over the Labor Day Weekend. It had to have been very difficult for you, and I am sorry that you had to face such a set of circumstances. How are you doing?"

"As well as can be expected, I suppose. I didn't sleep well last night and am a bit tired, but I do want to talk about how this episode has impacted Kenny, not about me. Since the ordeal, I never saw Kenny cry, which I find strange given all that he had been through. Why didn't he cry?" I asked.

"It is part of the post-traumatic stress syndrome. Tears are a normal way for the body to release turmoil. However, in your son's case, he is unable to cry because he continues to relive the incident with his father and the woods. It has greatly troubled him, and he continues to fade into a daze when reliving the event. With therapy, this will subside. Crying is the final phase of the syndrome and when that takes place, Kenny will be well on the road to healing."

"This breaks my heart to hear this," I said. "However, it is important for you to know that his father is currently in the Maine Cumberland jail and was denied bail until his trial at which point he is looking at least a year or two in prison. He also faces similar charges in Massachusetts which also involve prison time. This being the case I feel Kenny will have a decent chance of healing without any further interference from his father."

"That is both good and bad news and let me explain," the doctor said. "No further interference from the father will be beneficial for healing; however, facing Kenny's father's imprisonment most likely will be problematic for Kenny. Having his father in captivity will be a tough pill for a young boy to swallow. Luckily, we do not have to grapple with that issue at this time. We will cross that bridge when we need to."

The meeting continued on a good two hours with me sharing my narrative about how events unfolded over the weekend and Dr. MacHaskell sharing the process of getting Kenny well. It was a good meeting, and I left the doctor's office with a much better attitude than when I had first arrived for the conference. I was encouraged that the doctor could help Kenny, and he assured me that home visits would be taking place shortly, that it would be an important and integral part of Kenny's healing process. Little did I know then that Kenny would be living at Nazareth for another year before he would officially be allowed to come home to stay. That's a long time for healing but apparently necessary given all that Kenny had been through in his young life.

• • •

Hank is in Cumberland County Prison awaiting extradition to Massachusetts where he faces criminal charges. A new charge has been added on to the already long list of offenses he is being charged, that is threatening to kill a judge in writing and then mailing said letter through the federal postal service. What was he thinking? Did he actually think that threatening a judge in writing would change anything in the divorce case or the custody of the children? How stupid. He is in so much trouble with the law right now, I can't imagine him not serving jail time. He has committed a number of crimes in two states now and is still fighting the battle of 'might over right.' I don't think he will ever learn until he is incarcerated. He truly believes he is above the law. Nobody is going to tell him what to do. I think he has finally met his match. I can't imagine any court in the land allowing him to make bail given the many offenses he has committed in both Massachusetts and Maine. I have to believe that this time the system will do what is right and not be lenient with Hank. I'll just have to wait and see.

The next day, all the newspapers were reporting both the Massachusetts and Maine criminal offenses facing Hank. The reading was compelling. One article's headlines read, "Custody-obsessed dad's woes mount." The article read:

Last October, while Randolph police stood outside his bedroom door, divorced father, Hank Clark, allegedly handed his eight-year-old son a loaded shotgun and told the boy to "shoot the pigs." On Friday, after abducting the child from his mother in Ogunquit, Maine, Clark allegedly assaulted and tried to murder a Maine state trooper while the frightened boy ran into the woods.

Police found the child two hours later after an intensive search by helicopter. Yesterday, Clark pleaded guilty in U.S. District Court in Boston to mailing a letter threatening to kill a Middlesex probate court judge who ordered that the child be placed in state custody. Clark, 40, formerly of Randolph and now of Kingfield, Maine, has been in a custody battle for months with his former wife. Sources yesterday described him as "obsessed" with retaining custody of the boy who is under protection of the State Department of Social Services. After pleading yesterday, he was returned to Cumberland County Jail in Portland to face assault and attempted murder charges against the trooper. He also stands trial Sept. 28 for armed assault and attempted murder against the Randolph officers and will be sentenced in Sept. for the letter threatening to kill Middlesex County Probate Judge James Sweeney.

Another newspaper article read "U.S. marshals keep Clark confined," which read:

U.S. marshals of the federal justice department intend to maintain custody for at least the next month of a local man charged with the attempted murder of a Maine state trooper and assault with intent to murder a Randolph detective. Bernard Stone, the U.S. Marshall for the district of Massachusetts, said Thursday his marshals will "hold onto" Hank Clark, 40, formerly of 36 Maple Drive until he is scheduled for a sentencing in U.S. District Court in Boston Sept. 26. Clark, Wednesday, pleaded guilty in that court to a charge of threatening a judge who was involved in a civil suit between Clark and his ex-wife over the custody of their son. That charge was brought against him in November. Judge Walter J. Skinner Wednesday set Sept. 26 as the date for his sentencing. Meanwhile, Clark is expected in Portland District Court in Maine on Sept. 24 to answer charges of attempted murder of Maine state trooper and assaulting a police officer. Those charges were lodged against Clark after he allegedly overpowered a Maine state trooper Friday and held the man at gunpoint until the trooper talked him into giving up the gun, police said. In addition, he is expected in Cambridge Superior Court Sept. 28 on a charge of assault with intent to murder Charles Ryan, a Randolph police detective. According to police, those charges were brought against Clark in October, after he allegedly ordered his eight-year-old son to gun down Ryan. U.S. marshals picked Clark up Tuesday from Maine officials on the federal charge of threatening a judge. Federal authority supersedes state authority, and the U.S. marshals have no intention of giving up custody of Clark who is being held without bail until his Sept. 26 sentencing. When it is time for him to appear in Maine or Cambridge courts, Stone said, "Where ever he has to go, we'll be transporting him." Meanwhile U.S. marshals have locked Clark up in the Rockingham County Jail in Brentwood, NH. Stone reported.

Oh, I thought, the trouble Hank is in. He's been posting bail all over the place and yet, he can't give his kids enough child support to make their lives halfway decent. Finally, the U.S. marshals have figured out the only way to stop Hank from continuing criminal intent is to hold him in jail until his trial. Thank God, someone has finally figured this out. The judges have been granting bail for every offense Hank has been charged with. The U.S. marshals have more common sense than our courts do. I finally feel safer. Hank is behind bars where he belongs. It's a good thing that I have an unlisted telephone number, otherwise the phone would be ringing off the hook tonight from neighbors and townspeople. None of them know where I moved to or what the kids and I are doing. I am literally living incognito. Thank God.

Just then, the phone rang, and it was Mom. She read in the Boston Globe about Hank as well as the Portland Press Herald in Maine, and she was amazed at how much trouble Hank had gotten himself mixed up in. She was concerned about me and the kids and how we were holding up given the latest write-ups in the papers.

"I'm relieved," I said. "This is the first time in over a year that I feel safe knowing that Hank is locked up behind bars. I don't know if I should tell the kids or not. What do you think I should do, Mom?" Mom said,

"I don't see how you cannot tell them. Won't they hear about it when they go to school? You know how kids are. They can be cruel without realizing it."

"But how can I tell the kids that their father is in jail? I'm afraid to use that word because they are so young."

That's when mom said, "Why don't you ask your counselor, Barbara Kovar, how to phrase it to the kids? She might even advise you not to tell the kids. I don't know what to advise you, that is why you should talk to Barbara.

"You're right, Mom," I said. "First thing tomorrow, I'll call my counselor and ask for her advice. She knows all that has been going on, and I'm sure she will be able to help me work this out."

After the phone call, my head was swimming with information, too much to handle all at once, so I decided to take a nice, hot bath, sipping a hot cup of tea and just soaking until I felt calmed down. The hot tub felt wonderful as I lay there with my hands wrapped around a nice hot cup of tea. It felt good, better than crying myself to sleep. What is it about a nice, hot tub that can be so soothing? I moved my feet and listened to the water gently swish back and forth. It was comforting; so comforting that I decided to soak in the tub until I got sleepy or until the tub turned cold. I fell asleep in the tub. I awoke with a slight chill and turned in for the night.

• • •

As for Judy Costello, she also was arrested for aiding and abetting a criminal, claiming innocence and that she had no idea that Hank was even thinking of kidnapping Kenny, let alone actually doing it. She continued to claim she had nothing to do with this crime and that she was innocent. Needless to say, the district attorney didn't buy into this premise and she, too, was arrested as a material witness. She was livid and was forced to get a lawyer to defend herself in court. She was released on $5,000 bail and had to appear in court with Hank Tuesday morning to answer to charges of aiding and abetting in a criminal offense. She most likely will not get jail time, but she will be levied a hefty fine and be put on probation, which means she will have a criminal record. Little did I know then what Hank and Judy were planning. Even behind bars, Hank continued to strategize ways to get his son.

• • •

Judy Costello was found wandering the halls of Nazareth unattended, looking for Kenny two months later. She simply let herself into the building and began walking down the halls, looking for Kenny unattended and unannounced.

When the director found her meandering, she was furious saying, "Who are you and why are you here?"

Judy answered, "I was told I could see Kenny Clark, and I am going to his classroom."

"Who told you you could visit Kenny?

"The director of the facility," she said.

"I am the director of the facility, and I insist that you leave now under my supervision. I will escort you to the door. What is your name? Let me see your driver's license," the director insisted. Judy turned over her driver's license and once examined, was escorted out of the building. The director then locked the door so any further visitors, including deliveries, would have to ring the bell, the normal procedure. The door was always locked. This was clearly an oversight on one of the staffs' part. The director thought to herself, I will have to address this incident in my staff meeting as well as inform the police of this intrusion. This woman will be getting a visit from the police shortly. I was told a woman was with the father when Kenny was taken, but I never anticipated that she would have the gall to go after Kenny on her own, the director thought as she walked back to her office.

Coincidence had it that I had an appointment with the director, Mrs. Kathy Lawrence, the very same day. I was so upset to hear that Judy Costello had entered the building looking for Kenny. Kenny was supposed to be safe from harm, and this misstep was very worrisome to me. I irritably said, "What kind of security do you have at this facility? Why was the door unlocked?"

"I assure you, Mrs. Clark, that this is very unusual. This door is always locked, and there will be an inquiry into this incident. This should never have happened. I assure you this has never happened before, Mrs. Clark."

"I can't stress enough," I said, "that Kenny's father is extremely dangerous. He will stop at nothing to get his hands on his son. He believes he is above the law. And now that he is incarcerated, he is having his girlfriend do his bidding for him." I was furious. "What if this woman managed to find Kenny's classroom and convinced the teacher that she and Kenny had an appointment with the director. She could have walked right out of this facility, and no one would be the wiser. His father will stop at nothing to get his own way. Do you understand, Mrs. Lawrence?"

"Of course, Mrs. Clark, I understand that you are very upset right now, and I don't blame you, but let me assure you that Kenny is safe at our facility. This woman would never have been allowed to take Kenny out of the classroom. The entire staff knows that only the director in person can release a child from his classroom, no exceptions."

I couldn't continue to harp on this situation, so I simply nodded my head in compliance as we walked into Mrs. Lawrence's office for our conference. It had been several months now since Kenny had been kidnapped in Maine. Last week, Comprehensive Mental Health Services (CMHS) had performed psychological testing on Kenny. Our meeting today was to discuss the outcome of those tests. The tests administered were: Wechsler Intelligence Scale for Children-Revised, Family Drawing, Bender-Gestalt, Rorschach, and Trematic Perception Test.

Just then, the phone rang, and Kathy gave me the written report to review while she took the call. The report read Kenneth is a slight boy with blonde hair and hazel eyes. He was cooperative with the tester in an obedient way but appeared to find this cooperation a strain. He was guarded and had little to say outside of the testing. Kenneth is right-handed, and his attention span is adequate.

Kenneth has been visiting his mother and sisters and now says that he is ready and wishes to return home. Although he has been doing well at Nazareth and has been in therapy, he finds it difficult or impossible to talk about his experiences with his father.

His intellectual functioning I.Q. is 123 with a performance I.Q. of 132. Kenneth is currently functioning in the superior range overall. This classification is somewhat misleading, however, as there is a highly significant disparity between his ability to use verbal as opposed to perceptual-motor skills. It is clear that Kenneth finds it far easier to manipulate objects and to respond to visual-motor stimuli than to use words. His verbal skills are average to bright average while his visual motor skills are very superior. There are no outstanding weaknesses in Kenneth's performance. Neurological functioning is appropriate for his age.

Kenneth's personality has clearly been traumatized by the events of the past and is still very upset. His reality testing is adequate, but there are many areas of significant conflict. Immature, especially given his intellectual potential, Kenneth prefers to deal with animals or things rather than people. There is an absence of meaningful relationships on other tests. Relationships with other people are threatening to Kenneth, and he seeks to avoid them. In drawing his family, Kenneth included his father in the middle of the family, thereby expressing his wish to have his family all together. Whenever test material suggested interpersonal conflict, Kenneth denied or blocked out this aspect of the material. In response to a picture of a man and a woman, obviously in conflict he said, 'what am I supposed to say about this? I don't think anything. I don't know anything.' This response and others like it indicate how upsetting Kenneth finds the conflict between his parents and the effort he is making to block it out or deny it.

Extremely constricted emotionally, Kenneth is clearly making an attempt to keep strong feelings from surfacing. On an unconscious level, he is angry, sad, and extremely threatened by sexuality. In the drawing of his family, the figures are sexless, they all look alike. His response to sexual images suggests that he is experiencing castration anxiety. Kenneth's anger easily overwhelms him, and he becomes explosive. When he is angry and/or experiences strong emotions, he becomes overwhelmed and reality testing is poor.

Kenneth feels that he has been damaged or injured and is preoccupied with this feeling of injury. He is very angry that he has been broken and wants to be magically fixed. He feels he is weak and cannot do it by himself; he also cannot figure out how anyone else can help him. Perhaps because of his experiences before and during these experiences, Kenneth considers himself an important person and entitled to get whatever he wants/needs.

Kenneth is currently functioning in the high average range when using verbal skills and in the very superior range when using perceptual motor skills. Neurological functioning is age appropriate. Kenneth uses denial frequently and is very constricted emotionally. His defenses are often overwhelmed, resulting in feelings of anger and fear. Kenneth is aware of his difficulties and feels damaged. He wants help.

Diagnosis is: adjustment reaction to severe trauma and post-traumatic stress syndrome.

It is important that Kenneth continue in individual therapy, whether or not he returns home. He will need considerable help in order to resolve his conflicts and to function. He needs to blow off steam through physical activity. Eventually when Kenneth returns home, he should not be left to devise his own activities all day but should be enrolled in a structured program of some type, preferably involving physical activities.

By the time I finished the report, my eyes were filled with tears. My beautiful little boy had been ruined by Hank. At this point, I wanted Hank in prison for the rest of his life, never to be able to hurt my precious Kenny ever again. I knew Hank would never see this written report and if he did, he would call it hogwash. Our meeting lasted an hour. I couldn't think one more intelligent thought after the meeting. My brain was overwhelmed, my emotions were raw, and my heart was in tatters. All I wanted to do was go home and try to sleep off the pain. I would have to set the alarm though because I had to be awake when the girls came home from school.

When I arrived at home, there was a man ringing my door bell. I didn't know this man and couldn't imagine why he was trying to reach me. As I approached my apartment, the stranger asked if I was Mrs. Clark. I acknowledged who I was and asked who he was. He then served me with a subpoena and said good day. As he left, I was furious. Who could possibly be suing me? I immediately panicked and feverously ripped open the envelope. I couldn't believe what I was reading. Judy Costello was suing me for custody of Kenny, the gall! I was outraged and yelled out, "What? What is this? You've got to be kidding me!" I stood there in shock, talking to myself. I quickly let myself into the apartment and sat down at the kitchen table and began to read the decree.

In the matter of guardianship of a minor, Kenneth Clark, now comes the petitioner Judith A. Costello and moves that due to the emergency situation, which exists concerning the care and custody of the above-named minor, that the petitioner be given temporary guardianship until such time as the court can properly grant custody of the minor. The affidavit of Judy Costello then filled up two pages of lie after lie, stating that Kenny was allowed to remain at her home on weekends quite often, which never occurred. She further stated that after Kenny and his father were arrested on that dreadful Saturday morning that she went to the police department quite concerned to offer any assistance. After speaking with the social worker and attorney for the Department of Social Services, she was allowed to take Kenny to her home for the remainder of the weekend, taking on the responsibility of having him appear in court on Monday morning for his arraignment. What a pack of lies. I was outraged. Social Services took responsibility for Kenny at Nazareth, not Judy Costello. Lies, all lies. The affidavit further stated that when Kenny saw me Monday morning in court, that when I approached him to console him that Kenny punched me in the face twice, outrageous lies again. The affidavit finished, respectfully pleading that the court allow Kenny to return to her home and that she would welcome Kenny into her family. She further stated that Kenny would feel content to remain with her until he could be reunited with one of his parents. She then signed the document under penalty of perjury.

I immediately picked up the phone and called my attorney. Tom couldn't believe it either. Obviously, Judy Costello was in cahoots with Hank. He would stop at nothing until he had custody of Kenny. He wasn't even in his rational mind. How could he possibly raise Kenny? After all, he put a loaded shotgun in his hands and told him to kill the police. He refused to send him to school. He was dressing up as a woman in his presence, and he was currently in jail. The court would laugh this affidavit right out of the courtroom, I thought. Tom agreed. Unfortunately, the subpoena had to be answered, which meant another day in court, which was very upsetting to hear. I was terrified of court. I emotionally blurted out, "I'm scared to death, Tom. What if Judy gets custody of Kenny? I can't even get custody of Kenny, how can she?"

"Calm down, Mary. Of course she will not get custody of Kenny. I will petition the court to have Judge Sweeney hear the case since he is the judge who issued the Writ of Habeas Corpus. He has standing in the case already. Once he hears all the facts, he will rule against the petitioner. She was in the car when Hank kidnapped Kenny, for God sakes."

"I know, this is so insane," I said. "How can Hank even come up with these ideas?"

"This is so out there, it doesn't even begin to make any sense," Tom said. "Don't worry, Mary. I will make this all go away. Trust me, this woman will never get custody. I'll call you with a court date as soon as I hear back from the court. This is going to go away, Mary, so please calm down and don't worry."

Don't worry? How can I not worry, I thought. Not only was Hank after me, now even this other woman was out to get me. Hank was always one step ahead of me. When would this nightmare end? I immediately thought of Barbara Kovar and lunged for the phone to call her. I left a message that I was in crisis and needed to meet with her ASAP. I then hung up the phone and waited for it to ring.

Chapter XIII

The phone rang, and it was Tom, my attorney. He had good news.

"Mary, I have a court date for the Costello guardianship petition for next Tuesday. The good news is that Judge Sweeney has taken full jurisdiction over the matter. As you recall, he is the same judge that issued you the Writ of Habeas Corpus, so he already has standing in this case. He has moved the hearing out of the Cambridge Middlesex County Courthouse to Concord District Court where he will be presiding. I will be arguing that Judy Costello has no standing and that in fact, she was arrested with Hank during the 2nd kidnapping in Maine and is now subpoenaed as a material witness in Hank's sentencing trial slated for Sept. 26th at Federal Superior Court in Boston."

"This is good news," I said.

"Why don't we plan on driving together so you don't get lost? I know how anxious you get sometimes when you have to drive alone."

"I appreciate that, Tom," I said.

"Now there is another matter that I have to discuss with you," Tom continued explaining that the FBI would be contacting me as part of the process of determining sentencing for Hank. It's normal procedure to interview an array of individuals to get a clear understanding of what the defendant is truly like. Based on all their interviews, the FBI can then make a determination about the length of the prison term."

"Do I need to prepare myself for this meeting?" I asked.

"Not in the least. Just tell them what Hank is like, a control freak. I'm sure there are many incidences that you can remember that show Hank's arrogance and *'his way or the highway'* attitude. It's those kinds of stories they want to hear about.

"Now, Mary, I want you to understand that Hank may only get probation given the fact that he is a 40-year-old white male without a prior criminal record."

"What are you talking about?" I was very upset to hear that Hank might walk on all charges.

"He threatened to kill the judge. He tried to kill a police detective and a Maine state trooper, not to mention all the damage he has done to Kenny. If he just gets probation, Kenny and I will never be safe. Right now, Kenny is under protection by the Department of Social Services because they don't trust Hank. If he doesn't go to prison, then the Department will never release Kenny into my custody. "

"That isn't necessarily true. The Department cannot keep Kenny indefinitely."

"That's not true. The only reason Kenny is in their custody in the first place is because Hank is free to roam. It's not because I'm not a good mother. It's to keep Kenny safe under lock and key away from Hank. He is not a good role model. He's incapable of parenting. And he's dangerous. It's a miracle that Kenny hasn't been killed already because of Hank's misconduct. He has to go to prison, he just has to." I could feel my blood boiling and was beginning to lose it. Tom could sense my frustration and tried to settle me down.

"I'm telling you this, Mary, as your attorney. I wouldn't be doing you a just service if I didn't warn you that jail time may not happen."

"I understand, Tom. But please, don't say it again. You've done your duty, you've told me. Just please don't tell me again," I reiterated with a defiant voice. So, we finished up our phone call and when I hung up, I took a big deep breath to clear my lungs. I was nervous about the Costello custody hearing and upset about jail time. But when I thought about a meeting with the FBI, I was kind of excited. I had never met an FBI agent before and thought it might be fun. I knew exactly what I would say to the FBI. And I couldn't wait to spill the beans. Hank was going down!

• • •

Tuesday was a beautiful September day. Everything was deep green, and landscapes looked picture perfect. Everyone's lawns looked so green. I loved this time of year. The kids were in school, and it was still officially summer. The weather was glorious, and weekends in tourist communities were less hassled. Everything seemed less rushed compared to the month before when it seemed the whole world was taking their summer vacations.

Tom picked me up right on time. We chatted with light-hearted nonsense. There was no discussion of court, which was nice. I needed to remain calm and not get all churned up over court business. I'd been to court so many times now, you would think I would be used to it by now but instead, it was always nerve racking. Nobody wins when they go to court. It always costs money, and the innocent usually get slammed, the loop holes and the postponements and motions to dismiss and etc. Even the bible says don't go to court, but try to settle it yourselves. There's sound logic there. If there is one thing that I have acquired this year, it is perseverance. I do have staying power. But then again, I'm a mother fighting for her child, so I will fight until the bitter end no matter what.

Just then, I saw Judy Costello pulling up to the courthouse.

"Tom," I said, "wait until Judy gets inside before we go in. I don't want to run into her."

The Concord District Court was a newly built building and was much smaller than the Middlesex County Courthouse. Tom whisked me inside and brought me right into the courtroom where we could sit without having to observe Judy and her attorney. Court started right on time and before I knew it, we were all standing as Judge Sweeney took the bench. After seeing him, I remembered his face, and I was hoping that he remembered me. We were the first case on the docket, so my attorney started with his opening statement. Everything he said sounded wonderful. He laid out our case without a hesitation. He really knew his stuff. Then Judy's attorney began to argue his case. As he began, I couldn't help but wonder if he knew that everything he was saying was a lie. Do attorneys know when their clients are lying? After a brief two minutes, Judge Sweeney interrupted, asking if there was anything new he could present to the court today that was not already in his petition. The attorney replied, you have everything, your honor. That's when the judge said, "I'm ready to make my ruling. Your petition is denied." And with that, the judge banged his gavel and said, "Next case."

I looked at Tom and said, "Wow."

"I told you not to worry. The woman had no standing," Tom said. And with that, we left the courthouse.

When I got home, the phone was ringing. It was the FBI.

"Hello, Mrs. Clark, this is Mary McCabe of the FBI. I believe your attorney told you we would be calling you.

"Yes, Ms. McCabe. How can I help you?"

"We are presently conducting sentencing interviews and would like to meet with you concerning your former husband, Hank Clark. We were wondering if we could meet with you this coming Thursday at 7 o'clock."

"8 o'clock would be better. By then the girls are in bed for the night, and you will have my full attention."

"Then 8 o'clock it is. We look forward to meeting you soon. Thank you for your time."

Things were finally moving along. Judy Costello's petition was denied, Hank was in jail under U.S. marshal's control until his upcoming trials, and the FBI was actively interviewing to determine sentencing guidelines. I felt that if I could just get through this last interview, I would be able to dedicate all my efforts toward getting Kenny well and keeping the girls happy. So much had happened this past year. It was a horror story; one that usually was only told on a TV show but for me, it was reality up close and personal. I had lost ten pounds over the past year and was considered quite slender, skinny to be exact. My nerves still weren't as calm as they should be, but my depression was finally lifting. I rarely got a headache now, and the pins and needles in my left leg, as well as the tightness in my jaw. I was sleeping better now, too. Working full-time now didn't leave much room for worrying. The job took all my concentration. I was an administrative assistant working for the Director of Human Resources at GTE Laboratories. It was a large plant of over 1,000 workers, and the folks in my department were all great to work with. My boss was especially kind and knew of my situation. There were times when I would have appointments out of the norm, and she was always more than accommodating. She kept my situation highly confidential, which I greatly appreciated. A couple of the gals I worked with tried to befriend me, but I was always on guard. I still didn't trust anyone and was afraid to commit to a friendship; so, for now, we just took coffee breaks together.

I was really tired by the time Thursday rolled around. It was almost the end of the work week and it was a hectic one, more so than the usual. I had to put in eight hours of overtime and was allowed to work through my lunch hour to shave off one of those hours. Getting home at 6:30 instead of 5:30 really made a difference. I still had to play mother when I got home. Cooking supper on those nights was an easy supper of spaghetti with sauce out of a jar or a grilled tuna sandwich with a hot bowl of chicken noodle soup. The girls never complained. I still had time to help with the little bit of homework they got, as well as a bedtime story. Tonight, the story of choice was Robert McCloskey's classic, *Make Way for Ducklings*. The girls loved this story.

"Mommy, can we ride on the swan boats, too?" said Becky.

"I don't see why not. We live near enough to Boston to take a ride in," I said.

"Can we go this Saturday, Mommy?" asked Izzy.

"This weekend it is supposed to rain. But the first Saturday that it doesn't rain, I promise, we all will go in to ride the swan boats. How does that sound?"

"Yeah," chimed the girls simultaneously.

"Okay, you two. It's time for bed. Climb in. Oh, I love you so much," I said as I gave both of them a big fat squeeze and a kiss on their cheeks. Life really was getting into a regular routine now, and full-time work kept me out of debt. It was a tight budget though, and I was hoping to move up the chain of command so I could get an increase in pay, which would allow us to have some discretionary income. That would be a real luxury.

Tonight was my appointment with the FBI agent, and I knew I had to pick up the pace if I was going to have the girls all settled in for the night before the doorbell rang for our 8 o'clock meeting. I was really tired from working the overtime this week and don't know where I found the energy to get through the usual nightly chores but I did. I guess I was more anxious about this meeting than I had realized. My adrenalin was running high, which kept me energized. As soon as I shut off the girls' bedroom light, the doorbell rang. I was sure it was the FBI. However, when I opened the door, there was a man and a woman standing on my front stoop, and I was wondering if perhaps this was not the FBI. Mary McCabe announced herself and then introduced me to Jack Lowry, her partner, and I welcomed them both into my home. After we were seated in the living room, Mary got right to the chase.

"The reason we are here, as you already know, Mrs. Clark, is to determine an appropriate sentencing for your former husband. He has committed many offenses and is quite unpredictable. I was wondering if perhaps you could tell us something about Hank from your personal point of view."

I asked, "How many people do you normally interview during the course of your investigation?"

"As many as we think is necessary to get a true picture of the individual. So far in Mr. Clark's case, we have interviewed his coworkers, his mother, and sister and Kenny's godfather. Tonight, we would like to hear from you. What can you tell us, if anything?"

I then began to tell my story: "I can tell you that he is a very emotional and impulsive man and that he is a control freak. Things have to be his way. He is the boss. He has a college degree and feels that he is smarter than me since I only have a high school education. He has always thrown money around arrogantly, literally with the flick of his wrist, which I always found offensive. It made people uncomfortable, and I always bowed my head in shame.

I remember once when Hank was buying a car that he had signed the contract, and the keys to the new car were on the agent's desk. At the very last moment, the price of the car had changed and as Hank was writing the check, he became quite indignant and stopped writing the check to debate the price. The agent tried to remain calm and explain the slight increase, but Hank wouldn't hear of it. He took the check and threw it on the agent's desk with arrogance, grabbed the keys, and quickly started out the door, grabbing my arm as he pulled me along. As he hopped into the new car, the agent came running out of the showroom, calling after Hank to stop, but Hank just kept on riding right out of the parking lot. The agent followed him all the way home. Hank thought he was Mr. Big Shot, laughing that he never finished writing the check when he tossed it in the face of the salesman. He thought this was a big joke. He kept hollering, I just rode out of the showroom with a brand-new car for free. Let's see how the salesman reacts to this situation. I was humiliated. We weren't home for more than two minutes when the salesman's car hurriedly parked his car in our driveway and quickly jumped out of the car. Hank was laughing, playing Mr. Macho. I wanted to scold him but instead I disappeared into the house out of embarrassment. Eventually Hank did write a check for the full amount, but it was not until he made that salesman squirm a bit. I could hear their raised voices from inside the house and kept shaking my head in disgust."

I then shared another story that was just as arrogant, and the agents began to get the picture that there was no stopping Hank once he made up his mind. That's when I asked the agents if they thought he would go to jail because that was the only way the kids and I could live safely.

"I'm sorry to say this but unfortunately, all we can do is submit our recommendation. It is up to the court to decide how to hand down the sentence. They have to follow the law, and sometimes there are extenuating circumstances that alter our recommendation."

"But do you think he'll get jail time?" I asked

"There is a good possibility but then, he may only get probation."

"I'm afraid of him," I said. "I don't think I'll ever feel safe as long as he is free. He will keep trying to get Kenny. I'll have to live the rest of my life looking over my shoulder, wondering what and when will Hank do the next insane act. How can I let a transvestite raise my son?"

"Unfortunately, Mrs. Clark, with this kind of man, there is no way the law can protect you. They would have to watch you 24/7, and that is impossible. He is obsessed and will stop at nothing to get his son."

"So, how am I supposed to stay safe?"

"Don't tell anyone I said this, but I can give you a name that can take care of this problem. But you can't tell anyone I told you."

"Are you kidding me? If I were to do something like that, I would be the one who would be going to jail, then the kids wouldn't have a mother or a father."

"Then can you tell us anything else that will help us solidify our recommendation?"

"Of course, I could tell you a dozen more stories if you felt that would help."

"We have all night, Mrs. Clark, so begin telling us your stories," Jack Lowry stated.

And so, the evening progressed until I began yawning. I was really tired from doing the overtime, and the agents understood that I had work the next day, so they wrapped up the meeting. This is never going to end, I thought, unless Hank goes to jail. I knew I'd sleep well because I could hardly keep my eyes opened. That night, I slept like I was dead. If only Hank was.

• • •

Yesterday, Hank was sentenced to prison for threatening to kill a judge. The papers reported: Flanked by two marshals in U.S. District Court Tuesday, a Randolph man who pleaded guilty to threatening a judge was sentenced to serve six months of a three-year sentence in a federal prison. US District Court Judge Walter Jay Skinner slapped that sentence against Hank Clark, 40, formerly of 36 Maple Drive, Randolph for threatening Judge James Sweeney of the Concord District Court last November. Clark pleaded to that charge in September. Meanwhile, Clark still faces legal action in Maine on a charge of attempted murder of a state trooper and in Middlesex Superior Court on a charge of assault with intent to murder a Randolph detective. Besides handing Clark a six month prison term, Judge Skinner ordered Clark to be placed on probation for five years during which time, he must not own guns and during which time, he must submit to psychiatric treatment at the direction of the chief probation officer. According to the District Court grand jury, Clark mailed a letter to Judge Sweeney around Nov. 18 saying:

> "I'm a very patient stalker. I'm wanted 'Dead or Alive.' Time is on my side…if you choose to rectify the injustice, then I can live with this. If not, be prepared for a long and dying revenge. All I have to do is kill only once, and the system will come tumbling down on your heads, not mine. There are only two things I want, my boy and my gun collection. I'll kill for either one. I'll give you sanctuary from such … if you restate me as a law-abiding citizen. If not, suffer the consequences of stupidity. If you're a Christian, God will guide you, if not, the Devil shall own you. I will assist him in this goal. You are going down.

The attorney general requested that I appear in court on trial day to identify Hank's hand writing in court. However, that wasn't necessary since Hank pleaded guilty in court and accepted a plea bargain. I couldn't believe what I was reading in Hank's hand-written letter. It was so graphic. The best part of the sentence was that Hank would be undergoing psychiatric treatment for the five years he was on probation. Thank God. He still has two more trials coming up with sentencing scheduled next month. I know he'll get jail time. He's in a lot of trouble.

The news reported the story on TV tonight, showing Hank being led away by U.S. marshals flanking him on both sides. He was in hand cuffs. It was on the 6 o'clock news, and my girls accidently saw it while we were eating dinner that night. Needless to say, they were quite upset.

"Mommy, look, it's Daddy." Becky pointed at the TV.

"Why does he have handcuffs on?" Izzy asked me in a very upset voice.

"I know this is very upsetting to see Daddy like this. But you have to understand that Daddy has been very naughty. You cannot go around with a gun and threaten to kill people, which is what your father did. He is being punished for what he did. When grownups are punished for doing bad things, they go to jail; and that's why Daddy is being punished, because he did some very bad things."

"I hate him," Izzy said as she ran out of the room. Becky started to cry and believe it, so did I. Where was this emotion coming from? The ordeal was almost over. Maybe it was a sense of relief that brought on the tears. As for Becky, she was too young to understand, so I just let her cry it out while I rocked her in my arms. Later that night, I tried talking to Izzy, but she was pretty headstrong, claiming she never wanted to see him again, she hated him. There was no consoling her, so I just let things lie for now. Maybe someday she would be more willing to talk about it, which I was hoping for, but I wasn't counting on it. After all, she refused counseling and never participated in the family therapy sessions either. So why would she talk about it now? I wanted to comfort her, but she would have none of it. All I could do was tuck her into bed that night with a great big kiss and let her know how much I loved her. As I turned out the bedroom light, I thought, maybe this will rear its ugly head again someday like the psychologist had informed me way back when.

• • •

Another month has gone by, and Hank's trials have taken place. He was sentenced to a year in prison for attempting to kill a Maine state trooper, and he received a year's sentence in Massachusetts for attempted murder of a police detective. Because he took a plea, both Maine and Massachusetts agreed that he could serve both sentences concurrently in the Cumberland County Prison in Maine after which he will be placed on probation for five years. So for now, the craziness has stopped, and the kids and I can find some peace of mind and get on with our lives. Or can we?

Chapter XIV

It's hard to believe it's all over. Hank is away in prison, and the girls and I can finally breathe a sigh of relief. What started out to be an everyday divorce ended up being a nightmare of monumental proportion. I still have Social Services to deal with and the most important of all, I have Kenny to help get well. I thank God every day that justice has prevailed and continue to pray for his guidance in helping to get Kenny well. And Kenny is improving as each day goes by. Social Services allow Kenny to come home for supper once a week, as well as to spend one weekend a month at home with me and the girls. He is not as explosive as he used to be, which always upset him greatly. Kenny wants to come home, and I wish he could. He has been at Nazareth for such a long time.

It's been six months since Kenny was last evaluated. Nazareth wants to perform another round of tests to evaluate whether or not Kenny is ready to enter home life with his sisters and me. Social Services called to inform me that it was recommended by Kenny's psychiatrist that the department evaluate Kenny again to determine his progress. Kenny's doctor felt as though his test results this time would show remarkable improvement. Of course, Kenny doesn't realize he is being tested because of the way the tests are conducted. The evaluation is scheduled for next week, and Social Services have promised me that we will get the written results within the same week. I don't think I could wait much longer than a week for feedback. I thought I got good at waiting after all this time but now, once again, waiting has become very hard for me. I want so much to get on with my life with the kids now that Hank is out of the picture, and I finally feel safe again. So, I will patiently wait for the written report on Kenny. I know I can patiently wait. After all, it is only a week and with all I've been through, a week is a piece of cake. I know his progress has been phenomenal and only good can come out of the testing. So, I wait.

• • •

It's been a very long year now that Kenny has been at Nazareth, and it looks like he'll be coming home by Thanksgiving. I had to jump through hoops to get Social Services to issue the motion to dismiss custody but finally, on November 23rd, my last day in court would finally be taking place, motion to dismiss. Of course, there were stipulations. The Department of Social Services will continue to monitor Kenny's environment and reserves the right to bring to the attention of the court any actions of any party which are not in the best interest of Kenny. That should take care of the Judy Costello factor. I must ensure that Kenny continue in any therapy as recommended by the Department of Social Services. Therapy will be pro-rated according to my income, which will help tremendously. I further had to agree to cooperate with the Department of Social Services in its attempt to ensure that the welfare and best interests of Kenny are pursued. The department did agree that there be no visitation between Kenny and his father until all legal matters have been fulfilled by Hank, including probation. That should take care of at least five or six years that the kids and I can live a normal life. And so the Department of Social Services, after a full assessment of the Clark family situation, finally determined that the best interests of Kenny require that he be returned to the physical and legal custody of his mother, Mary Clark. Hallelujah!

It was November, the gloomiest of all the months of the year and yet, the sun was shining, and the sky was so blue without a cloud in it. Kenny was sitting by the window waiting for me. His favorite counselor, Neal, was waiting with him. This was the day Kenny would finally be going home.

"I'm tired of waiting, Neal. When will they be here," Kenny asked in an excited voice. He still had a real nice way of expressing himself when he was happy, and he sure was happy. Today Kenny was going home. Neal said, "Look up at the sky, Kenny. There is a plane sky writing in the sky. Let's wait and see what he writes."

As Kenny looked up, a big smile fell on his face and he said, "I wish I was riding in the airplane because then I would write, 'T o d a y I g o h o m e.'"

Neal knew how much going home meant to Kenny, and that's when tears came to his eyes. He was so fond of Kenny. He enjoyed his delightful personality and was going to miss his friendship. As they both looked up to the sky, the plane finished writing, and the word CONGRATULATIONS filled the sky. Neal silently thought to himself, how appropriate that such a message so close to heaven was in the sky for Kenny to see. Neal said, "Kenny, you have worked so hard all year at getting well and always obeyed everyone and everything that was asked of you. You are such a good boy. I am so proud of you, and I am going to miss you very much. I promise, once you're settled in your home with your family, I will come and visit you."

"Will you?" Kenny asked. "Do you promise?"

"I absolutely promise I will come and visit you. I wouldn't miss it for the world."

That's when Kenny let out a yelp.

"Look, there is Mommy walking to the front door. And I see Izzy and Becky too."

Neal knew this was his final goodbye to Kenny as he reached out to give him a big hug, wishing him all the happiness in the world because he deserved it. It was so hard to let go of that hug, but Neal knew he had to for Kenny's sake.

"Let's go to the front door to meet your mother," Neal said.

Kenny took off running as Neal quickly tried to keep pace and before you knew it, both Kenny and his mother were hugging and smiling and giggling and jumping for joy. What a commotion they both made but who cared. Complete happiness was so obvious for both Kenny and his mother that it was tough for Neal to hold back his tears.

"Time to go," Mom said as Kenny took off running as fast as he could to the front door and then through the parking lot to the car where his sisters were waiting. What a reunion was there. Could happiness get any better than this? Kenny was finally coming home and for the rest of his life, would be in my care. It was like a miracle had come true.

The first year having Kenny home was a tough one. There were quite a few explosive episodes. Kenny was extremely fragile, and it didn't take much to set him off. We were all walking on eggshells for a while. He had been lifted out of his depression but was still sad and missed Daddy. He understood that Daddy was in jail for being bad. He still had explosive episodes and outbursts when he became angry or could not handle his emotions. These episodes were quite upsetting to the girls and me. We hated to see Kenny in such anguish.

Kenny knew when he behaved badly and didn't like it. I remember once after one of those traumatic episodes when he ran out of the room crying. I found him in his bedroom, sitting on his bed, sobbing, and I sat by him with my arms around him when he said, "Why am I like this, Mommy?" My heart broke for him as I tried to console him and explain that it wasn't his fault. I tried to explain to him that he had been away from home for a very long two years, and that was a long time for anyone to miss their family, let alone a little boy.

"You must have been very lonely and wished that you could see and spend time with your family," I said. "Unfortunately, Daddy was very bad in sending you away. He should never have done that. You are not bad, Daddy was the one who was bad, and that's why he is being punished now."

I was running out of words. I was trying so hard to be so careful in my explanations; after all, he was only eight and a half. And after all that he had been through, he still wanted to live with Daddy. I suppose it is a natural thing for a boy to want to be with his father, but under the circumstances, it was hard for me to grapple with given all that his father had put him through. Is it a natural thing for a boy to want to be with his dad just like girls want to be with their moms? I suppose, but it sure did make things harder.

Adjusting to regular day life was a hardship at first. Kenny was still meeting with his psychiatrist weekly. Carol Daily was still in our lives. She met with

Kenny every two weeks; sometimes off site and sometimes at dinner with us at home. The meetings seemed to be going well, and Kenny's psychiatrist kept me updated weekly with Kenny's progress. It was a very long couple of years before Kenny finally settled down and began to live a more routine life. My little boy was growing up and seemed to be adjusting well to home life. He was doing well in school and had made some friends, which was a huge step forward for him. It was good to see him enjoy playing and enjoy friends again.

He still was under psychiatric care and both the doctor and I were encouraged that with time and lots of love, Kenny would get through this most difficult time of trying to reenter his life with me and his sisters. But as time went on, that's when Kenny began haunting me about living with his dad. I was hoping that the desire of wanting to be with Dad would pass as he became more settled in and comfortable with his life at home, but the persistence to live with Dad continued until I finally had to have a very serious conversation with him. He was now almost twelve and quite often would mention living with his dad. It broke my heart. He was glad to be home, but he sure did miss his dad.

One day, there was an outburst that Kenny just couldn't get under control and he blurted out, "I want to live with Dad. When are you going to let me live with Dad?"

It was then I decided to sit down with Kenny in private, just him and me, and really talk about how living with Dad right now just couldn't be.

"How can you live with Dad? He is on probation. You can't live with him right now," I insisted. My head was swimming with how to approach this in the right light so that Kenny would once and for all realize that living with Dad was not in his best interest. But no matter how much I tried to explain the situation, the harder Kenny persisted that was what he wanted. So I stopped talking and tried to think of a way to make this happen that would not hurt Kenny. It's then that I said, "When you are a teenager in high school, if you still wish to live with your father, I will let you."

Kenny stopped crying and then I was able to explain further that his father had to promise to be good and that Social Services would need to make home visits guaranteeing me that Daddy was being a good father to you and that you and Daddy were happy living with each other. Social Services would be like babysitting, checking in every once in a while so that I wouldn't worry. After all, you wouldn't want me to be worried about you all the time. Social Services would help Daddy be good to you, and that was what was important. Daddy had to be good to you. If he wasn't, then you could come back to living with me and your sisters.

"How does that sound?" I asked. My heart was so torn up by now, I had no more emotional strength to argue with Kenny about living with his dad. For almost two years now, Kenny had badgered me about living with his dad. I kept telling myself it was the boy in him. After all, a boy needs a father when he is a teenager, and I was hoping by that age Kenny would be mature enough to handle whatever life sent his way when it came to his father.

And so, the evening ended with me crying myself to sleep. The thought of losing him to Hank was more than my mind could handle. But six years can make a world of difference in Hank's behavior, especially because he would be under psychiatric care for five of those years. If I continued to raise him with strong values, then perhaps all would work out well. I had to believe that, or I would go out of my mind. I just had to believe. No one ever told me that being a mother would hurt so much.

Chapter XV

It was during this time that I met someone. He was a very kind and understanding man. We were deeply in love with each other, which surprised me because I thought I would never feel this way again. I was like a school girl, so giddy in love. The kids loved having their mom be so happy, and life was beginning to get good again. His name was Peter O'Connor and what a catch was he. He was an executive specializing in corporate taxation. He was six feet tall, smoked a pipe (very sophisticated), and had a mustache. He was a man's man, if you know what I mean. He lit up the room where ever he went, and there wasn't anyone I knew that didn't enjoy his company. He was just one of those people that where ever he went, everyone knew him and liked him. And I loved him, for sure. I was now thirty-seven, and I understood what marriage was. I knew he was the one. He proposed on Thanksgiving Day because he was so thankful that I had come into his life. We courted for three years before we were married. I didn't want to rush the kids. They needed time to adjust after all they had been through. If this marriage was going to work, it meant that Peter was marrying me and my kids. My parents loved him, too. They used to tease him and call him Saint Peter because he could walk on water; after all, anyone who would take on me and my three kids with all our baggage had to be a saint, right? He loved my kids, and the kids loved him. He was great counsel to the kids during their teenage years, and there wasn't a woman

I knew that didn't wish Peter was their husband. I was the lucky one…he was mine, all mine.

I remember once how he counseled my daughter, Becky, when she was just sixteen. They were sitting at the dinner table after dinner while I was in the kitchen cleaning up. Becky asked, "Peter, can I ask you something?"

"Of course you can. You can always ask me anything you want," Peter said.

"What do you have to do," Becky asked, "to be successful?"

When I heard this question, I was flabbergasted. What a profound question for a sixteen-year-old teenager to ask. I was thinking how I would answer such a question. I was in a quandary. What do you say, work hard, study hard? I didn't even know how to begin to answer such a question when all of a sudden, I heard Peter say, "Relationships," and then he went on to explain. The world is filled with people, and you are going to have to figure out how to get along with all of them. It begins with your family. You and your mom have a very special relationship different from any other relationship you will ever have with anyone else. It is special and should be cherished. She will always be there for you no matter what, giving advice, and loving you always unconditionally. Then there is your sister and brother. The bond you share with them will be stronger than any other person on earth. You will defend them to the ultimate; after all, they are family, which is everything! And then there are your neighbors. There are some you will love, and then there will be some that will challenge you daily, always complaining, or finding fault or simply annoying you to no end. There are your friends that you can confide in, and your best friend that you can trust with your life. And what about your boss? He is always hovering and micro managing you, driving you crazy. Do you quit because you can't stand working for him? No, you have to pay the rent. You stick it out. Try to get a promotion by working harder and learning all you can to improve your position, so then you can be working for someone else, hopefully better than the boss before. There are business associates and people in church or folks you take a class with. You have to figure out how to get along with all of them without making yourself crazy. It will take perseverance sometimes or tolerance another time or patience or understanding, all those intangibles that matter in life and make life worth living. If at the end of your life, all these individuals who have touched your life can hold you in high regard, then not only have you been successful, but you have truly been blessed.

"Wow," I said to myself. And I married this man. How lucky am I?

That was the kind of man he was. He completed my life and made the lives of my children better. It was this kind of man that was with me when Kenny turned thirteen and wanted to go live with his father. Peter helped guide both Kenny and me through the process of getting him settled with his dad. Of course, we had to work with Social Services to make this happen. I needed guarantees that Kenny would be safe, protected from harm, and happy. With Social Services actively in the picture, both Kenny and his father would be monitored closely. The first sign of trouble, Kenny would be brought back home to me and his sisters.

And so, Kenny went to live with his dad. At first, it was good. His dad bought him a dog and tended to spoil him his first year living up North with him. He attended the regional high school, which meant his bus trip was a 70-minute commute each way, which Kenny hated because it didn't get him home until almost 5 o'clock in the afternoon. He had to leave for school as early as 6:30 because classes began at 8 o'clock. That made for a very long day and by the time he got home, the last thing he wanted to do was homework. He did manage to get in some studying after supper but as for extra-curricular activities with the school, the time factor just didn't make room for any sports. I wanted Hank to enroll Kenny at Exeter School for Boys in New Hampshire. It was an exceptional school, but it meant that Kenny would have to board. Hank refused to even consider such a move because then he wouldn't be seeing him except for holidays, vacations, and the summer. The school would have done wonders for Kenny, and it would have kept him away from Hank for weeks at a time. I could always bring him home on weekends because the commute for me was only a two-hour drive. For Hank, it would have been a seven-hour commute each way. Hank and I always talked about Kenny attending Exeter but when push came to shove, Hank refused. So, Kenny attended the regional high school up North. It took its toll on Kenny and after a while, Kenny and his father began bickering amongst themselves. Kenny was tired and wanted to sleep in on Saturdays. Dad wouldn't hear of it. He wanted him up to go skiing with him. Skiing at Sugarloaf was a seven-month seasonal sport. The U.S. Olympic ski team trained there, so the long season was conducive for the training team.

Kenny's freshman year was a good year but by the time his sophomore year was wrapping up, he had had enough of his long commute to school. That's when their relationship began to become cantankerous. Once, Kenny told me that they actually had a fist fight when Kenny knocked his father to the floor. I remember saying, "Where has all the love gone?"

"He deserved it, Ma. He had it coming for weeks. He constantly is on my back, nagging me to do chores when I have to study. He just doesn't get how much homework I have."

"And the two of you can't resolve your disputes any other way?"

"You know what he's like. The only thing he will listen to is a punch in the face," said Kenny.

I begged him to come home, but he said he would try to stick it out and suck up to keep the peace. However, no matter how many times Kenny would try to suck it up, they always ended up hollering at each other and sometimes even hitting each other. I begged Kenny to come home, but he would not have it. That is until the end of his junior year. He showed up on my doorstep one day and ended up staying with us for ten days, trying to figure out what he wanted to do. He was so torn. He wanted to live with me, but he wanted to live with Dad as well. It was unsettling. He finally decided to stick it out until graduation and then the day after graduation, he was out of there. That's when he joined a construction company, which traveled all over the states. He loved that job, and I always called him my little vagabond. He needed a home, and I worried constantly about him. He would call every now and again, and he always made it a point to come home and visit with me every other year. Trying to get him to come home more than that was impossible. After all, he was a young adult now and 'mother' was not a priority in his life. His work was priority, as was his love life, as it should be. His birthday was Mother's Day weekend, and he always remembered me then. He was a good son, and I loved him dearly and was so proud of the work he was doing. Kenny had joined a nationwide construction company right after graduation, building hydro electro water plants across the country, and Kenny loved the work and the travel. He was gifted when it came to motor skills, and he loved dangling mid-air hovering over steel girders wearing a harness and a hard hat. He looked like quite the crewman. I remember once he mailed me a picture of himself in full gear standing in front of one of his projects. He had a huge smile on his face, standing in front of the construction site showing two huge girders that had been installed that looked like a crucifix. After all he had been through, he still had Faith. I was so proud of him.

Sadly, Kenny died when he was only 24-years-old. Peter was there for me unequivocally. It was Mother's Day, May 11th, when I got the phone call from the coroner's office out in California. It was the other side of the world as far as I was concerned. It was one o'clock, Sunday afternoon when the coroner told me that Kenny had drowned in the Pacific Ocean while surfing. He had been diagnosed with epilepsy just two years prior and had a seizure while surfing and drowned. He had never surfed alone before. It was his birthday, and he was waiting for his friends on the beach to go surfing. For some reason, he decided to take a surf alone that infamous day that cost him his life. He was so young. After all he had been through, he still had a charming personality and still had huge faith. He had learned all those lessons of kindness and love in spite of all he had been through. They say the good die young. Kenny was good, so good, in spite of his father. I was so proud of him.

That's when the coroner told me that I couldn't have his body flown home to me in Maine.

"Why not, I don't understand," I cried out.

"Unfortunately," the coroner said, "under California law, both parents have to agree to release the body and your former husband, Kenny's father, refuses to release his body."

"That cannot be," I said. "Why would he do that? It doesn't make sense. Surely his father would want to bury his son here in Maine where he lives."

"It's not for me to say how people think, Mrs. Clark. The law is the law and unless both parents agree to release the body, we cannot under the law release the body to your care."

"Then," I said, "I will fly to California, so I can hold him in my arms. I need to hold him to say my goodbye."

"Unfortunately, Mrs. Clark, I cannot allow that. Your son has had a full body autopsy and cannot be viewed in that state."

"Then put a sheet over him so that I can hold him. I have to hold him in my arms. Don't you understand?"

"I am sorry, Mrs. Clark, but I cannot permit that. It is not proper protocol."

"I don't care about protocol," I argued. "I just need to hold him and kiss him. I don't care what he looks like."

"I am sorry, Mrs. Clark, but as the state coroner, I cannot allow that, I am sorry."

"Then I am flying to California. One way or another, I will hold my son in my arms before he is buried," I said.

The phone call ended with my husband sitting at the kitchen table in shock. He could not believe what he had just heard.

"Honey," he said, "I can't believe it," as he held me in his arms. I began to cry in disbelief. After all Kenny had been through, to have it end like this, what a waste. And on Mother's Day, the greatest insult of all.

I knew what I had to do. I had to fly to California, and I had to leave now. No waiting, no packing a suitcase, just leave right now. I immediately called the airline and made reservations for the next flight out. It was departing at 3:30, so we had to hurry. I literally threw a change of clothes in a suitcase and said we'd get anything else we needed when we get there. We were out of the house in thirty minutes and on our way to the airport, a 45-minute drive to the Portland JetPort. We were at the ticket counter at 2:45 and were at the gate by 3:15. We made it. What a relief. If we had missed that flight, there would not be another one until 10 o'clock that night. We boarded on time and when I reached my seat, I literally fell into it and started to cry. My husband was there for me holding me ever so gently. Reality had finally hit home. My precious son was gone, and I couldn't bring him home.

Chapter XVI

It was a six-hour flight, and I cried off and on during the entire flight. My husband was like a rock, just like Saint Peter. I would never have been able to get through any of this without him. Thank God I had him. He truly was a gift from God and was sent to me during the most difficult time of my life. He helped sustain me then, and he helped to sustain me now. What would I do without him? I thanked God he was in my life and prayed to God to welcome my Kenny into his heavenly home.

By the time we all got to the hotel, we were all wiped out with nothing left to give. We all crashed, and none of us awoke until eight the following morning.

"Honey, it's time to wake up," Peter said softly as he gently tried to coax me out of bed. "It's almost 9 o'clock, time to get up."

"I'm so tired," I said. "My eyes are stuck close. I just can't open them right now."

"I know, sweetheart, I know, but you really should try to wake up now. Today, you get to see Kenny."

My eyes immediately popped open. Just the thought of Kenny made me want to get out of bed and go running to him, my precious Kenny. How could this be happening? After all he had been through. After all the family had been through to have it end like this seemed so unfair. Why, God, why, I kept asking myself. Why have it end like this when we all had worked so hard for so long to get Kenny well. Why take him now when his life was going so well. He had just met a girl and had fallen in love with her. Her name was Tracey. She was eight-years-older than he but in a way, that was a good thing. In a way, he needed to be mothered, loved as only a mother can love a child. But he was a young man now and also needed to love a woman as a young man in love. He and Tracey were very much in love and wrote love letters to each other all the time while Kenny was away on a project. Whenever the project wrapped up, Kenny would always fly home to California to stay with Tracey for the three-week break. He was happy and in love. His life was going well. He was making fantastic money and had already managed to save $40,000 of his salary. Life was good. Kenny was in love.

He called me one day to tell me that he had met a girl and that she was wonderful. He told me how they had met and what an amazing woman she was. She was everything that a woman should be, and he loved her very much. Kenny still had such a sweet way about him. While we were talking on the phone, I said, "It is so good to hear from you. I have been thinking a lot about you lately and was wishing that you might call home." I didn't always have the most current phone number to contact Kenny. He was traveling all the time and had already built plants in 13 different states. I was happy for him and so grateful that he was successful in his job and in his life as well.

That's when Kenny said, "The sound of your voice sounds so good to me, Ma." He called me Ma, and I always called him Kenny, not Ken or Kenneth but Kenny. What a sweet way to say hello to his mother, I was thinking. He told me all about Tracey: how old she was, what she looked like, what she was like, the kind of work that she did. It was wonderful to hear him share such a big part of his life with me. I felt blessed that Kenny might actually have a chance at a complete, happy life, being able to put all the emotional baggage behind him. I wanted to meet her, and Kenny promised me that someday soon, he would bring her home for a visit. He wanted me to meet her.

"She is the one, Ma; she is the one I'm going to marry," Kenny said.

Little did I know then that I would be meeting Tracey sooner than I had realized and under completely different circumstances.

It was time to get up, and it was already a little past 9 o'clock. I was in slow motion, but that was okay. We had all day to find out where the coroner's office was. While I was sipping on a nice, hot cup of coffee that Peter brought me, he was making phone calls to the police and the coroner's office to see if we could get an appointment to come in and view Kenny. Peter was able to arrange a 1 o'clock appointment with the deputy coroner, and he got driving directions to the facility while I was slowly waking up and listening intently to every word he was saying on the phone. He was a take charge kind of guy and took all the burden of finding Kenny away from me. He understood how fragile I was and was completely accommodating to every need I might have. I was still numb and couldn't believe that Kenny was gone. My precious little boy who had grown up to be a wonderful young man was now gone. This was an enormous void in my life, and I could not even begin to fathom how to move forward with my life from this point on. I had friends who lost children and was always grateful that it wasn't me. And yet, here I was, and it was happening to me; I had lost Kenny, forever.

Kenny didn't have much of a relationship with his father. He did keep in touch with him over the years, but they always fought over the phone. His father was still very angry about how his life had turned out, and he and Kenny had a pretty contemptuous relationship. Hank would always criticize him no matter what Kenny did. No matter how successful Kenny was, it was never good enough for his father. Hank was an impossible man to get along with now. He had turned into a very bitter man and continued to hurt everyone around him. He was set in this ugly mode of operandi and with each passing day, he became more self-absorbed and mean spirited. What a waste of a life he had made for himself. What started out to be a very promising life was now only a shell of a man. No one respected him in the community, and he had quite a reputation of always being in drag up in northern Maine. All the police knew him to be very emotional and over the years, there had been many skirmishes with neighbors and strangers that were all documented on the police record. He still was not allowed to own guns, so his hunting days were over. He constantly complained about it. Hunting was a macho thing for Hank, and he could no longer be macho, which was extremely frustrating for him. He now signed all his checks Cochese, the great Indian warrior. This made him feel macho because hunting could no longer fill that bill of superiority. And he still called himself Joanna Carr when he was in drag. Go figure. He was extremely discontent with his life. What a shame that all his psychiatric therapy during his probation never really took effect. Five years of therapy, and he still was living in drag more than he was living as a man. The obsession had now become his normal way of life, and no one respected him in the community. They all thought he was a weirdo of the greatest magnitude.

"Breakfast is here, honey," Peter said as he brought me an Egg Mc Muffin. While I was slowly waking up, Peter had gone out to get me breakfast. He knew I had no appetite, so the Egg sandwich was just enough to get me started for the day. Izzy and Becky were with us, thank goodness. We all needed toiletries as well as makeup, so Izzy and Peter went out shopping while I got dressed for the day. When they got back, I was ready to begin my day and was anxious to get to the coroner's office. I finally was going to be able to hold Kenny in my arms, and I couldn't wait to get there.

It was a thirty-minute drive to the coroner's office. All the way there, none of us said a word. We were all in mourning, and the sensation that flooded over us was a complete washout of emotions, so much so that none of us could speak.

I remember what a beautiful day it was. It was much hotter in California than in Maine for this time of year. It was still early spring back in Maine and yet, here everything was a full six weeks ahead of schedule. There were flowers everywhere you looked, and all the trees were dripping with blooms of every color. There were flowering trees here that I didn't recognize and wished that we had them back home. The sunshine was glaring off the windshield of the car, and I found myself squinting constantly. So, I asked Peter to stop at a drugstore along the way to get everyone sunglasses and to get me and Peter some cigarettes. Peter and I walked around the parking lot, smoking a cigarette, which helped me to get a handle on my emotions. I was beginning to well up in tears and knew that what was facing me was going to be the toughest thing I would ever have to go through. I was not sure what to expect and of course, I was worrying about how the day would turn out. What was running through my head was the thought that maybe they wouldn't let me see Kenny. The phone call I had had with the deputy coroner was racing through my mind.

"It's against our protocol to allow you to view Kenny in the state that his body is in. He has had a full body autopsy, and I cannot permit you to view his body." What if I had come all this way for nothing? But of course, I had Peter with me, and he would help make everything right. Surely, if I was saying yes to release Kenny's body and was sitting right in front of the coroner, my yes would prevail over Hank's no, which was in Maine. Kenny's father never made any attempt to travel to California. After being obsessed over all those years of having Kenny live with him, now was his final chance to say his goodbye, and he chose to stay home in Maine. What kind of man had Hank become? He would not even attend his son's funeral.

We all got back into the car and continued on our way downtown. Peter was driving slowly so that he could read directions and find his way to the city morgue and was not talking. We all sat quietly as we drove with none of us saying a word. We were all in grief, and grief leaves you mute. So, we all drove in silence wearing our sunglasses.

"There it is," Peter said. "Oceanside City Morgue."

My eyes opened up wide as I stared at the sign leading to the facility. I had never been to a morgue in my life and didn't know what to expect. The building looked quite ordinary but then again, why wouldn't it? My mind began wondering now. What would it be like to be standing in the morgue with Kenny on a slab? But what if they still didn't let me see him? A chill went through my body just then, and I let out a little moan.

"Are you alright, honey?" Peter asked.

"What if they don't let us see Kenny," I said.

"Now, Mary, don't think that way. We have come too far to be turned away. I promise you I will make this happen," Peter said. Just then, Becky started to cry.

"Sweetheart," I said, "I know this is hard. Just let it all come out. If you have to cry, don't hold back any tears. Just let the tears flow." I couldn't reach into the backseat to comfort Becky, so I asked Izzy to give her a hug, but Izzy was frozen and couldn't offer Becky any comfort. She just sat there, numb in silence, and still. Both my daughters were hurting. Becky was now 26-years-old, and Izzy was 28; both beautiful, young women who were doing well with their careers. Becky worked with physically impaired individuals designing programs that would help strengthen their impairments, and Izzy was a pianist and was playing a full schedule all the time. They both were pursuing their careers, and both were dating very nice, young men. Their lives were good. Now they were hurting puppies. Their brother was dead, and they were in mourning. This was a brand-new emotion for them, and I wished with all my heart that they didn't have to experience such a painful one in their young lives. But sometimes, earth beats us up pretty badly, and this was one of those times.

"Here we are," Peter said as he steered the car into the parking lot. As he turned the key, we all just sat there in silence for a very long few moments.

"It's time, honey," Peter said. "Let's go."

I just sat there, frozen, as Peter circled the car to open my door. As the door swung open, there was Peter's hand to guide me. What would I do without him? I could never have gotten through this without him. He was such a beautiful gift and now, I was losing my most precious gift of all, Kenny.

As Peter guided me out of the car, I stumbled a little but did manage to stand my ground. The girls were right behind me. As we all slowly walked into the morgue, I was hit with a sense of horror. Seeing Kenny at a funeral home was one thing but seeing him on a slab was a moment I didn't know how I was going to handle. Peter could read my mind as he gave me a hug and said, "It's going to be alright. I'm right here with you."

He then took charge and directed all of us the right way to the deputy coroner's office.

The deputy coroner was waiting for us as we entered and ushered us all into a conference room. Once we were all seated, the coroner offered her condolences and then went on to say, "I'm very sorry to have to tell you this, but the father has still refused to release the body; and under California state law, both parents must agree to release your son; otherwise, your son's body will remain in the coroner's office until burial."

That's when Izzy spoke up, saying, "He hates us all. He blames all of us for his miserable life. If he was here, he would think nothing of threatening us with a gun and probably would even shoot one of us before he would let

Kenny's body be released. Don't you see? This is the ultimate punishment for us. We left him, so he is punishing us now by not releasing Kenny's body. What kind of a man does this? He would rather see Kenny lay on a slab than bury his own son with dignity. I hate him. I hate him."

"Izzy," I said, "please don't."

My mind was so convoluted, just then, I found myself tongue tied. That's when Peter spoke up and in his very calm way, went on to explain what this man was really like. He spoke for a good five minutes explaining Hank's exploits and prison record. That's when I spoke up saying, "I have flown 3,000 miles from Maine to San Diego to hold my son in my arms. I am sitting right here before you saying yes, and you mean to tell me that his father's no carries more weight in Maine than my yes in California?"

"That's right," the coroner stated. "His no prevails. I am very sorry to tell you that, but the law is the law, and I must follow it, like it or not."

"Please," I said, "then just let us say our goodbyes to him here. Please, I'm begging you. There doesn't need to be a funeral. We will all just say our goodbye's here, and it will be done. I just need to see him for closure."

"Mrs. Clark," the coroner said, "your son has had a full body autopsy, and I cannot allow you to see him in that condition. It is against all protocol to let you view him in that state." The coroner continued to talk, but her words fell on my deaf ears. I didn't hear anything she was saying. Peter began talking again, and it was surreal. I was looking right at him, and it was like he was talking in slow motion, and I couldn't hear a sound. It was a nightmare, and I had all I could do to maintain my composure. Just then, Peter looked at me, and I began to cry. The tears just flowed, and I had no control over them. That's when Peter took the lead and asked if we all could take a break before continuing on. The next thing, Peter was holding me and leading me out of the conference room back into the sunlight of the day outside. There were two picnic benches about fifty-feet from the building, and that's where we all ended up. Peter got us settled and then went back into the morgue. The girls and I just sat there, crying.

"I can't believe this is happening, Ma," Izzy said. "He's a convicted felon, and he's still winning. When will it ever stop?"

"I know," I said, "but trust me, we are not going home until we see Kenny. One way or another, we will say our goodbyes to Kenny. Maybe we will have to get a lawyer or pay a surgeon to put him back together, so they will let us view him, but we are not going home until we see Kenny." That's when I saw Peter walking toward us. He had made arrangements for us to go back to the deputy coroner in one hour.

"So," Peter said, "we are all going to just sit here and try to calm down. We all need to breathe in the fresh air and regain our composure. Otherwise, we will never get to see Kenny."

"Do you think we should call a lawyer?" I frantically asked.

"That's a good idea," Peter said. "It certainly wouldn't hurt to get some advice if our next meeting with the coroner doesn't go well. Let me go inside and get a phone book."

"Mary, will you be alright?" Peter asked.

"I'm alright now. Please, get the phone book," I said.

And so, the next half hour, we searched the yellow pages looking for an attorney who would help with a case like ours. Suddenly, "Hello, are you Mrs. Clark, Kenny's mother," a young woman's voice said as I looked up. I was looking at a young woman, about 30-years-old, and was wondering who she was. She introduced herself as Kenny's girlfriend. She was just as Kenny had described her to me, so yes, I did recognize her.

"Are you Tracey?" I stated.

"Yes, are you Kenny's mother?" asked Tracey. "You're so beautiful, just like Kenny said you were," Tracey said. "I am so glad that you are here. I have come to see Kenny, and I thought I would have to do it all alone. But now that you are here, I feel so much better." As Tracey began to cry, she said, "I love your son so much, I don't know what I am going to do without him." It's then that I got up and put my arms around her. We both were crying, trying to console each other. Neither one of us could stop crying. We finally regained our composure, and I introduced Tracey to my daughters and Peter. Peter assured Tracey that we would all be seeing Kenny soon to say our goodbyes. He then went on to explain the complexity of the situation and what some of our options were if things became difficult. Tracey hung on his every word and could not believe that the coroner would not let us see Kenny.

"But I have to see him, I just have to," said Tracey. "What if they don't let us see him? I can't stand this. I simply can't go on unless I can see him," Tracey cried.

That's when Peter said, "We have 30 minutes before we can see the coroner, so let's all try to calm down and get our emotions under control. Tracey, what can you tell us about the accident?"

Tracey then began her heartfelt story of what happened. She had seen him at her house just before he had left to go surfing with his friends. He was going to meet them at the beach, and they all were going to surf for a while. After surfing, he would be back home, and I had baked a birthday cake for him while he was surfing. His friends would be joining him, and we all were going to be celebrating Kenny's birthday. He was going to be 24-years-old.

I knew something was wrong when four hours had passed, so I decided to take a drive down to the beach to see if I could hurry them along to come back to the house for cake. When I got there, the police and ambulance and red rescue trucks were there, and the paramedics were loading Kenny into the ambulance. I began running as fast as I could. I didn't know if it was Kenny or maybe someone else, but my heart was pounding out of my chest as I ran to see what all the commotion was about. All Kenny's friends were crying, and I couldn't find Kenny. They all saw me with horror written on my face as they all began talking at once, explaining what had happened. They said the paramedics worked on Kenny for over an hour trying to revive him, but in the end, they were not able to save his life. Kenny was gone, and the ambulance was taking him to the coroner's office to order an autopsy. I didn't understand why Kenny needed an autopsy until his friends explained to me that when they all arrived at the beach to go surfing with Kenny, they found Kenny floating in the Pacific Ocean unconscious. They all ran into the ocean to rescue him and thought he was dead, but they still called 911 to have the paramedics come and try to save his life. They worked on him for over an hour and then called his death at 1:10 pm, Friday, May 9th. Kenny was gone, and they were all in shock.

That's when I said, "But I don't understand. Why does Kenny need to have an autopsy? We all know that he drowned," Tracy cried out in anguish.

"I can't bear the thought that they will be cutting Kenny open for no reason. We all know that he died from drowning."

That's when his best friend, Johnny, spoke up, saying that Kenny was alone when he died. We found him like that, so no one knows for sure what happened. Maybe he had a fight with someone, and they wrestled with each other in the water, and Kenny died in the scuffle. Or maybe Kenny tried to commit suicide and swallowed some pills and then fell asleep in the ocean. None of us know what happened. We found Kenny dead, and we don't know how he died. So, the police told us that, by law, an autopsy had to be performed by the state, like it or not. Tracey came to a sudden stop and began weeping uncontrollably. Then we all started to cry after hearing such a horrific story about our Kenny. He didn't deserve to die like this. He was all alone.

"Why, why did God allow this to happen?" I cried as I began to hug Tracey. The girls were still sitting on the picnic table listening to Tracey tell her story. They were hugging each other, crying so deeply hurt. Peter let us all cry it out as he paced back and forth. After a very long five minutes, Peter broke in trying to offer us comfort, and we all took a seat at the picnic table. Peter took charge and began to explain how the meeting with the coroner was going to go down and how each one of us had a role to play in this meeting. We were all silent as we listened to Peter take charge. He laid out the strategy we would be taking and assured all of us that everything would be all right. We were going to be able to see Kenny and say our goodbyes, one way or another. Thank God he was with us. He was so strong, and we were all so weak with grief and worry. As we passed the tissues around, Peter got us all a bottle of water and asked us to drink the entire bottle. It was very hot, and we all needed to stay hydrated. The last thing we needed was for one of us to end up fainting from lack of water. We had to remain calm during this meeting so that our point of views could be clearly understood by the coroner. If we were all crying, logic would be difficult to achieve. So, we all drank water, wiped our eyes, and blew our noses to get ourselves ready for this heartbreaking meeting.

It was now 2 o'clock, and the sun was beating down on us relentlessly. It was so hot, it must have been 90 degrees. Since we were not use to such hot temperatures this time of year, the heat was taking its toll on us. I was thinking, thank goodness Peter had us all drink water. I was in a daze looking at the traffic rushing by. The humdrum of the cars was hypnotizing and for a while, I was lost in a wide-awake sleep, all pain gone, just completely relaxed in another world…a world that didn't hurt. Just then, I felt Peter's hand on my shoulder saying, "It's time, honey, to go in. Let's go."

We all walked in with austere faces so grim that they felt as though they never would be able to express anything else but hardhearted reality. The coroner was waiting, and we all entered the conference room together, ready to take on battle. The coroner had no feeling here, but we all did. Our hearts were full of love, and emotional trauma usually takes a front seat. We had uncompromising resolve on our side, so our chances of winning this debate were on our side, not on the side of California law.

The coroner opened the meeting by introducing herself to Tracey and then began to explain to Tracey the situation as it pertained to the law. Tracey listened intently, never batting an eyelash. I was amazed at her steadfastness. Being Kenny's sweatheart, I couldn't even begin to imagine the grief she was going through. I don't think I could have been so strong if it had been my Peter. The hurt for Tracey must have been debilitating.

After the coroner finished her expletive clarification, Peter piped in and began his dissertation on our behalf. He explained in a much more rational voice than Izzy had about just how bad Kenny's father was and that this was just another way of reaching out to hurt Mary. Even after all these years, he still had a vendetta to achieve. How could the state in all sincerity allow such a vendetta to take place given the fact the Kenny's father was a convicted felon? With a loving family all seated here after traveling 3,000 miles to bury their precious son, to not allow them to see him was the cruelest blow of all. All we wanted to do was bury him in peace. After all, doesn't any individual deserve to have a decent burial? Certainly, a son as good as Kenny, after all he had been through, deserved to be buried in peace.

The coroner was dead silent after Peter finished his narrative. We all sat in total silence, our grief not allowing any of us to speak. When would this silence end? It seemed to go on without end, perpetual silence. I remember thinking the coroner has to break the silence. Surly after hearing Peter's heartfelt account of both Kenny's life and the hateful life of his father, the coroner had to realize that what she was insisting was unreasonable. That's when at long last, the coroner broke the silence with this statement, "The only way I will consider releasing Kenny's body is if he does not have a will. Does he have a will?" the coroner questioned.

"Of course not," I said

"No, he does not have a will" Tracey acknowledged. "He is only 24-years-old. Why would he even think of making a will at the age of 24? Don't be ridiculous!"

Suddenly, there was a knock on the door. Knock, knock, knock. Three knocks on the door. The door opened and in came a secretary holding a four-page fax that had just arrived from Kenny's father, stating that a will of Kenny's had been received. I couldn't believe it!

"A will!" I said. "What will?"

"Where did you get that will?" Tracey demanded. "He doesn't have a will."

The coroner turned the will over to me and asked me to read it. I was shaken and in shock. Why on earth would Kenny have written a will? It must have been his father's insistence that he write a will. Kenny would never have thought about writing a will. Why would he? He was in the prime of his life. As I took the will from the coroner's hand, I began to read it out loud. It started by saying, "I, Kenneth J. Clark, hereby give permission to only my father that only he can have possession of my body for…"

Suddenly, I heard Peter demanding that I stop reading the first page and go to the final page of the will and look at the signature. I began flipping page after page after page of the document until I came to the final page.

"Oh, my God," I said. "This is not Kenny's signature. It is his father's signature. I know his signature because I had to testify at one of his trials about the threatening letter to kill a judge that he had written. I know his writing like I know my own."

Just then, Tracey grabbed the will and ripped it out of my hands. I was startled. I was afraid that she was going to rip it and then what kind of discussion would we be forced to have. Tracey glared at the last page of the will and started to scream,

"This is not his signature. I have proof. I have his driver's license with his signature on it."

She began to fumble through her handbag, searching for Kenny's license, which took forever, she was trembling so hard. Finally, her hand emerged from the bag with Kenny's license, and she forcefully placed the license right in the eyes of the coroner to see. Slowly and methodically, the coroner took the license and then began to compare it to the signature that was on the will. Clearly, it did not match and yet, she still did not say anything. She looked intently, glancing back and forth from the license to the will and then the will to the license and then yet again at the license, placing it face up next to the will as she lay both side by side on the table. Examining it carefully, comparing each signature meticulously to the letter we all watched attentively. After making us wait and wait, finally, the coroner stated that clearly the signatures did not match and that it was obvious that the will was a forgery.

"So, you see," Peter said, "his father will stop at nothing to punish us. What are you going to do about this?"

The coroner said, "Let me talk to the Chief Deputy Coroner and see if we can release his body to a funeral home. However, let me be clear. His body cannot be flown out of the state of California. If his body is released, it must be released to a funeral home in this city. You must have his funeral in California, not in the state of Maine. Do I make myself clear?"

As I nodded my head in compliance, Peter said, "Yes, we all understand."

The coroner left the room, stating, "Wait here while I try to reach the Chief."

"You did it, Tracey," I said. "If it wasn't for you, we would never have been able to prove Kenny's signature. Thank you," as I grabbed at her to hug her. The torment was almost over. Now all we had to do was wait for the coroner to return. In my heart, I knew we had won our argument but, in my mind, I was scared to death. The law was never on my side when it came to fighting Hank, so why should it be now?

And so, we waited until the coroner returned quite quickly.

"I am sorry, but the Chief cannot be reached right now. Why don't you all go and have some lunch and when you return, I should have an answer for you."

And with that, we departed for lunch.

Part IV
Bringing Kenny Home

Chapter XVII

There was a McDonald's across the street. None of us were really hungry, so we all just went through the motions of getting some sustenance into our bodies. Izzy was being cranky, and Becky was tearful. Her voice was quivering sometimes when she talked, and I was just filled with sorrow. I ate quietly, thinking all the time about how to convince the coroner to let us view Kenny. How cruel the world can be some times. Can you imagine losing a loved one and not being able to bury them? After all these years, this man was still inflicting torture on his family. He was punishing me but in reality, he was torturing his own children, inflicting pain on them at a time when they were not capable of dealing with their own grief. I wish he was dead. When will this relentless pursuit end?

"Are you all right, honey?" Peter said. He could sense that I was pensive and someplace else, not in the moment.

"I just don't know how we are going to figure this out. All I want to do is bury my son. Is that so unreasonable? How much suffering does God expect me to bear because of this man. I know Hank was very angry when Kenny joined the construction company and decided to leave home. I guess I'll never understand this man as long as I live. He continues to be relentless when it comes to his son. He'll never let go."

"Try to eat something," Peter said. "I'm worried about you."

"I'll be alright. Let's just finish lunch and get back to the coroner's office."

And so, we all tried our best to eat and drink something. Peter bought us all our own bottle of water. It was so hot, and we were not use to this humidity so early in the season.

So, we all trudged back across the street to the coroner's office and were told that the Chief Deputy Coroner would not be back in the facility for another 15 minutes. That's when we all were ushered once again into that small conference room, which was right next door to the coroner's office and that infamous fax machine. I remember staring at the fax steadfastly as I slowly walked past the machine thinking, I hate you, which was ridiculous. How can you hate a machine and yet it was the machine that delivered the news of a Will. I wasn't looking where I was walking and almost bumped into the door of the conference room. Peter stopped me in time.

As we waited, Izzy began to strategize about how we might be able to see Kenny. While we are waiting here, I'll pretend to use the rest room but instead, I can search the facility for the morgue.

"It is probably down stairs, don't you think, Peter?"

"You will do no such thing," Peter argued. "The last thing we need is to tick them off at us. It may come to that in the end but not right now. For now, we are all going to just sit quietly and behave ourselves."

Just then, we all jumped and were startled when the door to the conference room abruptly opened quickly and in came the deputy coroner, looking stern and serious as she took a seat at the table.

"I have talked to the Chief, and he has given approval to have Kenny's body released to the Oceanside Funeral Home. Under no circumstances is Kenny's body to leave the State of California. I have already been in contact with the funeral home, and they will be served shortly with papers clearly laying out what they can and cannot do. So, if you all agree, I will begin to make arrangements to have your son's body transported to the Oceanside Funeral Home. Do you all understand the gravity of this situation, and do you all agree to comply with the law?"

We all nodded our heads, and Tracey said, "Yes, yes, we will have his funeral at Oceanside"

"Thank you," I said. That's all I could muster. I remember thinking, 'Thank God.'

• • •

Tracey was amazing. She took charge immediately. We decided to all go back to the motel where we could all share our thoughts about the details that would make this funeral beautiful.

"Kenny always picked me wild flowers everyday when he was on work break," Tracey said. "He loved flowers."

"Then we will fill the funeral home with flowers, tons and tons of flowers no matter what the cost," I said. I looked at Peter and he nodded approval. "I want a heart of flowers in his casket, all yellow, his favorite color," I said.

We all began talking at once then and before we knew it, everyone's suggestions were wonderful and all was planned.

By this time, Tracey was exhausted. She told us all that she was going home to take a nap and that she would call us later. I was spent, too and sat down on the bed. Before I realized it, I was lying on the bed, and Peter decided to let me rest while he took the girls out to the florist. I fell asleep immediately. If only I could stay asleep forever, then this pain would go away. This gut wrenching pain hurt so much.

The funeral was beautiful. The room was filled with flowers, and they were breathtaking. The home was situated on a rolling green with trees and landscaping so beautiful, it took my breath away. It was a beautiful sun-filled day, and there was not a cloud in the sky, warm and sunny, just perfect. I was surprised to see so many people at the funeral; after all, we were so far from home, and all our friends and relatives were back in New England. Where did all these people come from? Tracey did a great job getting the word out. I got the chance to meet all Kenny's friends. They were all wonderful young men, and they all individually introduced themselves to me with quivering voices and tears in their eyes. So many people that day described my son as a sweet and gentle, young man. I found that amazing. To hear sweet and gentle so many times from so many different people was heartwarming. Everyone who knew Kenny loved him. His best friend broke down, and Peter was like a rock, taking charge and staying with him until he could compose himself.

And then I met his boss.

"Your son was a hell of a man," he said. I wanted to talk more with him, but the line kept moving along, and that was the only time I heard from him. I was disappointed because I was sure that would have been a wonderful conversation. But I was too heartsick to seek him out in time before he left the funeral home.

Kenny was so handsome. He was blonde and tanned and had a crew cut. He looked just like Brad Pitt, the movie actor when he was 20. I touched him all over and held onto his hands for a long time. Then I bent down and kissed him on the cheek, leaving my red lipstick kiss on his face. I said a prayer, asking God to please welcome my son into his heavenly home wearing his mother's kiss on his cheek. I knew God would understand that kiss. The Blessed Mother must have suffered more than me, seeing her son crucified. To stay with him, seeing him in such pain, had to be the greatest hurt of her lifetime. If God would allow his own Mother to have such heartache, surely, I should be able to get through this. My pain was so deep, but the Blessed Mother's pain had to be so much greater than mine. Death happens to everyone, and we still have a tough time accepting it. In a way our memory is a double-edged sword. It hurts to remember. And yet, if we didn't have a memory, death would be so easy. There would be nothing to remember, therefore nothing to hurt. So which is worse, not to remember or to remember? I can only hope that someday I will see Kenny again. One has to believe, otherwise, why bother living. Life is difficult but without hope, it would be impossible.

We all decided to have Kenny cremated, and Tracey and I would share the ashes. I've never been to a crematorium and would much prefer to visit Kenny in a beautiful grave yard with green grass and trees and shrubs and birds and whatever. Maybe we can arrange to have Kenny's ashes buried in a graveyard back home. A crematorium is so cold. At a graveyard, I could plant daffodils that would bloom every spring and they would be yellow, Kenny's favorite color.

"It's time to go," Peter said.

"No, no, it's not. I'm staying here until they close the doors," I cried.

"But they have shut the doors, honey," Peter said. "It's time to go home. Come on, baby, let me take you home."

• • •

All the way home on the plane, I felt so rattled and restless. I just couldn't sit still. My body was not cooperating. I couldn't stay in my seat and kept walking up and down the plane aisle trying to get a grip. When I did sit, Peter was right there by my side. I cried a lot during the plane ride home. I knew I would be seeing my doctor when I got home, otherwise I would never be able to get through a day, let alone sleep at night. Mom wanted to have a small family ceremony at the Franciscan Monastery in Kennebunkport, a twenty-minute drive from the house. That way my brother and sisters and some relatives would be able to say their goodbyes. So that was something to plan for when we got back home.

It's been three weeks now, and I am still waiting for Kenny's ashes. Tracey told me it would take about three weeks, so I have to trust that Kenny's ashes will be arriving soon. I haven't told Peter about what I want to do with the ashes when we get them. I know I don't want to have them scattered. That's for sure. I'm wondering if a graveyard will even let you bury ashes. Why not, why wouldn't they. That's what I think I want to do. We'll probably have to put the ashes in a casket, but that's alright. I need a place to go to visit him, and a crematorium is not going to work for me. Maybe it's time for me to sit down and have a talk with Peter.

Just then, Peter came in, holding a package in his hands that just arrived by the postal service truck.

"This just came from Tracey," Peter said.

"It must be the ashes," I said. "What else could it be?"

He carefully placed the package on the kitchen counter, and we both stared at it for a moment. I couldn't bring myself to opening the package, so Peter very gently took charge and opened the box. Sure enough, it was Kenny's ashes, and the container was sealed, so you could not open the urn.

Kenny's ashes were here, and I never got a chance to talk to Peter about what we were going to do with them. Just then Peter said, "Do you want to bring Kenny home?"

"You know I do," I said

"Well, what do you say we have a family graveyard on our property? I will take care of all the paper work and make this happen."

"Do they allow that in the state of Maine?" I asked

"They do," Peter answered, "and I am going to make this happen for you. Would you like that?"

"Oh, Peter, you know I would."

"What do you say we take a walk around the property and figure out where we want this graveyard to go. After all, we have 3 ½ acres to choose from."

It was almost as though Peter had read my mind. He was so in tuned to me. I never would have thought of having a graveyard on the property. It was the perfect solution. I always wanted to bring Kenny home. This way he would be home for good.